# HOWLING DESIRE

## HUNTER'S MOON RITUAL
### BOOK TWO

M. SINCLAIR

LOST & BOUND PUBLISHING

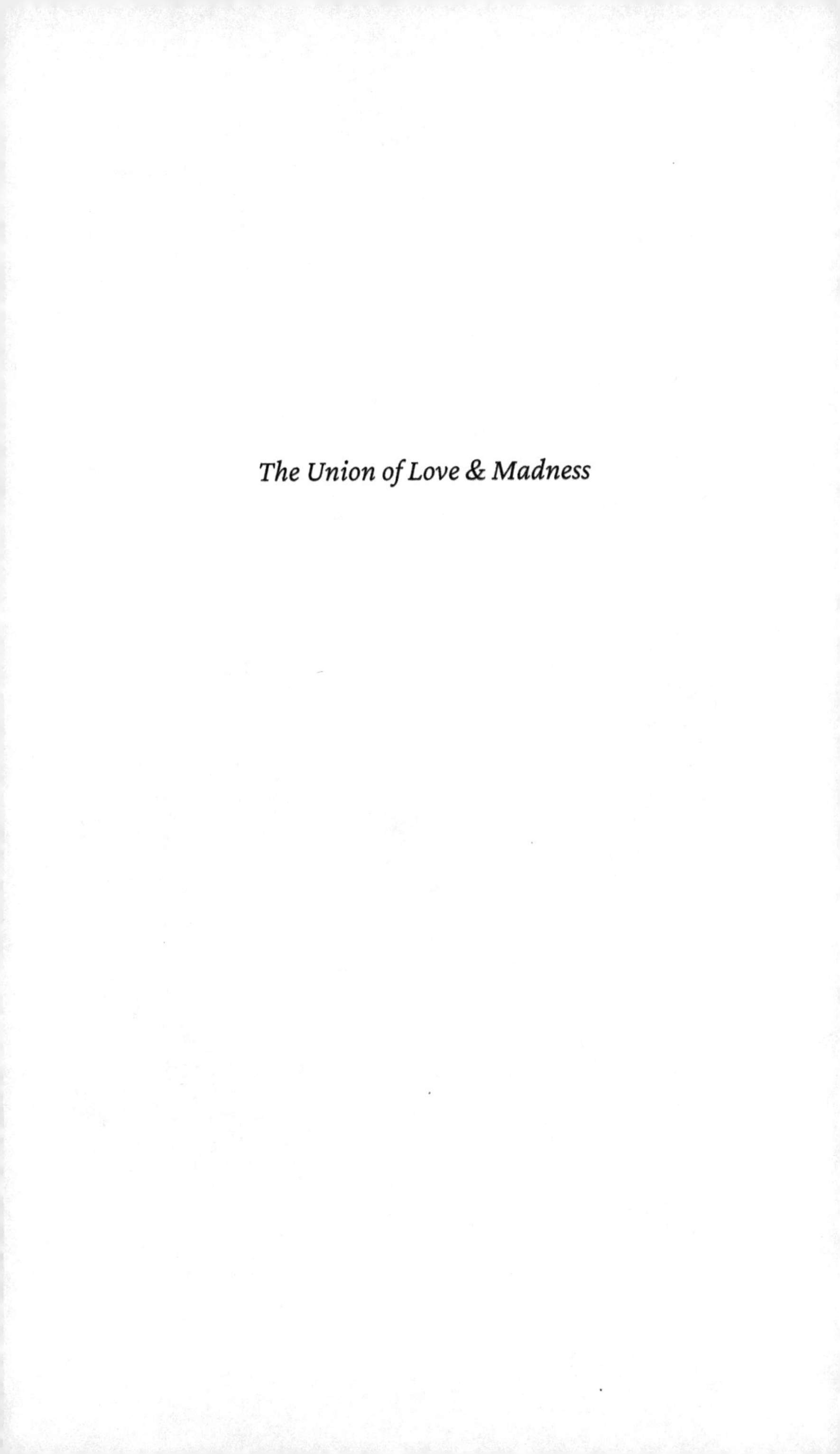

*The Union of Love & Madness*

# DESCRIPTION

**I survived. That was supposed to be enough.**

Freedom? Safety? Belonging? It felt like they were things that could still be taken away. The Cold Moon Pack had left marks on me that would never fade, and until Ivan Rivers was gone, I would *never* truly be free.

But my mates refuse to let my past define my future.

I found something in the three of them that I hadn't been allowed to want. The kind of belonging that felt permanent. The kind of love that felt real.

But our bond is so much more than a mate bond, and the future of Thornfell may be reliant on whether or not we complete it.

Something is building—a divine war. One that means traveling across Thornfell to secure alliances, all in the name of stopping Ivan's ritual.

The Hunter's Moon is coming. *Twenty days.*
And the key to stopping it?
Our mate bond.

~

**Howling Desire** is Book Two in the *Hunter's Moon Ritual* trilogy—a dark, steamy, why-choose wolf-shifter romance packed with fated mates, primal tension, found family, and dangerous rituals.

*The Thornfell Registry is located at the end of Howling Desire.*

~

*Content Warning: Contains explicit language, on page physical violence and abuse, adult sexual content (18+), PTSD, references to past abuse, violence, and other dark themes.*

# PROLOGUE
## GRACIE

*Twelve years ago...*

"WOULD you mind bringing these over to the shrine?" my dad asked, drawing my attention from where I was looking out the back window of our home.

I could see my brother and mother from here, both flipping through books she'd chosen for his lesson of the day. I was glad I'd gotten all of my work done early because in the summer months the last thing I wanted to be doing was sitting still. I had really only come in to grab a quick snack. I'd spent most of the day outside, underneath the golden afternoon sun.

I loved our home, but our garden was my favorite place to spend time. My mother and father had made beds of vegetables and flowers that grew huge throughout the season. Scattered throughout were wooden benches my brother and I had helped make before we painted them. There was only one place with shade—the large apple tree at the center of the garden—but I liked it that way. Even though we were wolves, most of whom liked the moon, my family had always loved the sun.

My wolf was practically begging me to go on a run. "Gracie?"

I turned and offered my dad a sheepish smile. "Sorry, I was thinking about going on a run," I admitted, taking the small basket of food he handed me to bring to the shrine. It wasn't much, but everyone in the village brought weekly offerings to show our thanks to The Eight.

"If you wait until after dinner, we could go as a family and maybe head further into the forest," he said, his eyes bright at the idea.

"Okay." I nodded eagerly, already halfway out the door.

Our village was one of the smaller ones in our territory, or at least that's what my parents always said. The few times I'd been outside of it, I mostly saw farmland stretching on forever, with one or two bigger cities along the way. Even so, our village was a place of trade where farmers brought their crops, and there was always a busy, lively feeling to it.

Greetings echoed through the air as I waved in passing to neighbors and to groups of women and men gathered within the town center. Most people were busy with their work during the day, but in the evening, as dinner drew closer, many slowed down to talk with friends or nearby relatives. It was a short walk along dirt roads to the village center, where a beautiful wooden shrine stood.

The hand-carved oak building had been there for decades, and though time had worn it down in places, it still showed the symbols of The Eight perfectly. Even the two unnamed gods were represented by empty spaces in the back, left open to be filled someday, as if the shrine were keeping space for them.

"I knew you'd be coming by," our town's priestess called out. I had known Tala my entire life. She was close friends with my mother, and I'd come to think of her as my aunt. Since she and my mom had grown up together, it didn't feel far from the truth.

"My dad wanted me to drop this off," I explained, looking around the inside of the hand-painted shrine.

"Tell him thank you," she said with a warm smile. "Are you planning to attend the ritual tonight? It will be a full moon."

I nibbled on my lip. I'd never been to one of the rituals to thank The Eight—they were way past my bedtime—but maybe this time... "I'll have to ask my parents."

"Even if you just come for the beginning, it's very peaceful. Mostly meditation," she said. "I wouldn't blame you if you found it a bit boring though," she added teasingly.

"That sounds really nice," I told her honestly. "Which of The Eight is it for?"

"All of them. We never tell people who they should pray to. It's a time to connect with one of The Eight, all of them...or even none of them. Some people have told me they don't believe in The Eight at all, but they like the sense of community the rituals bring."

Her words made my chest feel lighter. There was no pressure, no feeling like I *had* to pray to The Eight. It wasn't that I didn't believe in them, I just wasn't sure how I felt yet. My parents had always told us it was important to take our time when deciding things like that.

"I'll ask," I promised her.

After a few more minutes, I said goodbye and started toward home.

"Gracie!" a familiar voice called out. I waved at Nori, who was sprinting toward me, carrying a bundle of what looked like cloth.

Nori was two years older than me and a year younger than Owen, and we'd been friends ever since I could remember. I looked up to her like an older sister. She always seemed so confident, like she knew exactly what to do, and I thought she was amazing.

Right now, ink was smeared on her cheek, and her blonde hair was piled on top of her head like a crown.

"Hey! You coming over for dinner?"

Nori's family had passed away when she was very young, after a virus swept through our territory. Because of that, she spent a lot of time at our house even though she technically lived with Tala, along with two other children who had lost their families.

"Yes, and I brought those quilts your mom wanted," she said, holding up her bundle. "It feels good to finally be able to make something."

"They're beautiful," I said, admiring the shades of blue, purple, and creamy brown. "Did you do these all on your own?"

"Yes!" She shrugged. "Sometimes I can't sleep."

Owen had mentioned that to me before. In fact, most of the little things I knew about Nori came from my brother. They were best friends.

"You could try one of those sleep remedies my mom makes," I suggested, and she nodded in agreement. When we were only a few feet from the door, my brother stepped outside and offered Nori a gigantic smile.

"I was about to come find you. I finished my lessons for the day," he said, waving both of us inside —though his focus was completely on her. I wasn't surprised when they both headed out to the back yard, the quilts forgotten on the table.

"What are these?" my mother asked, shifting through the material and looking closely at each stitch.

"Nori made them."

"What an amazing girl," my mother said. "I'm going to be terribly disappointed if they don't get married one day."

My face scrunched up. "Nori and Owen? Gross."

My dad barked out a laugh while stirring the pot in front of him. "You don't think they like each other?"

My eyes moved to where they were sitting together outside, laughing, and I sighed. "I mean...I guess. I just...I mean, who's even thinking about getting married? Owen is only three years older than me!"

My mom smiled softly. "A lot can change in those few years. But anyway, I don't mean now—I mean when they're much older. I just think it's sweet they have a crush on one another."

"Your mom and I met when we were about fifteen. My family had just moved to a nearby village, but it took until I was eighteen before I finally asked her out on a date," my dad added.

"Apparently I was *scary*," my mom said, giving me a wink that made me laugh.

My dad continued his recount of the story. "Tala was the one who finally said, 'If you keep staring at her but not talking to her, The Eight are going to remove your ability to talk.' Felt like a bit of a curse." I couldn't help but giggle at that.

As we began to set the table for dinner, I thought about what they'd said. Would I want to get married one day? I didn't think so. At least not to anyone in this village. All of the boys my age were really annoying.

A few minutes later, the five of us were sitting down for a simple summer dinner of freshly baked bread, roasted garden vegetables, and grilled chicken. My dad offered a quiet word of thanks to The Eight, spoken softly in habit, before we dug in.

"So," my mother said as she passed Owen the bowl of vegetables, "are you still thinking about the ritual tonight?"

"Yeah." Owen nodded, looking at Nori who brightened immediately.

"I convinced him to go."

"What about you, Gracie?" my mother asked, making my brows lift.

"I was actually going to ask about it," I said. "Tala said it was peaceful. Mostly meditation?"

"It is," my dad agreed. "I know you haven't been before, and it's a bit past when you normally go to bed —but your mom and I are okay with you giving it a try."

"You don't have to stay for the whole thing, either," my mom added. "Only go if you want to. It's meant to be a gathering, not a command."

I glanced between them, thrilled they were okay with me staying up late, but thinking about what Tala had told me. "Wouldn't The Eight be upset if we don't go?"

"No," Nori spoke up. "The Eight don't need worship, but they appreciate it."

My mother smiled at her. "Exactly. True belief isn't something you perform."

I liked that. A lot.

"One of the soldiers passing through was talking about somewhere in the north of the territory where it's different," my brother said, frowning.

"There are places where rituals are...stricter," my dad said after a moment. "Where attendance is expected. Forced."

"That doesn't sound very nice," I muttered.

"It isn't," my mother agreed.

I thought about that as I ate, about the way Tala had spoken at the shrine, how calm everything had felt. No pressure. No expectations. Just...choice.

Outside, the light was already starting to fade, the sky shifting into deeper colors as the moon began its slow rise. My family talked about our plans for the next day, leaving me to think.

No one was watching. No one was waiting to see if I did the right thing. It was just a choice, and that felt like enough of a reason to give The Eight a chance.

# CHAPTER 1

# GRACIE

*IVAN RIVERS WILL BE a god of this world.*

The words settled over the room like a crushing weight, pressure erupting behind my ribs. I'd spent so much of the past decade feeling small—afraid to take up space—but that feeling didn't survive the thought of Ivan with *divine* power.

It burned away, replaced by something harder. Sharper.

Ivan Rivers couldn't be allowed to transcend.

I wouldn't stand for it.

I didn't know how I would stop him. I'd been powerless in his shadow for so long, but I knew the strength of those around me. I knew how capable they were, how intelligent, how prepared. Maybe...maybe together, we could stop him.

The thought felt unreal. Not long ago, my only goal

had been survival: keeping my head down, obeying quickly enough, and never giving anyone a reason to notice me. Power had always belonged to men like Ivan. Men who took and took until nothing was left.

But sitting here now, surrounded by people who waited for my thoughts instead of silencing them, I realized how much of that fear had been conditioned and cultivated.

Ivan didn't believe in the gods the way my parents or the people of my village had. He believed in obedience and control. The faith he had in Nyxarra was twisted into a weapon that slaughtered those around him.

The windowless room fell quiet in the aftermath of Ravik's declaration, all of us gathered around the circular table cluttered with artifacts and intel. Every piece hinted at a larger picture yet offered nothing solid to hold onto.

"Twenty days doesn't give us much time," Alpha Deegan said. His massive frame dominated the space across from us, dark hair and golden eyes lending him the unmistakable presence of a king. Although, I didn't think that was how he viewed the responsibility of being the Alpha for Ironsun territory.

Malara stood to his right, her calm blue eyes thoughtful as her hand rested possessively on his shoulder. "And we have to trust that he won't act irrationally or too suddenly."

"We can't trust that. He's insane," Thornar cut in, his tone deceptively casual. His deep voice drew my attention to where he stood only inches away, the steady presence of my three mates anchoring me in place.

"More than that, he views everyone in his territory as expendable," Ravik added. "It doesn't matter how many die or if *all* of them do."

"Especially if the ritual gives him more power," Basir said. My stomach tightened as fragments of my recent vision, a sacrifice of thousands under a blood red moon, pressed harder against my thoughts.

Elowen tapped the books laid out near her. Today, her willowy frame was clothed in dark wool that faded to cream at the edges, mirroring the pattern of her coiled hair—dark at the roots and honeyed at the ends. Her brown eyes, threaded with blue, remained fixed on the texts before her.

"I'll do everything I can to identify the ritual he's attempting—what he hopes to gain and who he intends to draw power from. Nyxarra, most likely. But I don't understand how this is possible. Drawing on a god who is imprisoned...or under duress..."

Even the soldiers lining the back wall shifted at her unsure words.

One of them exchanged a glance with the other, his hand curling into a fist at his side. They and their brothers in arms would be sent in first if things turned violent. And the idea of one of *The Eight* being bound or somehow part of this potential conflict? It was horrifying.

The thought of Ivan even siphoning power from them left my stomach roiling, so I'm sure they felt similar.

Thornar inclined his head toward his sister. "Allies and force will help, but without more details...if we can't stop the ritual..."

"All of Thornfell will fall," I said quietly. "Borders will mean nothing to him." He would justify *any* cruelty in the name of power.

"His goal is pure domination," Deegan agreed.

"We can't ignore the connection between your ritual being interrupted"—Solenne, Ravik's sister, spoke up from beside Isara, her golden eyes intense beneath painted sigils that marked her as a priestess—"the god scar placed on your mating mark, and the ritual being bound to a captured god."

Isara spoke up, dark braids framing silver-inked markings and an unreadable expression. "The four of you are connected to this as deeply as Ivan himself."

My throat closed as I looked at the three men around me, guilt coiling tight in my gut. They were involved because of me. *I had done this.*

Ravik squeezed my leg gently, sending a pulse of warmth through my tense frame. "Breathe, Gracie. This isn't something you can take the blame for."

I nodded, though the words didn't fully settle. This situation was layered with too many threats, too many moving pieces, and *I* had brought it into all of their lives.

Imprisoned gods.

Blood rituals meant to empower a monster.

An entire compound of enslaved shifters forced to serve the Cold Moon Pack's cruelty.

Anxiety crept higher, tightening my chest, but I forced it back. *Not now.* Not with so many eyes on me and decisions this important being made. I might not have been as strong as all of them, but I was strong enough to stay present.

"It's horrifying to consider—and not something he could do on his own," Isara pointed out. "He would need help. Divine help."

And somehow, impossibly, my bond was tangled at the center of it.

"Another god?" Deegan asked, concern flickering across his features.

"It's not out of the question," Elowen said. "In the past, there have been times when The Eight have fought one another...but they can't normally touch mortals. I'm not sure how Ivan would have become entangled in any of this."

"The one advantage we have right now," Basir cut in, halting the speculation, "is that his movements suggest preparation, not open warfare. If we strike soon, he may not be ready."

"So we prepare forces, then?" Ravik asked.

"Yes, but we don't move," Malara said. "We're waiting for those troops to return, and we need more ritual schematics, specifically timing and location. We can't act blind. We're assuming he's waiting until the full moon, but confirmation is necessary."

"Ivan has never strayed from his ritual schedule," I said.

"We know the compound is layered with fortified measures, and getting in will be much harder than before," Thornar said, then glanced at me with a quick wink. "Nothing we can't handle, though."

That sliver of humor eased some of the tension in my shoulders. "I know it may be naive, but I want to save as many of Ivan's prisoners as possible. Especially the children. Some of us escaped, but many didn't."

Isara and Solenne nodded as Malara added, "The goal would be to save everyone, while killing as many of his soldiers in the process. If Ivan is removed, there will be no one left to lead his men and they will scatter."

"And they aren't that large of a pack," I said. "Just a lot of—"

"Power-hungry men at the top," Elowen finished with a weary sigh. "I swear, history repeats itself in the most painful of ways."

"Is there any way to negotiate with him?" Solenne asked. "To stop the violence before it starts?"

"No." The word came out from me, both firm and unyielding. "No, there isn't."

"The only way to stop him is with force. And because of that, we can't ensure everyone will live," Basir said quietly, as if offering me a warning.

I looked up at him and nodded, squeezing his hand. I understood what he was preparing me for. War was rarely generous with survivors. Still, I accepted the reality he laid out. This wouldn't end without violence.

Even so, my goal remained unchanged: *to save everyone we could.*

"But what after?" Deegan asked. "What comes after we wage this war?" His gaze swept the table without settling on anyone. "Say we stop the ritual. Say Ivan falls. What comes next?"

Silence followed, thick with thought. The first part was easy—we try to save everyone—but then what? Move them? Leave them? While Deegan was asking, I had a feeling he already knew what he would do. The question was addressed to Ravik, which was good because I didn't exactly have an answer.

"We find a new leader, or we take over ourselves," Ravik said. "The first makes more sense, if we can find someone willing to lead after being freed from captivity. Someone they'll trust."

"They'll also need strength," Thornar added. "Otherwise the Grimfur Skulk will steamroll them."

"We could act as a temporary leading force," Elowen suggested. "Until they can choose a leader of their own."

"That means governance," Deegan said. "Stability. Protection for civilians. Rebuilding. Their territory is halfway across Thornfell from us."

*Stopping Ivan wouldn't be the end; that much was clear.* It would be the beginning of something much more complicated. Responsibility. Reconstruction. Becoming what replaced him, whether we wanted to or not. The act of stopping him suddenly carried a different weight, and that was *if* we could even stop him to begin with.

"We help remove him," I said softly, "then step back and let them choose their own leader."

Basir nodded in agreement.

"I don't disagree," Malara said.

"But if we're committed to helping," Ravik continued, his tone firm as he met his father's gaze, "then this stops being a discussion of hypotheticals and becomes a matter of action. We need to talk about how we get ourselves into position for quick action, especially while we wait for more intel. We may not have much time for planning after that."

"We don't have the numbers to do it on our own,"

Malara pointed out. "Even if everything goes perfectly."

"And it won't," Thornar said flatly. "The ritual could alter the balance of power."

"His generals used to shift on ritual nights and kill people," I said, my voice weighted with memory. "I never realized they might have been stronger because of the ritual...but they killed many."

Silence spread through the room. Basir's posture went rigid, and though I watched him carefully, waiting for a larger reaction, he only reached out and took my hand.

"Ritual-enhanced strength changes the equation," Isara agreed. "If Ivan gains even a fraction of what he's seeking, we'll be fighting uphill from the start."

The truth settled deep, heavy but unavoidable. Even with perfect planning, even if every piece fell into place, even if Ivan was weaker than we feared—this would still cost lives. Too many lives. And if we failed...

I didn't let myself finish that thought.

"Are there any other territories who'd be willing to help us?" The question left me before I could stop it, driven by the need for some kind of hope.

"We have many trade allies..." Deegan said.

"It just depends on whether they're willing to go to war with us," Ravik finished.

*Why did it feel like the war had already started?*

# CHAPTER 2
# GRACIE



"LITTLE FLAME?"

At the sound of Thornar's deep, honeyed voice, I turned my attention from the view of the Ironsun territory through the window. After living in the cold, sterile desolation of the Cold Moon Pack for so long, I was mesmerized by the mountainous skyline and all the trees—even after days of being here.

The meeting had concluded, and I'd escaped into the stone-covered hallway to grab some fresh air. I knew my mates would follow close behind, but I'd gotten what I needed: a moment to center myself.

"What has your attention?" Thornar asked, his warmth surrounding me as he closed the space between us, my back pressed against the window.

I tensed only momentarily. I loved Thornar's closeness. I loved the way our bond vibrated beneath my skin, and I loved the way he smelled like brown sugar and expensive bourbon. I just still wasn't used to anyone being in my space without it being a threat.

He clocked the tension almost immediately and paused before he set his hand on the windowsill.

"I'm fine," I said, placing my hand delicately on his chest. "I promise."

Thornar's chocolate brown eyes, circled with gold, darted over my face as he settled his hand on my waist instead of the window. Then in a quick move he switched our places, leaning into the window so that I stood in front of him, no longer trapped between his massive frame and a wall.

"Now." He brought a hand up to a strand of my hair. "What had your attention?"

I tried to focus on his question, but the way he so effortlessly navigated *me* truly amazed me. The appreciation I felt for Thornar was more than words could explain. I stepped into him, dipping my head and resting it against his chest.

"Thank you," I murmured. I felt his lips brush the top of my head before I pulled back, trying to shake the overwhelming affection the man inspired in me. Emotion wasn't the only thing he inspired, though. My pulse stuttered at how unfairly handsome he was.

Everything about Thornar was warmth and light, from his bronze skin seemingly lit with golden fire, to his playful humor. The way he heated my skin with just a look made it feel like he was my own personal sun. I almost felt possessive over that.

It was a feeling I'd never experienced before.

"I was just looking at how beautiful the day was," I said. "It was a nice break after the meeting being so..."

"Heavy," he agreed, running his free hand through his coiled onyx hair. "Far heavier than what you should have to deal with."

"Me? I'm the one who brought all of this on you!"

Thornar's chuckle this time made my muscles tense as I examined his expression with caution. "I wouldn't be so sure about that, little flame. Ivan Rivers has been a poison to this country for far too long."

My brows dipped as I considered what he was saying. "Why...why did no one stop him?"

"Stop him? When he took over the Cold Moon territory?"

"Yeah." I nodded, my voice a whisper as if I was worried about speaking it out loud.

"I know why we didn't. But for the other territories? I don't know," he admitted quietly. "Most likely because it didn't affect them. Not truly. When you're half a country away, it's easy to turn a blind eye to someone's entire life being destroyed."

The way he said it was so simple but also heartbreaking. I'm sure that was exactly why the other territories just moved on. They may have disapproved of Ivan's actions, but wolves—shifters in general—

stuck to their own packs, their own territories. Why fight a war for others, even if you are in a better position to do so?

"Shit. I didn't mean to make you cry." Thornar's chest rumbled as he used one finger to wipe an unexpected tear from my eye while wrapping his arm around my waist.

"I didn't mean to," I sniffed. "I haven't cried this much in...a decade? More? Between Ravik's news about my brother this morning and what you just said, it just feels...overwhelming."

Which in itself felt like an understatement.

Thornar's fingers clasped my chin as he examined my face. "The minute you need a break, little flame, we can disappear. You just say the word."

Warmth exploded through my chest as my gaze darted down to his lips, my cheeks feeling hot once again. My wolf nearly jumped out of my skin in response to his, a low rumble breaking from his chest. I wanted to kiss Thornar. *So why was I hesitating?*

"Why is she crying? Again?" Basir's gravelly voice broke through the moment as he strode from the meeting chamber.

I swallowed, feeling a surge of nervousness at his intensity, a mix of excited butterflies in my stomach and adrenaline. Basir didn't mean to be scary. I knew that wasn't his intention, but it was almost impossible not to feel that way. He was deadly, absolutely lethal, and I knew that without ever having seen him kill anyone.

Dressed entirely in black, his clothes hid the gold-lined grayscale tattoos that ran down his arms and up his neck. The one I had seen peeks of when he decided to stay in bed with me as I practically wrapped myself around him. I had no idea what I was doing when it came to any of these men, but especially Basir.

Sometimes I felt a world away from him, but other times, like now, he made his feelings clear. As he approached, he looked me over for injuries, his emerald and gold eyes flashing with frustration toward Thornar.

"She's fine," Thornar assured him before giving me a big smile and taking a step back. "We were just talking about the Cold Moon Pack."

"I'm fine," I assured Basir, stopping my hand from going up to touch his soft, shoulder-length black hair.

"*You* crying is never fine," he murmured, then heaved a sigh. "Ravik is almost done, and then we can get away from this for a bit."

"I am hungry," I admitted. Basir locked onto that, looking toward the exit. "We need to wait for Ravik, though."

"He might be a moment." He looked back toward the meeting room, which Thornar was moving toward. "He's discussing travel plans with his father."

With his gaze not directly on me, I was able to find

the courage to move closer to him and slide a hand up his chest, strumming my fingers there. He froze and looked down at my hand, heat filling his gaze. He wrapped his hand around mine before I managed to clear my head enough to ask him about what he'd said.

"Travel plans? For allies?" I asked.

"Yes. We may need to separate—"

"No."

The word left my mouth before I could stop myself, and I tensed up at his surprised reaction.

"No?" he asked softly.

It was hard to focus with the full weight of Basir's attention on me, but I managed to keep my composure. "I don't want to separate. I want...I *need* the four of us to stay together."

His emerald gaze darkened as he took in my words, and emotion clogged my throat as his silence wrapped around us. Part of my request came from my wolf, her outburst pushing past my normal control, but most of it was me. I didn't want to be away from any of them.

"If it's possible," I whispered when he didn't respond.

I almost tensed as his fingers slowly rose to wrap around the back of my neck. A position that should have caused me panic, but with Basir it didn't. Instead, I felt the urge to curl up against him.

My head tilted back, and he looked over my face

before leaning down. My eyes shut, and the breath between us nearly made me tremble.

He brushed his lips over mine, so faintly that it made me want more...but his words? They were everything. "If that's what you want, that's exactly what we'll do. We won't ever be apart, glow."

I nearly melted right into his arms.

I could feel the shift between us, despite not fully understanding *what* was changing, and when Basir pulled back, his protective and heated gaze wrapped around me like a secure blanket.

"Thank you." My whisper was hoarse.

"We'll just have to leave soon to make it work," Thornar called out. My cheeks turned bright red as I realized he'd been listening to our intimate moment while he waited for Ravik to leave the meeting room. Basir was startled as well if the low rumble that emitted from his chest was any indication.

I didn't even notice Ravik approaching until he was already there, moving with a quiet, determined stride. One second I was standing, and the next I'd been lifted clean off the ground, a small, startled shriek slipping from my lips.

I wrapped my arms around his neck on instinct as he turned toward the exit.

"Where is he going?" Basir demanded.

"Where *we* are going," Thornar called out as they followed us. "He heard she was hungry."

Oh. *That made sense.* Ravik's golden gaze was on me when I looked up at him, and the sunlight that shone through the windows in the corridor made his chocolate brown hair shimmer faintly. His tan skin was warm beneath my touch as my gaze traced his beard and the dark, tailored clothes he wore. He was the image of a perfect Alpha.

So how was I in his arms? I was still figuring that part out, to be honest. All I knew was that there were cords tethering me to each of these men, coated in magic that changed my perspective on everything. All I knew was that the closer we grew, the even *closer* I wanted to be to them.

"Should have had more breakfast," he pointed out before adding, "And I would never separate the four of us, *lux mea.*"

I didn't doubt his sincerity. From the very start, from the first time I saw him walk into the room, I knew I could trust the man. I'd just been terrified Ivan would hurt him. I still worried about that with all of them.

But now I also understood how powerful they and the Ironsun pack were.

"How will we gather all the allies we need then?" I asked as the other two caught up, and Ravik kept me in his arms, ignoring any passing looks we received.

"We travel to them. All of us together," he stated simply.

My eyes widened. "Like all around Thornfell?"

I knew that they could feel my surprise and nervousness through our bond, their wolves pressing toward me in comfort.

"Once we receive the intel we need, we leave," Basir agreed. "If you want to, Gracie."

"I do," I said. "I'm just nervous. I've never left the territory I grew up in, not really, and now I've gone to two other territories within the span of the past month... and now more. I want to do this. I won't hide from it, but I am nervous."

A small surge of pride strummed through me at my ability to so openly express that to them.

"We will be there next to you, and I think having your voice—as long as you're comfortable with it—to explain what is going on in Cold Moon will be invaluable," Ravik pointed out.

"Just think of it as a vacation," Thornar offered with a wink. I let out a small laugh. Thinking of it that way did make me feel better...sort of. The last trip I'd taken was with my parents to one of the territory's larger cities for a week. It had been over a decade since I'd even considered the concept of a vacation.

"So where are we going to have lunch?" I asked.

"The central gardens," Ravik answered. "We have something we want you to see."

～

"They come here every day?" I asked softly. I sat on a patio between Basir and Ravik, with Thornar across from me, his feet locked with mine so we were still touching as I ate my sandwich.

"Ever since the group of you arrived," Basir explained.

Nearby, about twenty people from the Cold Moon Pack had gathered, enjoying the fresh air of the garden. It was a beautiful place, a winding stone pathway lined with trimmed hedges and garden beds surrounding fountains.

"I get it," Thornar said. "It's easier to get through shit when you can talk about it with someone who went through it with you."

I had a feeling he was remembering what Elowen and him had gone through before coming to Ironsun territory.

"I'm glad they're safe," I whispered. "I hope they're adjusting..." My words drifted off in thought. The transition to Ironsun was a lot, even with the help and support of my mates.

Ravik's gaze shifted to me. "We made sure they have places to stay and work."

I recognized the faces I saw, but I didn't know any of them well. They knew me, though, and I felt the urge to go talk to them. What would I say, though? Would they expect me to have answers because of the company I kept? To have some sort of comfort to share? I could see it in the glances they sent my way, the questions they had about their loved ones who were still trapped with Ivan. I truly believed we would try to save them all, but it felt ridiculous to tell *them* that.

Who was I to promise that I could bring their children back? Their partners? Their parents?

Trapped in thought as my mates talked quietly around me, I let the gravity of the mission we were embarking on sink in. It would have been easy to hide away, to wash my hands of this. To bury that part of my life and replace it with the happiness and comfort that these men brought me. I had been through so much...but I couldn't do that. That wasn't true healing, and if there was a chance to stop more suffering at Ivan's hands, I had to help.

That was all I needed to remember when I doubted myself.

My wolf suddenly surged forward. I let out a sound of discontent, rubbing my chest as my head began buzzing. My wolf had been hidden for so long that having her so vibrant and powerful inside of me was frustrating at times.

We hadn't fully learned to coexist again. I could feel she wanted to shift, but that wasn't possible. I wasn't ready to be that vulnerable with so many eyes around. More so, the color change in my wolf felt significant—something to keep quiet for now.

Unfortunately, I realized too late that it wasn't really about my wolf.

*"Child of shadows and moonlight."*

The world around me swarmed with darkness as a voice echoed loudly in my head. I gasped under the pressure of pure, raw magic as a cold wind whipped past me. The taste of power—of Nyxarra—but something even *more* filled the air. Silence rang in my ears, and my eyes leaked with tears before I finally landed on a hard, cold floor.

At first there was nothing, but slowly my vision filled with a dim light that highlighted thick bars that disappeared up into the sky. Behind them stood Nyxarra, her chains broken and on the floor. She stared at me, a single hand extended.

Was this what her words from before had meant? *"You freed me from my chains, but I am still held prisoner."*

Trying to find my footing, I stood and walked forward, but the liminal space in front of me seemed to stretch and stretch, her name for me echoing on repeat in a soft whisper. There was fear threaded through her voice, and I could feel something else moving behind the bars, the sound of shuffling causing my stomach to sink.

When I fell to my knees, realizing I wouldn't reach her like this, I saw it.

Two gigantic shadows shifted behind her, their

forms abstract yet terrifying. I could feel their gaze. I could feel malice leaking off of them.

"Help me," she whispered, her eyes widening in horror as a massive hand came down on her. A physical shockwave radiated through the room, her scream ripping through the air as I was thrown out of the vision.

Voices and hands surrounded me, my mates asking me in low and urgent tones what happened and if I was okay. I couldn't answer because no, I wasn't *okay*.

"We were wrong," I said, my voice shaking as I tried to sit up. "It isn't just Nyxarra. There are...others."

# CHAPTER 3

# THORNAR

GRACIE WAS ABSOLUTELY NOT FINE.

I might not know everything about the captivating woman across from me. I didn't know much about god scars or what even had the capability to capture a fucking god. But what I did know? Gracie's soft "I'm fine" as we rushed her back to the privacy of our room was absolute bullshit.

I didn't care who you were, no one was "fine" after a seizure like that. She'd fallen from her chair and nearly cracked her head open on the stone patio.

I watched Gracie closely as she stood, tracking the way her weight shifted. She shouldn't have been on her feet yet.

Despite that, I knew I had to sit back, even if only for a few moments as she gathered herself. Our mate was still learning to trust and open up to us, and while

I wanted to demand answers, I also knew that it could have the opposite effect.

"Ravik and Basir will be back soon. They just wanted to update everyone on the vision so we can move the timeline forward," I said when I saw her eyes roving the room. I leaned back against the counter, watching her move through the kitchen like she'd done it a thousand times before. Opening cabinets. Pulling down bowls. Measuring without a second thought.

"Okay," she mumbled, completely occupied in thought. I decided to just watch her work, curious what she planned to make.

For the next hour, I watched Gracie move like an artist. She lined ingredients across the island in neat rows, flour dusting her fingers as she kneaded and mixed, her focus narrowed on the task in front of her. The chaos from lunch—the darkness, the gods, the way her body had hit the floor—seemed at odds with the steadiness in her hands.

There was only a slight pause when she reached for the wrong cabinet, her brow furrowing before she corrected herself and kept going. She didn't miss a beat. Part of me wished she'd rearrange the whole damn kitchen just to make it hers. She deserved to claim space like that. To take something and bend it to her comfort.

A softness settled in her expression as she handled

the ingredients, a quiet contentness. But it didn't reach her eyes. It wasn't until she placed a mound of dough underneath a cloth for the second time and stepped back that she seemed to register that we had been sharing the space in silence.

"I should make something else for dinner—"

"Gracie, come here." My voice made her tense, but I knew it wasn't about me as much as the questions she thought I would ask.

She hesitated for half a second before stepping into my space.

"Sorry, I was caught up in my own head about everything going on and I lost track of ti—"

I brushed a finger over her lips, and she closed her eyes in frustration.

"You don't owe me an explanation for not wanting to talk," I said. "I am curious about what has you so wrapped up in thought, though."

Gracie let out a long exhale before deflating, her head dropping as I resisted the urge to pull her completely against me.

"I just don't understand *why.*"

"Why what?" I frowned.

"Why...me?" She opened her eyes and held mine. "Why would she pick me? Why out of everyone that follows her would she pick me...*us*, actually? Why make us her champions? And what does this god scar mean for us?"

It meant we were mates but so much more. Before I could answer, though, she continued.

"And who is behind the gates? Why do we think we can go against Ivan, let alone the gods? Just...why? Why for any of this, Thornar? I just don't get why she would choose me."

By the time she was finished, there were tears in her eyes. My heart clenched painfully, needing to fix her pain and confusion. Unfortunately, my solution for fixing it included the violence that she no doubt feared would soon come to pass.

Pulling her forward gently by the waist, I brushed some flour off her cheek before speaking honestly. "I don't know. I don't know why she chose you or us. I can guess, though. I'm sure she saw the same strength I see, little flame. But I don't know for sure. I just know she didn't make a mistake."

Gracie inhaled softly before moving to rest her head in the crook of my neck. My hands smoothed over her waist as I held her against me. I managed to keep my thoughts calm, not violent, despite the rage that threatened to rise up at Gracie not being happy in every way possible. I knew she would feel it if I let it through.

"What I do know," I finally offered, "is that we have options, especially with traveling. In Nightstar Flight territory, on the west coast, there is an institute. If there are answers, they will be there."

Gracie pulled back, her gaze filling with hope. "What type of institute?"

"I believe it's part of the university, but it acts more as a library with archives, high-level scholars, and lots of research. My sister goes every few months. If we can get into their archives, maybe we can get a feel for where this started and how a god could even end up imprisoned."

"You're right, that would be a good place to start," she murmured.

When a timer went off, she moved out of my arms as I tried to hide the rumble that threatened to escape my chest. It was easy when Gracie was against me to forget.

To forget the way I needed her close at all times. To forget how easily that need slipped past reason when it came to my mate.

I watched as she placed the bread in the oven before looking around the kitchen with a renewed interest and lightness, my words seeming to have their intended effect. So why wasn't she back in my arms?

"This is a beautiful kitchen. I've never cooked anywhere like this."

"I'm guessing you've cooked a lot?" I asked.

"Yeah...it was actually my job," she said with a sad smile. "Every night for Ivan and his men."

My vision flashed red. The idea of her being forced to cook for any man, let alone that bastard, was unacceptable. That wasn't her fault, though, and I knew she was watching for my reaction. "I can't wait to taste it."

Pushing off the counter, I walked toward my little flame and took her hand, nodding toward the living room. I already had an old show going, but I wanted nothing more than to just sit next to her, to take the quiet moment while we had it.

Gracie seemed to love the idea because the minute I sat down and pulled her toward me, she melted into my side and pulled a blanket over us. She may not have realized it yet, but I could feel the tension leaving her, hour by hour, while in the safety of our home. Thirty minutes later I realized that she was breathing deeply and had fallen asleep.

After everything her body had just gone through, this was what she needed.

The door clicked open, and I slowly turned my head to signal to Ravik and Basir to be mindful of her sleeping.

"What's that smell?" Ravik asked quietly, looking around in confusion. The scent was mouthwatering, the fresh baked bread making our home feel like it'd been wrapped in a warm fucking blanket.

Basir was already at the oven, looking through the glass. "Did she make this?"

"Yeah. I think it's almost done, but I didn't want to wake her up."

"It's fine." She sighed contently, her eyes fluttering open. "I shouldn't sleep anyway, and I want to see if you like the bread."

I had zero doubt we would love it.

A few minutes later, as she pulled the bread from the oven, I entertained her with a story of when my sister had tried to bake bread and nearly burned down the kitchen. The minute a slice of bread with butter was put in front of me, though, my attention was captured. It was easy to see the artistry and skill it took to pull off something that appeared to have come right out of a bakery.

Even so, I still didn't expect the reaction I would have when I took a bite. The taste was fucking amazing, and I couldn't help but add a "holy shit" as Gracie's smile grew. I didn't even bother listening to Basir's reaction or Ravik's, who grabbed a second piece, because I was so busy enjoying the delighted smile on her face.

"This is amazing, little flame," I told her seriously. "Best bread I've ever had."

"Stop it," she teased, her cheeks pink.

"I'm serious." I lost my smile. "This is real talent, Gracie."

"It's damn good," Ravik agreed. "We almost never cook besides the occasional breakfast. You are welcome to take over the kitchen any time."

Gracie's eyes lit up. "You wouldn't care? If I added or moved stuff around?"

"We would love it," I said as Basir nodded sharply.

I wasn't sure what about our words affected her so much, or maybe Gracie was just realizing how serious we were, but the heaviness of the day lifted as we ate dinner the other two had brought back and finished damn near an entire loaf of bread. It wasn't until a yawn broke from Gracie's mouth that I realized how exhausted she had to be.

Slipping from the room, I went into her suite to get it ready, closing the windows and turning on the bath to the correct temperature. It may have been presumptuous to draw her a bath, but she had lived without comfort for so long that I wasn't about to question my instinct to do so.

When I walked back into her room, I found Gracie putting something away in her closet and offering me a curious look. I nodded toward the bathroom before placing a kiss on her forehead and leaving her to it. Mostly because if I thought about her naked, I wouldn't be able to leave.

Back in the main room, I found Basir and Ravik in the middle of a serious conversation.

"What's the plan?"

"We don't know yet. Intel is set to arrive tonight," Ravik said. "It's possible we'll have to leave as early as tomorrow."

"Shit," I murmured. I hated that we'd be so rushed, especially when Gracie was finally getting settled.

"If not tomorrow, then the next day," Basir said. "We have five territories to cover in twenty days."

I nodded sharply. "I'm going to check on a few things before we leave."

I didn't wait for a response before pulling on boots and a jacket. If we were going to be gone for the better part of a month, there was some shit I needed to lock down.

"You want us to double shift numbers?" Commander Dain asked as I looked up from the somewhat disorganized desk. The third floor of the compound was designated for our units, and we had an office that really only Basir used. It was why he hated when I came down here and messed up his organized shit.

It was also entirely too far from Gracie, and I wasn't sure why this man was repeating something I'd already made clear.

"Yes. For the next week. After that, I want you to start giving units a day or two off in between to rest. I also instructed the trainers to focus on combat readiness rather than general training."

The older commander stared at me, frowning. "This about the Cold Moon Pack?"

"Does it matter if it is?"

"I just think it's fair to know what we're walking into."

I studied his expression for a long moment before offering, "Yes. It is."

"And the individuals brought from there? Is that why we are facing conflict?"

"No. We are facing conflict because Ivan is messing in shit that he doesn't know how to handle." I paused. "And because he hurt Gracie."

Dain leaped at the opportunity. "The woman who's been accompanying you, I assume?"

"Yes. My mate."

"I see. Then we will await your direction beyond current orders."

With a quick salute, he was off.

When I was finally done tying up all the loose ends I could before our absence, I stood and made my way from the room, only stopping when I heard muffled whispers through a barracks door.

"I'm telling you, it's because of her. There is no threat. They're just tossing us into their fucking problem because they found their mate."

"I've heard Ivan is pretty fucking brutal, but I agree. It does seem out of nowhere."

"I don't want to fight a war for some wh—"

I kicked the door open with my boot, leaving it to

swing on its hinges. The three gathered soldiers sat frozen in the middle of their card game to stare at me in shock before quickly gathering their wits to stand at attention.

"Don't finish that sentence," I advised flatly, one of the men turning a sickly shade of green.

"Are we going to have a problem following orders?" I asked each of them calmly. "Has your allegiance flown because you don't understand every minute detail of what's going on?"

"It's not—"

"It is," I said evenly. "You have no idea what is going on with the Cold Moon Pack, nor do you understand why we are moving against them. So I highly suggest you shut your fucking mouth before it gets you in trouble. Understand?"

"Yes sir," the men said in unison.

"I don't want to hear another word out of any of your mouths about our mate. If I do, if I hear you utter one syllable—" I spoke in a cold, hard whisper. "Fighting Ivan's sickly pack is the last thing you'll need to worry about."

"Yes sir."

I turned toward the door, resisting the urge to pull my gun just to scare the living hell out of them. My wolf had other ideas as he howled over the idea of anyone even alluding to our mate as anything but absolute perfection. I was thankful that I had a hold on him. After all, slaughtering our own soldiers wasn't great for morale.

As I passed one of the officer's suites, I peeked my head in. "The three in that room."

"What did those bastards do now?" Sergeant Rigg asked gruffly, almost making me smirk.

"Assign them to the first unit out when we deploy."

"Got it." He sighed, shaking his head. "Absolute dumbasses."

The walk back home was long, the cool night air of the Ironsun territory nearly silent. I knew Gracie would most likely be asleep, but I still wanted to see her.

When I walked inside, I walked straight past Basir and Ravik and into Gracie's bedroom. She slept in the middle of her bed, wrapped in blankets, her red hair spread around her.

"Hey, we have to talk," Ravik called from down the hall.

"When do we leave?" I asked, begrudgingly walking back into the living room, finding Basir already in the process of gathering bags.

"First thing in the morning."

So much for giving Gracie time to get settled.

# CHAPTER 4
# GRACIE

The balcony doors swung open silently as I stepped out into the bright morning sunlight.

A cool wind brushed over my skin, and I tugged my robe tighter around me. The sky was a brilliant shade of cornflower blue, white clouds drifting lazily over the mountains, and the crisp, clean air was something I would probably never fully get used to.

For a moment, I just stood there before stepping to the railing.

Unlike the first time I'd woken here and came to stand on the balcony, I felt no confusion or panic. No fear. No unease. Just awe and a steady sense of growing calm as I got used to living in Ironsun's territory.

My fingers wrapped tighter around the tea mug I'd found next to my bed as I took a long sip, peppermint blooming across my tongue. *I knew we would have to leave soon, but every part of me was pushing back.*

I was finally comfortable, and that wasn't something I was ready to sacrifice so easily.

I hadn't realized, until I started living in the world—truly *living* in it—how numb I'd become. The silence that had infiltrated our pack when the Cold Moon Pack invaded was oppressive and harsh. Here, it was a peaceful luxury I'd never expected from life.

I hadn't expected *them* either. It would take time for me to fully come to terms with all of this—my mates, this new life, the idea that it could truly be mine. Still, I was adjusting faster than I would have expected.

My gaze drifted downward, drawn to movement below. A small group of soldiers trained in the court-yard, their motions sharp and controlled, while civilians moved through the yard with easy conversation and quiet laughter. No one hesitated. No one waited.

They just...lived.

My fingers tightened around the mug once more as the realization settled in. A slow breath left me as my shoulders eased, something deep in my chest loosening.

No one was watching me.

...well.

Except for maybe Basir.

And somehow, that didn't make me nervous at all.

I didn't need to turn to know he was there. I could hear him, feel the brush of his wolf against mine as he moved in close behind me. His right hand rested on the balcony railing, somehow completely taking over my space without even touching me.

Tilting my head up, I stared into his emerald gaze as he studied my face intently, seeming to gauge my emotions before dropping his eyes to the tea in my hands.

"I'm glad it was still warm."

Had he gotten it for me? I turned slowly to face him. "It's perfect. Although I may have slept a bit longer than planned."

It had to be almost ten at this point.

He nodded slowly before looking out toward the mountains, his expression tinged with frustration. "We don't need to leave before you're ready, glow. Take your time."

My pulse quickened with a sudden rush of tension flooding my body. "Leave?"

Basir's gaze moved back to mine as he spoke in a quiet, relaxed tone—as if trying not to worry me. "We received intel about Ivan's plans and the steps he's been taking."

"Yeah?" I whispered, anxious about what he'd say next.

"They've pulled most of the territory into the Northgrove compound and started moving people out of Grimfur Skulk territory. Our soldiers think the numbers are well into the thousands."

At first, Basir's words didn't fully register. Then my eyes widened, my mouth dropping open. "From the other territory as well?"

"Continuously bussing people out," Basir confirmed sadly. "Gracie?"

My chest felt like it was going to explode, and my hands shook around my mug. Somehow, the fact that Ivan was pushing beyond the Cold Moon Pack territory made it all so much worse. It wasn't just isolated to his current victims. He was expanding, and it would never be enough for him.

Ivan would take and take, and my newfound safety and security would end up as dust. I was spiraling, panic clawing its way up my throat. But what about all those people? What would we do when he came here and spread his blight on the land? *This was supposed to end where it had started—the Cold Moon Pack.*

"Ivan will never let me be free," I whispered. "I can't be safe in a world with him in it."

Basir's reaction was immediate, a deep rumble breaking from his chest. I wanted to press my ear to it —to listen to the comforting sound and absorb the protective aura he presented.

But he hadn't touched me, and I didn't want to assume—

Basir's hand came up to my cheek, his thumb

brushing just beneath my eye before his grip shifted, steady but careful, to pull me closer.

There wasn't any hesitation.

Just certainty.

Even if the look in his eyes said he wasn't sure how to handle what I was feeling, the way he touched me didn't. One of his hands slid to the back of my neck, not forcing—just there—as his forehead pressed to mine.

That deep rumble didn't stop. If anything, it strengthened.

When I'd been with Thornar in the kitchen yesterday, it felt easy to express my thoughts—almost as if his warmth had coaxed it out of me. With Basir, it was different. His quiet restraint and cool distance pulled answers from me because I felt like I *had* to tell him. The pure intensity of his will through our bond tugged the words from me.

"I just started to feel safe." My voice seemed weak even to me, and I kicked myself internally. The last thing I wanted was for my mate to see me like that. "Now he's going to spread through all of Thornfell, and what we're trying to do just feels...impossible."

Basir didn't interrupt. His thumb brushed beneath my eye again, slow and deliberate, before settling against my cheek, steady and grounding.

"I don't want to face him. I don't want to have to feel that fear again..." My breath hitched. "And I feel guilty about that, because it's the only way to stop him. To save everyone he's trapped."

The moment the words were out there, something in me eased. Relief and guilt tangled together, impossible to separate.

"I could tell you to stay here while we handle it, but I know you won't." Basir's voice stayed low and steady, his breath cool against my skin. "You're going to face it head-on. I can't promise it will go the way we want—"

I swallowed, dread curling in my stomach.

"But I can promise you this." His thumb brushed along my cheek again. "We'll do everything we can to make sure Ivan doesn't survive this. He won't be there to be something you fear…and we're never letting you be a prisoner again."

I didn't move for a long moment, soaking and savoring in his promise. I so badly wanted to believe him, even if my hope still felt fragile.

"I can also promise you that we won't leave until you are ready."

Having that control over my future, even knowing we had to leave, meant everything.

"He's right." Ravik's rough voice broke through the quiet, cutting the fragile stillness. Still in Basir's arms, I turned my head to look at him. "Everything else can wait."

I appreciated the sentiment, I really did…but I also

knew the truth. Time was everything when it came to stopping Ivan.

"Where exactly are we going? All of the territories?"

"Nearly," Ravik said. "Everywhere except for the Grimfur Skulk and Cold Moon Pack. We've sent word ahead of us, so they're expecting our arrival. I'm hoping it'll make convincing and negotiating easier."

"I think your testimony, glow, will be the most important," Basir said seriously.

I swallowed, feeling a prickle of pride at his words. Unlike with Ivan, I wasn't being brought along to be shown off or bargained with—I was going because I played a part in this.

"That is a lot of travel," I murmured. "Where first?"

"Nightstar Flight." Ravik approached, reaching out to tilt my chin up and examine my expression fully. "West coast. It holds the archives that Thornar mentioned."

I nodded, a surge of hope moving through me as Thornar joined us, leaning in the doorway. "The Solkaran Archive. My sister plans on coming with us."

"And Banthor."

That made me smile. I didn't fully understand the dynamic between Thornar's sister and Ravik's brother yet, but I had a feeling it would be interesting to travel with them.

The lighter moment lingered for a second longer

before reality settled back in, the weight of what was coming next pressing in on me.

I drew in a slow breath and stepped back from Basir's hold. "I should get ready."

"Take your time, little flame," Thornar said as I passed him.

Somehow, their relaxed attitudes as they broke into quiet conversation only made me want to go faster. Probably because I knew they were doing it for me.

Knowing that we would be traveling, I made sure to take a long shower, savoring it, unsure what conditions would be like on the road. I even took the time to dry my hair and apply some light skincare products that had been left out for me. I didn't know what half of them did, but after not using anything on my face for so long, it felt good.

It reminded me of the tinctures my mom used to keep in our bathroom—ones she'd handmade from the herbs in our garden.

After my shower, I pulled on a fitted long-sleeve shirt in a muted purple, the fabric soft against my skin as I tucked it into high-waisted black trousers. Practical boots followed before I pulled on a light, tailored jacket that would keep me warm.

When I left the bathroom and stepped into the closet, I realized pretty quickly that my mates had already packed. A good amount of the clothing was absent from the shelves.

"Already packed your stuff," Ravik said.

I smiled up at him. "You mean the stuff I'm borrowing," I said, a hint of teasing in my tone that had him narrowing his eyes.

I couldn't help it, though. There was no way I would admit to owning any of these clothes. They were far nicer and more expensive than anything I'd worn before.

Instead, I was choosing to see them as a gift. Or something I was just borrowing.

I stepped out of my room, the door clicking softly as Ravik and I moved down the hallway. For a brief second, the memory hit me—being marched through a different set of halls, wrapped in stiff clothing, my body already bracing for Ivan's cruel words on the way to the Thornfell Trade Conference.

This felt nothing like that.

I turned into the foyer, my gaze lifting instinctively to the stained-glass ceiling. Light filtered through it in fractured colors, spilling across the stone floor and softening the space. The hall stretched out ahead, lined with doors I now knew led to bedrooms.

I glanced left as the other two joined us, my gaze drifting back to the main living area. The wall of glass poured light into the space, the polished wood and soft seating giving it that same lived-in warmth I'd noticed before.

"Ready to go, little flame?" Thornar asked.

My hand paused on the handle as I considered his question. I wasn't sure if I was ready...but I was the one choosing to walk out that door.

No one was dragging me.

"Yes." I pushed the door open and stepped forward, ready to face Ivan head-on.

# CHAPTER 5
# GRACIE

THE LAST TIME I'd been on a jet, I hadn't been focused on the details; I'd been focused on surviving. On trying to make myself as small as possible to avoid Ivan's wrath or Marek's intense stares and obscene comments. I'd been trying to gather any information I could about the outside world, even if it was delivered through Velina.

This time, though—this time I could actually take it in.

The jet was huge, even larger than Ivan's. The interior stretched out in a series of plush seating areas instead of tight rows. Soft leather chairs faced one another near the front, while a longer couch sat further back, the low lighting and steady hum of the engines creating a space that felt quiet and contained.

Basir sat across from me, his hands folded over his

abdomen as he stared out the oval window, the afternoon light bright compared to the cozy cabin. Ravik sat beside me, leaning into the aisle to speak to his brother in the back with Elowen, while Thornar lounged across from me, completely at ease.

Everything about this kind of luxury was foreign to me, but I loved the quiet and peace that came with it. I pulled the blanket that had been placed over my lap closer, allowing my body to melt into the leather chair beneath me.

I didn't mean to fall asleep, but my eyes grew heavy as the adrenaline from leaving the Ironsun territory seeped out of my system. The entire car ride to the airport I'd been on edge, feeling as though something bad was waiting just outside my new sanctuary.

Instead, I'd been met with a view of the lush, mountainous landscape—the homes nestled into nature outside the city, the small villages filled with movement and life as people went about their day. It reminded me of the village I'd come from.

The memory softened something in my chest, the tension slowly unwinding as the steady hum of the jet filled the silence. My grip loosened on the blanket, and my eyes slipped shut before I could stop them.

WHEN NYXARRA'S *magic reached out to me this time, it was a gentle call. Coaxing. Welcoming enough that I found* myself searching for her, the darkness of my subconscious shifting into the cavernous room that held her cell. Except... it was different.

The room was filled with a smoky fog, and above us, stars twinkled down, shadows moving quietly in the corners. I made my way across the space, not expecting to reach her...but I did.

Something about our connection had shifted. She felt more real now, more solid, like everything around us had come into clearer focus. Or maybe it was just how intently she was looking at me.

Suddenly nervous, I came to an abrupt stop. Nyxarra stood over ten feet tall, cloaked in black, the shadows behind her shifting and dancing under her magic. I couldn't see her face, but two moonlit eyes stared at me, tracking my every movement. Despite the softness of her call, I couldn't help but feel the weight of her power pressing down on me.

"You come willingly now, child of shadows and moonlight."

Nyxarra's voice filled the space, the ground trembling beneath me as chills prickled across my skin. I wasn't sure I even had a voice—let alone know how to answer her—but somehow, I managed.

"I didn't mean to fight it before," I said honestly. "I just never expected to talk to you."

I hadn't even been sure she, or any of the gods, existed until recently.

*"You did not free me purposefully, I know. Your actions, however, have sent ripples through the shadows. They have altered what was once set in stone."*

*That didn't sound good.*

*"I'm not sure what you need me to do. I want to help, but I know I haven't freed you completely."*

*"My freedom pales in comparison to the blood that will spill at that revolting creature's hand." The words came out like a growl, and my eyes widened. "You must stop him. You must stop him and the one who controls him."*

*"Do you mean Ivan?"*

*"I do not care for the mortal's name," she snarled. "He believes he can use me for his worship—to kill my children!"*

*The room shook under the force of her anger, and I fought to keep my composure as true fear threatened to rise.*

*"Who—who controls him? Who controls Ivan?"*

*Nyxarra fell silent, her anger receding into something colder.*

*"The one who has been pulling his strings. Feeding him power... Two have been imprisoned here. One brought me forth, and the other used me."*

*A pause.*

*"You may trust one of them. One of them will help you."*

*"How do I get their help—"*

. . .

"Gracie!"

Elowen's panicked voice ripped me from the dream.

My eyes snapped open, my heart galloping in my chest as I inhaled sharply, trying desperately to pull in air. Disorientation and dizziness hit me all at once as my mates spoke in low, concerned tones, trying to figure out what was happening. My hands shook as I clutched the blanket in my lap, forcing myself to focus until I found Elowen's gaze.

"You were seizing and talking in your sleep. What happened?" she demanded. "Was it..."

"It was Nyxarra again," I said, my voice still unsteady. "But it was different this time. She wasn't... breaking through. She was there, waiting for me. She said something's changed—that my actions had changed fate—and that Ivan isn't acting alone. That someone's controlling him. She mentioned two gods being held with her...and that one of them might help us."

My explanation immediately sent everyone in the jet into a full-blown discussion of possibilities, but I could barely hear them. Instead, the overwhelm of speaking to a literal god sat heavy in my chest. My eyes squeezed shut before I forced them open again, looking out the window and trying to ground myself. We were already descending, the plane preparing to land.

"*Lux mea.*" Like a moth to a flame, I turned toward Ravik. Whatever he saw on my face made his jaw clench.

"I'm fine."

"You're not, and I can't fucking stop her from hurting you. It's infuriating."

It also meant I ended up not being able to ask Nyxarra everything I needed. But would I be able to stand by as my mates' were physically injured just so they could talk to a god? I honestly didn't think so.

I melted into his side as I listened to Elowen.

"I'm glad we'll be able to visit the archives," she confessed. "I may know a lot—but *this* is out of my wheelhouse. I'm glad she gave you more than just cryptic messages."

I nodded in agreement.

"We need to find out about these other gods," Thornar added.

"I would assume it's the two unnamed gods," Banthor said. "If she didn't name them...it could be them."

"That's a great point," Elowen agreed enthusiastically, a proud grin pulling at her lips. Was he right? Was it possibly the unnamed gods?

A soft light and chime filled the cabin, signaling that everyone should get into their seats. Banthor and Elowen stepped away as I looked across to Basir, who was watching me closely, his fingers twitching as if tempted to reach for me.

"The Nightstar Flight territory..." I drew in a breath, trying to shake myself from the vision and focus on the present. "Known for agriculture and led by Alpha Haiden Murphy, a dragon shifter."

"Studied up?" Thornar mused, attempting to lighten the mood.

"Sort of," I admitted. "They made me before going to the trade conference."

Thornar let out a low rumble as Ravik shook his head in my peripheral, not loving that answer. I leaned forward to look out the window, knowing that if they knew the truth about that plane ride, they would be even more upset.

As the jet descended, the coastline came into view in breathtaking detail.

Steep cliffs rose straight from the ocean, waves breaking hard against the rocks. Structures were built into the cliffs themselves, extending outward in layered sections of stone and glass, with bridges spanning the gaps between.

Domed rooftops caught the sunlight, flashing gold against the surrounding greenery, and terraced levels carved into the cliffs held dense vegetation. The architecture followed the natural shape of the coast instead of forcing itself onto it.

It was *gorgeous*.

"This is beautiful," I said, completely in awe.

"Just wait until you see the city." Basir's voice carried a soft promise that surprised me. I didn't fully understand what he meant until we had disembarked, settled into a large, dark SUV waiting for us at the airfield, and started the drive toward the city in the distance.

The road we followed curved along the cliffs, moving inland and upward through the territory. All of our eyes—except for Ravik's, who drove—were fixed on the passing landscape in the quiet comfort of the car.

The land rolled past in layered terraces, rows of trees and greenery blurring together between stretches of stone. People moved through the fields, carrying baskets and calling to each other as they worked.

Homes were tucked into the hillsides, and along the edges of the terraces, close enough now that I could see open windows, were shaded balconies and signs of a comfortable life in every direction.

The world felt...so much bigger than I'd been led to believe.

"You said Alpha Haiden knows we're coming?" Banthor asked, turning in his seat to look out the back window.

"We sent word," Ravik said.

"That explains the escort."

Turning fully in my seat, I saw what he was talking about. The road around us had cleared, and three blacked-out SUVs followed closely in our wake.

I knew it was probably normal, if not polite, to receive an escort. Still, it felt like we were in trouble. My hands tapped restlessly until Basir covered them with his, the weight and warmth pulling a quiet sigh of relief from me.

It wasn't enough to fully relax, but it was enough to let me focus on the world around me.

The capital city was something else. If I thought the land around it was impressive, it didn't even come close to this.

As we moved closer to the center, the buildings grew larger and more intricate, pale stone rising up with arched windows and columns. Bridges and elevated walkways connected everything, stretching between levels so people could move easily across the different heights.

Green banners marked with a gold dragon crest hung from buildings and entryways, shifting in the wind. The streets were busy, people moving steadily along the main paths, the whole place alive in a way I couldn't look away from.

At the highest point of the city stood the building I assumed we were heading toward, where Alpha Haiden lived. It rose above all others, with wide terraces, tall columns, and open balconies that over-looked both the city and the ocean.

"Not only an escort..." Elowen leaned forward to look out the window. "But the Alpha herself coming to greet us."

As we pulled into the circular drive and the car came to a stop, I realized Haiden Murphy was already waiting at the entrance, surrounded by other Flight members. Even from this distance, there was something about her that drew the eye.

As we stepped out of the vehicle, that feeling only grew.

She was striking, her dark eyes like burning embers beneath strong brows. Her sun-kissed skin caught the light, gold woven through her hair and marking her skin. Everything about her was powerful and intentional. She didn't seem afraid of us, or anything else, and the loose red dress draping around her underscored that.

"Welcome to Nightstar Flight, Ravik Gentry." She inclined her head in greeting as Ravik rounded the car and slipped an arm around me, her gaze shifting down to me. "And you—I remember you."

I couldn't help the wince that crossed my face.

Her formality slipped as we reached the foot of the stairs, her gaze flicking across my features. "Am I correct in remembering you accompanied Ivan Rivers?"

"Imprisoned by him," Ravik corrected. I was thankful for his words, cutting through the noise of my insecurity and the feeling of being unsure on how to answer her.

Her eyes widened before she nodded in understanding. "That doesn't surprise me. I am relieved to see you here. What's your name?"

When she'd asked me that question at the TTC, Ivan had stopped me from answering. But this time Ravik simply squeezed my waist in encouragement.

"Gracie Holloway."

# CHAPTER 6
# RAVIK

I BEGAN ASSESSING our safety from the moment we stepped into the guest suite.

The Nightstar Flight were allies in the most traditional sense, but being under their roof came with risks. I tracked Gracie as she moved about, her attention drifting over a space that was entirely too polished. The room was a mix of dark stone and glass stretching across the far wall of the living area.

One entrance. One exit. No balconies.

*I didn't like that.*

I might not have officially taken on the role of Alpha for the Ironsun Pack yet, but I didn't do well in territory that wasn't mine. And I liked relying on other Alphas even less.

We just didn't have a choice.

"Well, this is nice," Elowen said as she walked

down a narrow hallway. "Looks like the bedrooms are split. Three this way and—"

"Three over here!" Thornar called back.

Gracie was still studying the carefully arranged furniture in the common area. Low seating at the center, open space on all sides.

Comfortable enough for most. Not for her. And not for me.

"You doing alright?" Banthor asked, approaching from my right. Despite his usual easy disposition, he was on edge—especially with his mate here.

"Not entirely," I said. "I'm surprised you came."

"Are you actually, though?" he mused, his gaze tracking Elowen, who'd joined Gracie in the sitting room.

"No," I admitted. "I suppose not." I glanced at him. "Are you two finally going to figure your shit out?"

My brother went still. I felt his wolf shift just beneath the surface, bristling at the comment—at anything that touched on him and his mate. When he finally looked away and shrugged, I had my answer.

The delay wasn't on his side.

"I could ask why you haven't marked Gracie yet," he said, his voice edged with irritation. "But I won't."

I didn't respond. I had no interest in killing my brother today, and the idea of anyone speaking about Gracie like that, about her being claimed, was enough to push me.

"Our bond isn't typical," I said instead. "It was sudden. Unexpected. I'm not rushing her." *And I wasn't letting her go.*

In the short time we'd spent together, something in me had locked into place—protective and possessive in a way that left no room for doubt. *Lux mea.* Everything about her was mine to guard.

Thornfell would change for her after the war. I would make sure of it.

"Fair," Banthor muttered, the tension easing from his shoulders. "Elowen and I are heading to the archives during dinner. We're not needed at the dinner, so we'll get a lay of the land. Start pulling information."

Elowen stepped up beside him. "He'll take ritual history and political context. I'll focus on magic. The gods. Anything tied to Nyxarra."

"I feel bad you're working already," Gracie said as she approached, slipping her hand into mine. "You just got here. You should rest."

Elowen smiled. "This *is* rest."

As the two of them left, I looked down at Gracie and tipped her chin up. Her cheeks flushed, soft pink spreading across her skin.

"You should rest before dinner. I'll talk to the others about security."

"We do have time before dinner," she agreed, her gaze dropping briefly to my mouth.

A low rumble built in my chest.

I nodded toward the bedrooms. "Go. Before I get distracted, *lux mea.*"

Her flush deepened as she slipped from my grasp with a small smile. I held my position, forcing myself to stay put.

"Do we think Alpha Haiden is actually going to make a decision over dinner?" Thornar asked.

I considered that.

During our conversation as Alpha Haiden led us to the guest suite, she kept her cards close to the vest. She acknowledged why we were here—the situation, the rumors—but didn't commit beyond that.

So would she decide over dinner? Or would we need to push, even disclosing our issues with The Eight? Possibly. Or she'd drag it out.

More politics. More delay.

"I'm not sure," I admitted. "She may want more time."

"Could be a power play," Basir agreed.

"Either way," Thornar drawled, "I want to sweep the area near the dining room. Outside the property too." He shrugged. "I trust them as much as I trust any of our allies."

Which wasn't much.

"I'll come with," Basir said. "I want to see the kitchen."

Even if we found nothing, the message mattered:

we were watching. It was usually enough to make people think twice before doing something stupid.

"Don't take long," I said. "Gracie will worry."

They left a moment later, silence settling over the suite as the door shut behind them. I moved before I thought about it. *Gracie shouldn't be alone.*

Following the pull of our bond, I stepped inside one of the bedrooms down the hall. The door had been left cracked and I found my mate immediately, afternoon light catching in her bright red hair.

Gracie sat on the edge of the bed with her back to me, her posture curved as if she carried something too heavy to set down. Her head was bowed, her earlier curiosity gone.

Through our bond, I felt confusion.

Given what she'd been through, I couldn't blame her. The image of her seizing on the jet surfaced without warning: her body locking, her breath uneven, something tearing through her that I couldn't stop.

I could control almost everything...except for the god trying to reach her in her own damn head.

Taking another step inside, I let the door close softly behind me. Gracie turned and looked up at me, warmth filling her gaze in a way I had come to recognize.

Slowly crossing the room, I knelt on the floor in front of her, bringing my face nearly level with hers.

"Ravik," she whispered, her cheeks turning a soft pink.

My hand lifted, slow and deliberate, as I closed the distance between us. Cupping her cheek, my thumb brushed along the high arch of her cheekbone. She didn't flinch from my touch, or any of our touches anymore. She leaned into it instead, her eyes slipping closed.

*Mine.*

The thought was unavoidable. Primal yet...certain. Gracie was mine.

Her breath hitched as I lifted my other hand to mirror the first, framing her face. I held her there, steady between my palms, and let my gaze move over her. At some point since coming in here, she'd changed to accommodate for the warmer weather. The heavier fabric she'd worn earlier was gone, replaced with lounge shorts and a thin tank that left her shoulders bare, the line of her collarbone exposed.

A beam of sunlight lit her skin, catching along the left side of her neck, sliding over her collarbone and down the slope of her shoulder. There the light revealed something I hadn't seen before.

Scars.

They weren't clean. The skin along the left side of her body was uneven, warped where it had healed from an obvious burn. Some areas pulled tight, others rough and ridged, the faint sheen catching the light differently than the rest of her skin.

This hadn't been a surface injury.

My jaw tightened as the realization settled. Someone had done this to her on purpose. It hadn't been an accident—not a fucking chance. My fingers pressed slightly firmer against her cheeks before I forced the tension back, keeping my touch consistent. The anger didn't fade, though.

*I would find out who did it.*

*Lux mea* felt the emotion through our bond. Her eyes opened, searching my face. "What?" she murmured, suddenly nervous.

"Your scars," I said, my voice low and controlled. "Who did this?"

Her expression shifted, something haunted appearing. "The soldier who pulled me from the house the night of our capture. They're just...what's left. Much better than before."

My gaze dropped, following the marks to where they disappeared beneath the thin fabric of her tank. The material offered little cover, and I could see that the damage continued underneath. My hands slid from her face, down her neck, until my fingers brushed the hem at her hips. I paused, watching her.

"Let me see."

Gracie hesitated, glancing down at herself. At the simple bra beneath the fabric, at how exposed she already was. Then she nodded, those pink cheeks deepening in color.

"Okay."

I moved slowly, lifting the fabric just enough to reveal more of the damage along her left side. The scars stretched further than I could have imagined, pulling across her ribs and covering half of her back. My fingers hovered, then settled lightly against her skin, careful of the raised edges, the places where it had healed unevenly. Her breath hitched.

"They're beautiful," I said. The rage they inspired was less beautiful, but something in my voice pulled a soft, wounded sound from her.

Her voice shook as she replied, "I don't feel that way."

I wanted to show her she was wrong.

I leaned in slowly, giving her time to pull back. She didn't. Her breath caught instead, her fingers tightening on my shirt.

My mouth pressed to the scars beneath her shoulder, slow and deliberate. Not claiming. Just there. My hand shifted at her side, easing the fabric of her tank higher.

*I could mark her here.*

The thought came sharp and immediate as I traced the scarred flesh. It pulled from something deeper than instinct, something possessive and unrelenting.

My teeth ached with it, my jaw tightening as I forced it back down.

No. That wasn't mine to take. She wasn't territory. She was Gracie, and she was letting me close. That mattered more. When I marked her, it would be in a moment of absolute trust. I buried the impulse beneath the slow, deliberate worship of my mouth on her scars.

I traced lower, toward the curve of her breast. The soft bra she wore did nothing to hide the way her body reacted to my touch, the way her skin pebbled and her nipples hardened. I didn't push further though. I stayed with the scar, my lips following its path, my breath cool against her warming skin.

Her fingers slipped into my hair hesitantly at first, then tightened. "Ravik..." she breathed, the word sounding like a plea.

I lifted my head, our eyes meeting. The heat between us was undeniable, tension building to the point that the control I'd been holding onto began to slip.

I kissed her before I could stop myself.

It wasn't gentle or careful. My mouth took hers, and she answered just as intensely. Her breath caught as she leaned into me, closing the last distance between us. My hand stayed at her jaw while the other slid along her back, pulling her fully against me.

Her hands moved from my chest to my shoulders,

gripping, pulling at my shirt as the kiss deepened. We broke apart, breath unsteady, only to come back together again, harder.

My hand slid lower over the curve of her hip as I guided her onto her back, bracing myself above her. My mouth left hers, trailing along her jaw to her throat. I pressed a kiss to the pulse there, feeling her heartbeat hammer beneath my lips. My teeth grazed the skin, the urge to bite rising again, primal and instinctive. I forced it back, swallowing it down with a low sound against her neck. Gracie arched into me, a soft moan slipping free.

"More, Ravik. Touch me, more," she said, the words muffled against my shoulder.

I knew what she needed. And I knew exactly what I wanted to give her.

My hand slid down her stomach and lower, over the front of her shorts, settling at the apex of her thighs. I could feel the heat of her through the fabric, the soft curve of her body beneath my hand. My own need pressed insistent, but I ignored it.

*This was for her.*

My hand moved in slow circles over her fabric-covered core. She gasped, her body tensing before melting into it, her head falling back as I found a rhythm. My finger pressed and circled over her sensitive clit. Gracie moved with it, rocking subtly against my hand as her legs opened on either side of me.

"Ravik…" she breathed again, a broken chant.

I followed it, kissing my way back to her mouth, taking her lips as my hand kept moving. The fabric between us was a barrier I was starting to hate.

When I broke the kiss, my gaze dropped to my hand before lifting back to her face. Her eyes were half-lidded, dark with need.

"I need more," I said, my voice rough. "Can I?"

She nodded, fast and urgent. "Yes. Please."

I hooked my fingers into the waistband of her shorts, dragging them down with a shift of her hips until they were gone, joining the camisole she'd already shed.

Yet *lux mea* didn't shy away. She stayed where she was, exposed, her gaze locked on mine with a trust that had my heart beating rapidly in my chest.

I didn't rush. I leaned in, kissing her again before moving lower, my mouth finding the cotton of her bra, drawing the peak of her nipple into my mouth.

My hand followed, sliding down her stomach and lower, until my middle finger slid through her slick heat, finding her entrance before gliding higher to the sensitive peak above. I circled there, slow at first, then faster as her breathing broke into ragged pants. Her fingers gripped my arms, nails pressing into my sleeves.

I pulled back far enough to watch every expression

that crossed her face. Every flicker of pleasure. Every clench of her jaw. Every soft sound she made.

*Mine. Absolutely mine.*

I added a second finger, not entering. Just pressing, increasing the pressure. My thumb moved lower, finding a rhythm that completed the motion. Gracie arched into it, her back tightening, her head tipping back. I kept teasing her breasts, drawing small gasps from her as I watched, unable to look away.

"Ravik!"

"I want you to come, *lux mea*," I growled as I kept my fingers moving in a relentless rhythm. My focus was completely on her reactions—the shifts that made her jerk and the ones that made her tremble.

The urge to bite surged back. As she tightened under my hand, I moved to her shoulder, to where her scar met clear skin. My lips parted. My teeth pressed against her flesh—not biting, just holding.

A promise.

Gracie cried out, her hips bucking against my hand. I pulled back, releasing the pressure, replacing it with a kiss. *Not now.*

She was close, trembling, her words breaking apart. "Don't...stop...please..."

*Lux mea*'s climax hit.

Her body seized beneath my hand and she clenched around my fingers, a cry breaking from her throat.

*Fuck.*

Gracie collapsed back against the bed, her body shuddering through the aftershocks. I pulled her into me, my fingers stilling as I withdrew them, denying myself the urge to taste her, to lick her wet heat off my fingers.

Gracie was breathing hard, her entire body flushed pink.

She spoke first after a long, comfortable silence, her voice muffled against my shirt. "You didn't... don't you need to..." Her words trailed, uncertain, like she wasn't sure how to ask.

My own need was an untouched knot, but it didn't matter.

"This was for you," I said, my voice rough.

Everything was.

# CHAPTER 7

# GRACIE

"It's nice to be around people who actually eat," Alpha Haiden mused.

Cole, her mate, huffed a quiet laugh. "Most events in this damn city have nothing but finger food." He dragged a hand through his black-and-silver hair, expression faintly annoyed.

"That doesn't sound enjoyable," Thornar said from next to me. "We eat a lot in Ironsun territory—maybe even more than we should."

There wasn't a piece of food I'd come across that I hadn't liked. And whatever we were eating now, it was melting in my mouth. I'd never get used to such an array of flavors. Despite having cooked almost everyday for the past few years, I hadn't eaten my own creations, outside of a taste here or there, in over a decade.

The bread was still hot when I picked it up from my plate, soft so that it tore in my hands instead of cracking apart like the rations I was accustomed to. Steam curled from the dishes in front of us, the air thick with spices I couldn't name—rich and intense, with something almost sweet beneath it.

I hadn't reached for anything at first, just stared at the feast in front of us. Ravik's thumb pressed lightly into my thigh to gain my attention.

"Eat," he'd said quietly.

So I did, because he said it like I was allowed to. I needed that reminder.

The eight of us—including Haiden, her mate, and two advisors—sat at the table while my mates carried most of the conversation. The two groups exchanged stories about their territories and what was happening with the harvest season underway, stories of festivals and celebrations I'd never even heard of traded easily between them.

I hadn't celebrated Yule in a decade, let alone anything else.

"What do you think of the food, Gracie?" Haiden asked, her expression friendly beneath the amber lights flickering through the dining space. The table we sat around was large, the chairs plush velvet cushions I nearly sank into.

"It's delicious," I said honestly before adding, "It probably helps that I was starving."

I hadn't eaten since this morning. I'd passed out after the...amazing *peak* Ravik had brought me to, and between the lingering heat of his touch, Thornar's closeness, and Basir's gaze from down the table, I hadn't noticed the hunger at all.

Not until now.

"Not feeding you enough, are they?" she teased.

My eyes went wide. "Oh, they are," I said quickly. "I just..." I hesitated. "This is better food than anything I'm used to."

"If you don't mind me asking," one of her advisors said, "where are you from if not Ironsun?" Haiden hadn't introduced her or the woman who sat next to her.

I could tell that the question wasn't merely to satisfy her curiosity, and Ravik's hand tightening on my thigh confirmed it. This wasn't small talk anymore.

"The Cold Moon Pack." My voice was steadier than I expected. "My family and I were forced to join when Ivan River invaded."

Haiden straightened, her attention sharpening fully on me. "Your family—are they still there?"

"No." I took a deep breath, steeling myself. "Both my parents are gone. My brother escaped, but I haven't found him yet." Then my voice cracked as my control slipped. "I was at the Northgrove compound for nearly a decade before we went to the TTC."

"And found your mates," one of the advisors pointed out.

"Yes," I whispered.

Ravik pressed a kiss to the top of my head. "She's ours."

"Well, that explains why you chose to go back to Northgrove. I was surprised when Alpha Kaliyah told me about your plans, but...that makes sense." Haiden nodded slowly. "It makes me wonder...this war..." She trailed off, studying me.

"Is it strategy, or revenge?" she finished, not unkindly.

"Both," Basir said, surprising me.

"There's a personal element," Ravik agreed. "He was at the trade conference to traffic Gracie to another alpha." His hand tightened on my thigh before he continued. "But beyond that, we uncovered something bigger. It's not just the rumors of abuse from those who escaped when we got her out. It's worse."

"Explain," Haiden commanded.

I was thankful for my mates, who moved the conversation forward with ease. As they spoke, I took note of what they chose to tell her—and what they didn't.

"The night we broke into Northgrove, we inter-rupted a ritual," Ravik said. "Gracie was the sacrifice."

The words settled heavily over the table. I didn't react. After so many years of pain, I'd learned not to.

"What type of ritual?" Haiden asked.

"A sacrifice to Nyxarra," I explained. "They did it every month. Every full moon."

Saying it out loud still felt...wrong. How had something like that been allowed to happen? Why had no one stopped them?

"If he's been doing this for nearly a decade—even with proof," Haiden added, offering all of us a pointed look, "why does that involve us? I understand wanting him removed from power, but why the urgency? Why call for support now?"

"Our intel shows he's pulling everyone from his territory and the Grimfur Skulk into Northgrove for a ritual," Basir said.

The table went completely silent. "Everyone?"

"Buses of people," Ravik said. "Thousands."

"*By The Eight*," her other advisor murmured.

"Why?" Haiden asked.

"Power," Thornar said with a shrug. "Who knows. But he has to be stopped. Slaughtering thousands is..." His jaw tightened. "Insane. No matter the reason."

A flicker of something unexpected cut through me at the way they explained all of this without a single mention of Nyxarra's deeper influence, of fate or of the gods. It was a skill that I was only just starting to understand. And somehow I was part of it now. Not just a pawn being moved.

Haiden studied each of us in turn before nodding

slowly, her gaze going distant. "I see why you're concerned."

Then, in the blink of an eye, she refocused. "If we take military action, what kind of threat are we facing?"

"Unstable. But organized enough to be dangerous," Basir said.

"Numbers?"

"Thousands," Ravik answered. "Not all trained. Not all willing. But enough to cause chaos."

"And Northgrove?" Cole asked.

"Fortified," Basir said, "with increased patrols and reinforced inner sections."

"And he's expecting interference," Thornar added. "He knows we won't let this happen."

"What are you asking for?" Haiden said.

Ravik's hand stayed steady on my thigh. "Support, strategic and tactical. Your aerial defenses would give us an advantage."

Cole's mouth curved slightly. "Our skies are *well* protected."

"We know," Ravik said. "That's why we're here."

Silence filled the room once more, but I found my voice. It didn't shake with nervousness this time. "If Ivan completes this ritual, it won't stop at Northgrove. It won't stop anywhere."

Haiden's gaze was completely on mine as I continued. "Even if he kills everyone he's gathered, there's no controlling what comes after. Not with a man like him."

The Alpha looked between us, considering. Then she nodded once. "I'm glad you came to me with this. I may not care for many of the territories, but I care enough about Thornfell to protect the people of the Cold Moon Pack and the Grimfur Skulk from mass slaughter."

I hadn't realized how tightly I'd been holding myself together until that moment.

Hope bloomed in my chest—quiet, cautious.

Maybe this would be possible.

"Tomorrow we'll talk more. For now, rest. Being on the road is never easy," Alpha Haiden said with a friendly smile as we exited the dining room an hour later.

Hope still buzzed in my veins, and despite the discussions about logistics and Ivan's plans, the space felt lighter than before. As we parted ways, I turned toward my mates and offered a small smile. "That... went well?"

"As well as it could have," Thornar agreed. Basir nodded, reaching forward to adjust my sleeve where it had twisted slightly. I'd worn a dark dress for dinner, a soft, deep purple that covered most of my body. Now, with how full and tired I was, I was glad I'd chosen something comfortable.

"I'll take it," Ravik rumbled. "I'm curious what she'll think come morning, after she's had time to think about how she wants to approach this."

"Or what she wants in return," Thornar murmured.

I frowned. I shouldn't have been surprised there was more to consider, but now I wasn't sure her agreement meant as much as I'd hoped.

"There you are!" Elowen appeared from down the hall, her body swallowed by a thick, dark coat that looked like a robe. "I wanted to show you something before bed."

"Where in The Eight did you come from?" Thornar demanded.

"We've been searching for all of you," Banthor said around a yawn. "She wants an early start tomorrow and insists you all know where to go."

Elowen hooked her arm through mine and pulled me away with an eager tug. She dipped her head close, ignoring the men behind us. "How did everything go?"

"I think...I think good?"

"I'll take it," she said enthusiastically. "Now, since you haven't been to the university archives before, it might be a bit overwhelming when you go in tomorrow. But whatever you're looking for, it can be found with the help of an archive keeper."

I didn't understand what she meant until we were standing at the entrance to the archives.

In the evening hours, the tall windows of the archives were dark, the halls between the books and desks quiet, but there was a thrum of power that made the floors and walls shimmer.

This wasn't...this wasn't a normal place.

I could see figures moving through the shelves in the distance, but they didn't quite seem real. The four men behind us kept their distance, but I wondered if my mates saw *them* as well.

"At night, they look like ghosts," Elowen said. "Much better to come during the day. I promise it's wonderful, and after looking around earlier, I'm hopeful we can find some answers."

"I would second that, especially the part about going during the day." A new voice, feminine and edged with soft amusement, came from in front of us.

A woman appeared. Literally *appeared.*

Or she had just moved so fast that she was suddenly there, standing in front of us, drawing a small smile from Elowen.

"Charlie!" Elowen smiled brightly. "You're out late!"

Charlie was taller than me, built long and lean with an effortless grace that felt more fox than wolf. I was almost certain that was exactly what she was. I didn't recognize her scent the way I did with other shifters, especially wolves.

Her skin looked kissed by the sun and her rich brown hair fell in loose waves, threaded with strands that caught the low light like fire. Her eyes were amber, flecked with green, tracking everything. Sharp. Calculating. A sly, almost playful smile curved her lips. Leather wrapped her form in shades of black and brown, fitted for movement and meant to blend into the space around us.

"I could say the same to you, though my reason is a bit more dull." She flashed a quick smile. "Giving a tour?"

"Sort of." Elowen shrugged. "Gracie, this is Charlie. She's a university student at the branch here. Second year, preparing for trials."

Charlie grimaced. "Don't remind me."

"Trials?" I asked, trying to sound relaxed. I didn't often talk with other women like this, easy and teasing.

Her eyes flickered with frustration, though not at me. At least, I didn't think so.

"The university allows anyone to attend for two years. After that you have to compete in the Solkaran Trials to prove your competence and keep your place."

My eyes widened as I looked at Elowen. "Did you have to do that?"

"Um…" Elowen winced. "Sort of? Not the physical part. I was exempt."

Charlie huffed softly. "The Gentry family got her out of it, I heard."

"It's true!" Thornar called out.

Elowen scrunched her nose. "Not all of us are knife-wielding badasses like you. Some of us prefer knowing the closest I'll come to danger is a paper cut."

I caught the smallest flicker in Charlie's eyes before she smiled again. "I get it. Some of us live for the thrill of it. Sneaking around, stealing, fighting bad guys…all the fun stuff."

But it didn't sound fun. Not the way she said it. I didn't think she quite believed her own words.

"Honestly," she added, "I'd take that over this bull-shit I'm studying for now."

As she and Elowen kept chatting, I couldn't help but think that there was something dangerous about Charlie. Beneath the easy smile and the way she slipped into conversation, there was a calculated control. A lethality.

I didn't have that, but I'd seen it before. In my mates.

"Alright, well, I need to get some sleep." She sighed and looked at me with a faint smile. "It was great to meet you, Gracie. I'm sure we'll see each other back in Ironsun territory. I'll be there at the end of the school year."

"It was nice to meet you," I said, though she was already gone, slipping from the room with the same easy, unsettling grace she'd entered with.

"Charlie is great," Elowen said. "Brilliant, actually. And despite her...background, she's risen to the top of her class."

"Her background?" I asked, concern slipping in.

Elowen shrugged. "She grew up different. Not my story to tell."

I understood that. I wouldn't want anyone telling mine without permission.

"She seems nice," I offered.

Elowen smiled. "Oh, she's nice! She's also terrifying. One of the most dangerous contenders this year. No one will train with her here. Not even the teachers."

Oh.

"Which probably means she'll survive the trials," Elowen added, turning to lead us out of the archives. "And succeed. Which is awesome because I need her around. She keeps me company when I visit."

I followed, my gaze drifting back to where Charlie had disappeared. If someone like her was only *expected* to survive...

Then the trials weren't just difficult.

They were deadly.

# CHAPTER 8

# GRACIE

"I THINK our question may have broken the library," I murmured.

The past three hours had dragged. At first, the shadowy figures lingering between the archives' shelves had unsettled me, but now they'd become just another part of the scenery. I still hadn't seen an actual archive keeper, but every time we spoke aloud what we needed, a book would slip free and drift down like it had been waiting. It was fascinating.

It was also a problem.

The second we'd asked about the two 'unnamed' gods, the six of us—Elowen and Banthor included—had become buried under a pile of books. Now, after hours of digging through brittle, dusty pages, I'd hit a wall.

I needed a break and some fresh air.

Luckily, a long corridor stretched from our work area to a terrace overlooking the coastline. The warm afternoon sun settled against my skin, easing some of the tension from my shoulders.

"Possibly," Ravik admitted, stretching his arms over his head. "I know the history of the unnamed gods has always been considered taboo, but you'd think it would be easier to find in a place like this."

Basir made a low sound of agreement, his hand grazing my back as we both looked out over the balcony. The wind against my face had my wolf perking up, a surge of energy rising in me that pushed for release.

"Glow?" Basir prompted, already catching on to the shift in me.

"My wolf wants out," I said. "I haven't shifted since the garden."

"Then shift," Basir suggested. I looked up to see the heat and anticipation in his gaze, and as I weighed the risks...I realized there really weren't any.

"I agree. I think you need to shift as much as possible to get used to it," Ravik added.

"Okay," I murmured, stepping back. Ravik's smile told me he liked the idea more than he was letting on.

This time, when I let go, it wasn't like falling.

It felt like something had opened up before me, and my wolf surged forward to meet it head on. Heat flared from the center of my chest and the world snapped into focus all at once—every sound and scent pressing in on me as my body transformed.

The shift felt effortless as Ravik's grounded strength, threaded in gold, and Basir's dark pull, laced with silver, danced across my skin. Even with Thornar back in the archives I could feel the vibrance of his bright, electric presence. Our bond had grown in power since the last time I'd shifted.

*Except it wasn't just me.*

A small yip of surprise left me as I backed up with urgency, realizing a gigantic black wolf stood in front of me, facing toward Ravik. I was so startled at first that I didn't realize it was Basir until our bond pulsed with fury. He was snarling at Ravik, who was staring at him in blatant surprise.

When I tried to move forward, Basir turned his head and nudged me back, so hard that I nearly tumbled. My wolf let out a huff as Ravik's voice broke through the tension.

"Basir, you need to shift back. Now."

The tone wasn't one I was used to, and it only made Basir angrier, the energy through our bond turning volatile.

"What is going—*shit.*" Thornar's tone darkened as he stepped into the doorway, his gaze landing on Basir, who was crouched defensively in front of me.

My gaze darted between them with panic. I wanted to shift back, but my wolf wouldn't allow it, our focus completely on the intensity moving between my mates and the closeness of them.

"He didn't mean to shift. It happened the minute she did," Ravik explained carefully. "I'm guessing it's because of the bond. I felt a similar pull the first time she shifted."

"So why is he so pissed?" Thornar arched his brow before his gaze slid back to me. "Little flame, you are beautiful."

If my wolf could blush, she would have. Instead, a bark of happiness burst out of me, drawing a chuckle from Thornar. Basir didn't like that, backing me up even further as if trying to hide me from him.

My mate's bright smile disappeared. I didn't like that at all.

"He's defensive because he thinks we're a threat to *our* mate." Ravik emphasized the 'our.' Basir took their momentary distraction of conversation to turn, using his nose to bump me lightly again and back me up further into the corner of the balcony. I let out a frustrated sound but he immediately turned back to face the current 'threat.'

"I think we may need to be careful in the future about where we shift if we're going to be this interconnected," Thornar said seriously.

He was right. If we weren't somewhere safe this could easily become a liability.

"Here's what we're going to do," Thornar said, clapping his hands. "Ravik and I are going to leave—"

"No." Ravik's tone of voice, the power imbued in it, made my wolf want to surge toward him, but Basir was not budging. I even tried to hit him with my paw on the back of the head a few times, but he just ignored it.

"Come on, you know he won't shift back until we do." Thornar gave Basir an exasperated look, then glanced at me. "Little flame, remember when you asked me about being alpha? Why I wouldn't want to be one? This is exactly why."

Anticipation was snapped tight between Basir and Ravik, power and dominance colliding in a silent standoff—and I didn't know how to fix it.

Using my smaller frame, I crouched low and darted forward, slipping between Basir and the railing in a quick, fluid movement. I landed a little unsteady, but the second I turned toward him, his snarl died.

I nudged my nose against his, holding his gaze until the tension slowly melted from his body. I stayed there, keeping his attention on me, until the aggressive edge between the four of us softened into something more familiar.

Suddenly, a soft white glow surrounded Basir, his wolf form disappearing and leaving him as the man I'd spent every day with since being rescued. His emerald gaze looked a bit wild as he stared at me in surprise before looking up at the other two, opening his mouth even though nothing came out.

"Don't think about it too much," Thornar said with a shrug.

"Ravik..." Basir's voice was a bit unsteady as he straightened up. "I had no idea—"

"Just glad you shifted back," Ravik said easily, the tension between them gone.

Feeling as though the problem was resolved, my wolf backed down enough to let go of the reins, allowing me to shift back as well. I stumbled to my feet as Basir caught me around the waist, pulling a smile to my lips.

"I know you didn't mean to shift, but I loved seeing you like that."

Basir gave me a tight nod, but I could feel the near panic surging through his part of the bond. I was realizing that Basir craved control, and shifting without meaning to had clearly shaken him. It reminded me of when he took on the guilt for my vision in front of the Solspire, as if his touch would ever cause me to be in pain.

*This time, though, he wasn't trying to run away afterwards.*

"That shouldn't have happened," he said, his gaze averted and focused on the ground.

My worry for him grew as I buried my head against his chest, hoping to ground him and to give him comfort. All I wanted was to make him feel better.

"Guys!" Elowen's voice echoed down the hall. "I think I found something!"

That was enough to break the moment. We moved toward the door, my hand slipping into Basir's for support. Despite the darkness still drawn across his face, he didn't let go.

When we turned into the archives and made our way back to the table, it was clear Elowen had found the book we were looking for. She held it up like a prize, the cover so worn it was nearly falling off, the pages hanging on by a thread.

"Well, what does it say? Because it sort of looks like every other book in here," Thornar pointed out in amusement. Banthor scowled at him, and Elowen offered her brother a narrowed look.

"I'd never given much thought to how they managed to hide the names of two *entire* gods—after all, not exactly my field of study. But considering this is the *one* book I found them named in, I'd have to guess they got rid of the rest." She shook her head in disappointment. "This book is nearly four centuries old and references The Eight: including the *Father of War and Chaos* and the *Mother of Fur and Claws*."

"Interesting," Ravik said, sitting back. "So these two are the ones no one wants to talk about. Do they have names past their titles?"

"And what did they do that was so terrible?" Thornar asked.

"Especially to get locked up," Basir added. "And to essentially be erased, except in some imagery where their spots are left open."

"Mother of Fur and Claws," I mumbled. Something about that title drew my interest more than the other.

"Vaelithra," Elowen said. The god's spoken name summoned a soft wind that made my skin prickle as it brushed through the archives.

"Weird, but okay…" she continued, her brow frowning in confusion. "The goddess of shifters, pack bonds, and transformation."

Banthor shook his head. "So we erased an entire god that is connected to our literal essence as shifters? Sounds right."

"It is a bit odd," Elowen admitted. "And if that's what she symbolizes, shouldn't we all be 'worshipping' her on a daily basis, even if her name isn't being said?"

No one had an answer to that.

"She didn't just aid in the creation of shifters, she was the one who—and this is only according to *this* text—designed the original pack bonds, hierarchy, and even mate bonds."

If we were right about them being the two who were with Nyxarra, then maybe she had something to do with our unusual mate bond.

"And the Father of War and Chaos?" Ravik asked.

"Kaevorak," Elowen said. "He embodies chaos, war, bloodshed... He was pure destruction, and according to this text, he took part in the unraveling of some of the earliest societies."

"Were gods always so integral to daily life?" I asked, unable to stop myself. "I know they exist, clearly, but for them to affect life so directly...what changed? Why did they withdraw to the point that we never see them?"

To the point that I hadn't known if they were even real or not.

"Maybe whatever led to them being locked away," Thornar suggested as his sister nodded. "Maybe it made the others choose to withdraw too."

"I would assume so," Elowen murmured, finally finding the page she was looking for. "The two of them apparently acted as a pair for most of our history and were the main forces behind the creation of shifters. She built on instinct and unity while he drove society forward through conflict and dominance."

"Then the bastard took it too far?" Banthor assumed.

"Yes. He began encouraging shifters to slaughter for the chaos of it, for the sense of victory rather than survival. To form bonds out of possession instead of unity...and you can imagine how that ended. His influence spread, and it led to widespread war."

"Did she try to stop him?" I asked.

"According to this? She tried, but it wasn't enough, so the other gods stepped in," Elowen explained. "They created a ritual that combined their power to seal the two of them away. I assume they couldn't destroy them—their existence was too fundamental to shifters—but they could imprison them. Nyxarra oversaw and maintained their prison."

Silence settled over us before Elowen added, "This is just one text—a fable, a story. The truth could be different, of course. But it may explain why the other gods pulled back from interacting with the world."

"So how did she end up on the other side?" Thornar leaned forward, his expression sharp with curiosity.

Elowen shrugged. "I'm not sure, but I'd guess one of them either tricked her or dragged her in."

Fear rippled through me. What kind of power did you have to have to imprison a god who built the cell around you?

It was a long moment before Ravik spoke. "Ivan thinks he's serving Nyxarra, which clearly isn't true. So which of them is he serving?"

And more than that, how were they influencing anyone if they were locked up? Were they just that powerful? Or were they gaining power?

Images slammed into me, different from before. Tall bars. Shadows pulling Nyxarra back, her cries ringing in my ears. I forced the vision away before it could take hold, blinking hard. The visions were coming easier now.

*Almost too easy.*

"Ivan's not worshipping Nyxarra. He's feeding something." Basir's words rang true.

"We were probably right, then," I said. "Ivan's rituals are fueling at least one of them. And what would that mean for the next ritual he has planned?"

*Absolutely nothing good.*

"Nyxarra said you could trust one of them, though." Thornar's attempt at positivity was appreciated despite the situation growing more and more dire.

"Vaelithra, probably?" Elowen's answer was the most logical conclusion. I had a feeling she was right, but it didn't make me feel any less uneasy.

"She may be reaching out to Gracie through Nyxarra," Thornar agreed. "But that doesn't mean it's not for her own means."

After all, an imprisoned god wasn't exactly the safest ally to trust.

# CHAPTER 9

# GRACIE

"I REALIZE you can't stay longer," Alpha Haiden said as I lifted a fork to my lips. "But I do hope all of you return—especially you, Gracie. Elowen visits often. Next time, come with her."

"I would love to," I told her, and I meant it. Thornar squeezed my leg gently but didn't say a word as Basir took a long sip of his drink. Ravik and Haiden's mate stood talking nearby, already having finished the light lunch we were sharing before leaving for the next territory.

After everything we'd discovered earlier in the day, I was eager to keep moving—so much so that we'd already packed the car before being invited to join Haiden for lunch. Now, sitting on the stunning patio which was draped on all sides with soft ivory curtains that billowed in the ocean breeze, I was glad we'd taken the time to do so.

"Where do you go next?" Haiden asked.

Thornar responded, "Blazefur Pride."

Haiden's expression scrunched up slightly before smoothing. "I wish you all the best. I fear you won't find nearly as easy an ally as you did here."

"I really do want to thank you," I said, a small smile pulling at my lips despite everything waiting ahead. "For hearing us out—and for recognizing how important this is."

"Of course." Haiden agreed. "I've already begun readying our flight units. I did think of something last night, though. I'm not sure if it's something you've considered."

Basir immediately focused on her, a silent question in his gaze.

"You won't be able to reach the Cold Moon Pack easily. You'll need to travel either through Grimfur Skulk territory or go into Silverpine. The mountains between Scarlet Sloth and the Cold Moon Pack are too unpredictable to move units through."

"If Alpha Graeme Sharp is transferring people from his territory into Ivan's, it'll be easier to go through there." Basir's voice was rougher than normal, and I glanced at him with concern. "Unfortunately, I know the lay of the land."

Basir's history and the drug-running his parents had been part of within the territory came rushing back to me. I hated the idea of him having to face a place that had caused him so much pain.

"Noted." Haiden nodded in understanding before looking toward Ravik and her mate, both of whom had made their way over. "Before you leave, I wanted to discuss something—although I know an answer may not be possible today."

Ravik rested his hands on the back of my chair and waited, clearly prepared for this.

Haiden continued smoothly, "Your territory possesses a mineral—Korite—that allows for armor transition between shifted and non-shifted forms, specifically for dragons. I also know it's not much use to wolves."

Ravik nodded, unsurprised. "You want access to it?"

"At a discounted, ally-friendly rate," Haiden's mate said, earning a quiet chuckle from Thornar.

"We can make that happen," Ravik agreed.

Watching politics play out between them was fascinating. My mate didn't question why she would want something from us, but since we were asking for help, it made sense. Even knowing this would eventually affect her territory if Ivan wasn't stopped, Haiden still treated it as a negotiation.

Following that, we slipped back into casual conversation until the end of lunch. The serious tone eased, smoothing into something lighter, almost normal.

It didn't last.

Before long, we were standing to leave. The good-byes came easier than I expected. Ravik shook Haiden's hand, Thornar flashed an easy grin as he traded an amused quip with Cole, and Basir dipped his head in quiet acknowledgement.

Haiden offered a small smile. "Safe travels. Our units stand by, awaiting your signal."

"Thank you," I said sincerely.

Then we were moving. The patio gave way to the inside of the estate, then to open air. The ocean breeze followed us, and I glanced around one more time before we left, taking in the beauty of the territory.

I held onto that sense of awe for a second...and then refocused.

The drive to the jet was quiet. Books that Elowen had gotten special permission to borrow sat heavy on our laps, and I listened as my mates discussed what we would face next.

*The Blazefur Pride.*

I didn't know much beyond what I'd learned on my way to the trade conference: their Alpha was Chace Wall, they traded in gas and oil. That was it. I shifted in my seat, watching the estate grow distant behind us, replaced by stretches of land that blurred past the window.

By the time we reached the jet, the conversation had shifted into something more focused and urgent. Ravik moved ahead, already speaking with the crew, while Thornar walked with his sister and Banthor, carrying the bags to be loaded.

Basir stayed close. The tension from the morning still lingered in our bond, unspoken but impossible to ignore. So before I could overthink it, I led him toward the back of the jet once we stepped into the cabin.

I dropped onto the couch beside Basir, and immediately he filled the space so that I felt completely insulated and tucked away in the back of the jet with him. Elowen and Banthor claimed the tables up front, already spreading out books and notes, while Thornar and Ravik settled into a conversation of their own after a quick check to make sure I was comfortable and had everything I needed.

"Basir." I softened my voice when he looked down at me, something unsettled moving through his emerald eyes. "Are you okay?"

His jaw tightened. "No."

"Because of earlier?" I asked, slowly shrugging off the cardigan I'd been wearing. I was turned toward him, cushioned by the couch, while he now sat rigid beside me, his back tight with tension.

"Yes."

I frowned, frustrated. I didn't know how to pull more out of him, but I knew I needed to.

"I need you to explain," I said quietly. "I don't understand why you're upset."

Basir's head snapped toward me. Before I could fully register the movement, he shifted position, pulling me into his lap in one smooth motion.

And then Basir's hands were gone.

They dropped away from me like he hadn't meant to touch me at all. I boldly placed my hands on his chest, both to steady myself and to keep contact with him. Because I wanted to touch him. I *needed* to, until I understood what was going on in his head.

Even on his lap, he still dwarfed me. He studied my expression, visibly struggling with what to say.

"Can I try to guess what's wrong?"

Basir closed his eyes and shook his head, like he was disappointed in himself. "I'm not upset. Not at you, glow. I'm upset at my lack of control. You could have gotten hurt."

"You were protecting me—"

"You still could have gotten hurt."

But I could tell there was more to it than that. The restraint, the way he held himself, keeping me close but denying himself any touch...denying himself *me*.

Was that what was happening? Just like the night in my bedroom?

A wave of realization rolled over me.

Basir wanted me. I could feel it, steady and contained beneath everything else. But he would keep himself at a distance unless I made it clear that I wanted him close. My hands trembled just a tiny bit as I lifted them, bringing them to either side of his face.

The moment I touched him he shuddered, his eyes closing as a low rumble broke from his throat. My instinct was to pull back, worried I'd overstepped with my boldness—but as if he'd anticipated it, his hand shot out, gripping my hip in a firm hold.

Not trapping.

Just...keeping me there.

"I loved seeing your wolf," I said, my voice thick with emotion. "And I know this bond is a lot...and it's not something you asked for...but the connection I feel to you—and the other two—it's nothing I've ever experienced."

My fingers tightened slightly against him as I spoke.

"I know you're worried about hurting me, but you shifting in response to my wolf...it just...it showed me how close we are." I closed my mouth before I could say anything reckless, my emotions rising too fast, too close to the surface.

But my words had already landed.

Basir's eyes opened slowly, something low and simmering building in them.

"Gracie..."

"I'm serious," I whispered. "I know I might not seem strong, but..." I paused, the truth of it settling deep in my chest before I forced the words out. "I've been through a lot. I'm stronger than I look. And for the past decade I've been around many that happily hurt me. I know what it feels like, what it looks like." My voice softened in the end but didn't waver. "You would never hurt me."

Basir's expression shifted, emotion cracking through the walls he kept trying to put between us. I didn't want to push him into something he didn't want, but with the way he held me, keeping me anchored against him with a firm grip, I didn't think that was the problem.

I just needed to hear it. And maybe he needed to hear it too.

"I want you close."

His hand flexed on my hip before tightening.

When he spoke, his voice was controlled but strained. "You don't know what that means, glow. I know your strength. I see it. But that doesn't mean I couldn't hurt you. *I could.* And the idea of that..." A wave of disgust rolled through our bond. "I don't have control when it comes to you. I could lose myself, and I don't trust who I would be in that moment."

"I trust you."

That stopped him.

Basir's entire body went still, his grip freezing as my hands softened against his face. He lifted the hand not on my hip, sliding it up to gently catch my chin. I shivered at the quiet strength in his touch.

"Why would you? Why would you ever trust me, glow?"

I knew we were stepping into something dangerous, but I was too far in to stop now.

"I can feel it through our bond," I said softly. "I can feel how much you care. I trust you not to hurt me."

Something in Basir shifted.

Not breaking.

*Unraveling.*

His mouth found mine in a sudden kiss that was intense and deliberate. I slid my fingers into his hair, holding him to me as the tension between us finally dissolved. His breath cooled against my lips even as his touch burned my skin, the balance between control and need pulsing through our bond.

But when I didn't pull away—when I pressed closer instead—the dam broke open.

Basir's hand on my chin slid gently around my throat while his other wrapped firmly around my waist, tugging me closer. A soft moan slipped from my lips when I felt his hardness beneath me. My legs straddled either side of him, letting me feel every inch as we devoured each other.

When he broke the kiss and trailed down my jaw, his teeth grazing my skin, heat pooled low between my thighs. The distance between us, both physical and through our bond, melted as I rolled my hips to grind against him.

Basir's fingers slid down the straps of my sundress, exposing my shoulder before slowly tugging the fabric lower, revealing the edge of my bra. An eager sound slipped from my lips.

"More. Please."

It was more than enough for Basir. His fingers tugged at the cups of my bra until my breasts spilled free, my nipples pebbling under the rush of cool air in the jet. I leaned into him, a pulse of need rising between us, demanding his touch.

"Careful, glow…" His voice was low, strained against my skin. "You're pushing me further than I should go."

Despite his words, his teeth grazed one of the sensitive peaks, and a whimper of his name spilled from my lips.

"There it is," he murmured, almost to himself.

The more he teased, the wetter I became, the friction of moving against his length making my mind go hazy with the overwhelming sensation of being so close—yet not nearly close enough. My hands pulled at the back of his shirt, wanting to run my fingers along his skin, to taste him the way he was tasting me.

"Gracie…" My name was rough on his lips, almost a warning. "Don't start something you're not ready to finish."

I didn't stop. I moved against him slowly, testing the contact, drawing a sharper reaction from him. His hands tightened, then loosened, like he was fighting for every thread of control.

A low growl left him, making my skin prickle with awareness. "I'm trying to hold back...you're making that impossible."

When his lips and teeth returned to my breast, I could feel the shift—his touch rougher now, more deliberate, almost punishing in the best way possible.

"I don't want you to hold back," I whispered. When his fingers slid down my back and cupped my bottom, I almost moaned at the shift forward.

Basir's voice brushed against my ear, sending a shiver through me. "Are you sure, glow? Do you really want me to let go? Or do you want to just grind this pussy against me while I tease you? Make you see stars before I pull back, burying my dangerous need for you?"

"I want more," I promised, breathless as the pressure kept building, never quite reaching its climax.

"Show me you want more then," he demanded softly. "When I go to sleep at night, I want to imagine exactly what you'll look like coming all over my cock."

Basir's words pulled a moan from me as my head fell back, his lips finding my breasts once more. The sensation of his mouth, toying with the peak, sent shockwaves echoing through my body.

When he spoke again, his voice was edged with something darker—almost anger. "I want you to come, glow. Come *for* me."

His teeth bit down on my breast, and a tidal wave of pleasure crashed through me. A small cry left my lips as my clit pulsed, the climax breaking over me like a storm. Molten heat spread through my body, and my eyes fluttered shut at the intensity of the moment—at the way he still held me so close, so unyielding.

"Eyes on me, glow."

I opened my eyes and found him adjusting my clothes with slow, precise movements.

"You ask for more like that again... I'm giving it to you."

Somehow, he made it sound like both a threat and a promise.

# CHAPTER 10

# BASIR

GRACIE'S HAND tightened in mine as we hit a bump in the road, our SUV kicking up dust in every direction.

We'd only been in the car twenty minutes and already the oppressive heat bleeding through the glass was putting me on edge. The Blazefur Pride territory was one I'd avoided traveling to. Unfortunately, we didn't have much choice now.

Gracie let out a small yawn beside me, and my gaze snapped down to her, concern tightening in my chest. Was she tired? Clearly. I'd thought she'd slept well last night, but maybe there was something I'd missed.

"Glow?"

Her gaze lifted to mine, a shy smile tugging at her lips. "I'm just tired. It's been an eventful day."

A low rumble caught in my throat as I realized what she was alluding to. The moment between us had been equal parts blessing and curse. I would never regret touching her, kissing her—*tasting her*—especially now with her sitting closer than ever, her head resting against my shoulder.

But I also would never be able to forget it, no matter how hard I tried. The image of her coming apart on top of me. The soft sound of my name on her lips. Even after the way I'd spoken to her...or maybe because of it.

Even with her curled against me, I worried it had been too much.

Too intense. Too dark. Too possessive.

I existed in a state of control, and with Gracie that unraveled far too easily. I would always give her what she asked for. I couldn't deny her anything.

But how close I'd come to taking more than she offered...that was what sat heavy in my chest. Gracie deserved better.

"Is that where we're headed?" Ravik's brother asked.

In the distance, beyond the sparse desert growth stood a sand-colored stone city surrounded by a massive, fortress-like wall.

"We haven't received permission to enter the inner city, and with no response from Alpha Chace, the most we can do is make ourselves known by staying at a prominent hotel right outside the city," Ravik said. "There is very little chance he doesn't already know we're here, considering we flew in."

"Why do we need permission? Why the wall?" Gracie asked.

"No idea, but the Blazefur Pride is extremely private, and the city perimeters are heavily guarded with patrols. They don't just let anyone in," Elowen explained from the back row next to Thornar.

"My theory is resources," Thornar said. "Which is why everyone *outside* of the city tries to move as close as possible, hoping for a chance to be part of the luxury inside."

It was controlled entry to an extreme, and I had a feeling nothing got done around here without permission from Chace.

As we entered the city's outer district, the spectrum of wealth became clear. On the outskirts the houses resembled rock formations, but as we drove closer to the city's walls, glass and metal began to replace natural materials. So much so that the buildings near the wall reflected the stone in an almost blinding way.

I had to wonder what kind of reach Chace had out here when he was so exclusive about who he let into his city.

"We could bully them into letting us in," Banthor offered.

"But that wouldn't exactly lead to peace talks," I murmured as Gracie nodded in agreement.

I didn't bother speaking the quiet part out loud: Alpha Chace was going out of his way to ignore us. The question was *why*. I didn't like the fucking silence, and it made me ten times more suspicious about his thoughts on what was going on with Ivan.

Had we somehow missed that he might be aligned with Ivan? That seemed unlikely. More likely he just didn't want to get involved.

When Ravik turned toward a more luxurious section of the outer city, the buildings shifted to white stone and glass, many of their floors opening into wide balconies. As we pulled into one of the roundabouts, suited hotel staff stepped out to greet us.

Banthor and Ravik made arrangements as Gracie stood to help with the bags in the back, only to realize the hotel had already brought a cart to load everything onto. Her brow furrowed in confusion as she gravitated back toward my side.

I understood why this felt so alien to her. We weren't dealing with an Alpha or an estate. These were normal people doing things she would have normally handled on her own.

After all these years it still felt unfamiliar to me, and

I'd traveled across Thornfell and even to other countries with the Gentry family. I had never been afforded luxury in my younger years, and while I appreciated the concept now, I still viewed it as...too soft.

*Too exposed.*

Especially in a place I didn't completely trust.

As we moved into the lobby, I watched Gracie, my focus honing in on her every reaction. The way her head tilted up toward the ceiling, her gold eyes sparking with interest at the water feature in the center of the room. The grand staircase with ornate carved wood railings particularly caught her eye.

I supposed this trip was worth it for her reactions alone. When she'd first come to Ironsun territory, I'd watched Gracie withdraw from things, like she was denying herself anything she thought she couldn't have. I knew what it felt like not to belong in places like this.

Something had changed, though, and instead of denying herself, I saw her allowing herself to be curious. Get excited, even.

As we stepped into the elevator, my hand settled against Gracie's lower back. I listened to her soft questions about the area and Elowen and Thornar's answers, but I kept watching her.

I might have hated that Ivan pushed us to this point, but I couldn't regret the chance to show Gracie more of Thornfell.

When we reached the penthouse suite—chosen to catch Chace's attention, given the price tag—I immediately began scanning the space. And though they were more subtle about it, Ravik and Thornar were doing the same.

I moved to the balcony and stepped out into the heavy heat, immediately missing the cool air of the opulent room behind me. My gaze tracked down and then up, noting how easily the stone exterior of the hotel could be climbed.

"I'm ordering food—Gracie needs to eat," Ravik said from inside. "What do you want?"

"I'm good," I said. "I'm going to take a walk after the food arrives."

Ravik nodded, his expression grim. He knew I didn't actually plan on walking—I would be gathering intel—but Gracie didn't need to worry about that.

Forty minutes later, the six of us sat in the living room, eating takeout. There was still a thread of watchfulness between the three of us, but we kept things light enough that Gracie didn't notice.

Or maybe she did. Maybe she felt it through the bond and just...trusted us to handle it.

After all, she said she trusted me.

I was already in too deep with Gracie. The attachment between us was growing into something beyond any mate bond I'd ever heard of. I didn't even let myself dwell on the insane shit I could justify in the name of protecting her.

"I'm going on a walk," I told her after another thirty minutes. Her sleepy gaze lifted to search my expression before her hand reached out to squeeze mine.

"Come back soon?"

I nodded because I couldn't find the words to explain how foreign that was—someone wanting me to come back. Ravik and Thornar would argue otherwise, but it wasn't the same.

Deciding to take something for myself, I bent down and brushed my lips across the top of her head before leaving her in the safety of the others. I knew they would protect her with their lives.

Hell, Ravik barely slept as it was.

I understood though. I didn't feel like I'd earned rest until Gracie could lay her head down without fear of what would happen next.

The hotel was seventeen floors, with the first few levels dedicated to the lobby, restaurants, and back-of-house operations. Staff-only corridors ran behind most of it, and it didn't take long to find a service staircase tucked out of sight.

By the time I reached the lower levels again, I'd mapped enough of the layout to move unseen. I cut through a staff hallway that ran behind the kitchen and toward the front offices, close enough to the employee lounge and ventilation access to observe without being seen.

For nearly an hour, I listened to bullshit conversations and complaints the manager on duty fielded, but it wasn't until the phone rang that I truly focused. I winced at the high-pitched falsetto of the manager's phone voice as he answered.

"Sir—yes, I contacted you right away once I realized...no, no, I didn't say anything. We sent them food... Yes, the presidential suite. There are six of them... Yes, of course, discretion is key. I'll make sure they're cut off at the hour exactly."

The cameras.

My gaze dropped to my phone as I pulled it from my jacket. Twenty minutes. Not much time.

"I'll make sure the door to the fire exit is left open —yes, the one on the seventh floor."

After a few more minutes of assurances and groveling, the call ended, and I was already on the move. It didn't surprise me they were sending someone. What did surprise me was that I was nearly certain the call had been placed by Alpha Chace himself.

Sending a quick text to Ravik and Thornar, I positioned myself on the seventh floor and settled into the shadows. A minute past the hour, unease crept in. By the third, it had morphed into something closer to premonition. I slipped to a nearby window, opening it silently and angling myself out just enough to see the fire escape from a distance.

What I saw turned my blood cold.

A figure scaling the wall to my right, bypassing the fire exit entirely. *Fuck.*

The next few minutes were a blur as I turned sharply toward the staircase and sprinted to the seventeenth floor, barely winded despite the pace. I moved straight for a set of windows several feet down from the balcony, easing one open with practiced care. The fire exit would have brought the intruder in from the opposite side.

Stepping onto the ledge, I slid my fingers into the grooves of the stone and moved like a shadow before landing silently on the balcony. My entire body went cold, the air unnaturally still as I listened for any sound or sign of the intruder.

The lights in the suite were off; Gracie was likely fast asleep, and I was determined to put myself between her and whoever the fuck was trying to break her peace.

After a long minute, a dark figure climbed over the railing and moved toward the balcony doors, sliding them open silently. I was there in an instant.

I didn't think or warn. I just moved.

My arm locked around his chest as my knife came up, slicing clean across his throat. A wet, choking sound followed before his body collapsed.

I stepped back immediately, checking for any sign of life. A heavy silence settled over the air as I wiped my knife and moved to put it away.

"Basir?"

My body locked, and ice rushed through my veins. My gaze lifted to the balcony doorway, where Gracie stood wrapped in a robe, her wide eyes fixed on me.

Glow had seen *all of it.*

# CHAPTER 11

# GRACIE

BASIR HADN'T BEEN HURT. I just had to keep reminding myself of that as I stared at him from opposite the body sprawled on the floor. Blood was already staining the stone of the balcony, but beyond that...it didn't feel real. Just a body. Empty.

I'd seen my father like that once. I'd covered my mother's face with a cloth before they burned her body—there had been nowhere in the compound to bury those we lost—but her eyes had looked like that too. Empty.

Death didn't shock me the way it should have—not after everything I'd seen. Not compared to what people were capable of when they were alive.

Something I was seeing in Basir right now.

Tears slipped from my eyes in relief that he was unharmed, but I could still feel pain through our bond.

He stood frozen across from me, his knife clattering to the ground. The unexpected sound made me flinch, and something cracked in his gaze. His foot shifted back, like he meant to put distance between us.

*Not again.*

I knew what needed to be said couldn't come from across the space. I stepped forward, moving to cross the balcony—

A massive arm looped around my waist, lifting me clean off my feet.

"Let's avoid getting blood on your fuzzy socks, little flame."

Thornar's wonderful scent wrapped around me as he carried me across the balcony, far from the body... and far from Basir.

Except Basir didn't move toward me either. No disgruntled rumble from Thornar's move came from his chest. Instead, he just stared at the two of us, choosing not to do or say anything.

"I have to admit," Thornar drawled, "I expected a welcome party, not a welcome assassination."

My head snapped up, surprised by his levity, but his gaze was filled with a seriousness that didn't match. His arm remained locked around me.

"I suppose this makes their message clear," he continued. "Basir, you may want to pick up your favorite knife though. Wouldn't want anything happening to it."

Basir did so in an efficient movement just as Ravik stepped out onto the balcony, his gaze dropping to the body before lifting back to Basir. Panic began to build in my chest, but when I tried to move forward again on instinct, Thornar's arm tightened.

His voice dropped to a low hum in my ear. "Give him a minute, Gracie. He didn't expect you to see this."

Thornar's words, mixed with what I already knew about Basir, made something click, and I nodded slowly. His nose brushed into my hair as I melted back into his chest, trusting his judgment.

I just wasn't sure how long I could stay there without being near Basir. Not with the agony and guilt still echoing through our bond.

"What happened?" Ravik asked calmly.

"The hotel manager got off the phone twenty minutes ago, arranging for them to use the seventh-floor fire exit. They chose not to. They scaled the wall instead and were headed for the balcony doors. So I stopped them. I'm not sure who the manager was speaking to, but considering the crest on the back of his uniform"—Basir nodded toward the body—"I have to assume it was Alpha Chace."

I peered at the body, barely making out the outline of the crest, blacked out but still visible. *A lion.*

"Do we know the target?"

Basir tensed. "I have to assume us. Or you."

"Or Gracie," Thornar hummed.

Basir's face didn't change, but the lack of reaction felt off. Detached.

I hated it. After everything we'd been through today, it felt *wrong*.

"Thornar." I looked up at him, his dark gaze flicking down to me. "I need you to let me go."

His jaw tightened. He clearly didn't like the idea, but he released me anyway. I crossed the balcony in a split second, ignoring the squelch of blood underfoot, my arms wrapping around Basir as his body went stock-still.

For a long moment, I wondered if it had been the wrong move. If, after all this, I hadn't understood what he needed.

Then a deep rumble built in his chest as his arms came around me. The way he held me was more than *need*—it was like he was grounding himself, pressing into me as if I could keep him tethered to reality.

"Well, now that that's handled," Thornar sighed happily, "I suppose we should dispose of the body."

"No," Ravik said decidedly. "We leave it. I want the message to be unmistakable."

"You got it, boss," Thornar said in amusement. "Well, let's get this show on the road."

"We're leaving? Already?" I looked up, Basir's grip tightening around me. I wasn't moving from him, though.

"Alpha Chace has made his feelings obvious—and

if it's a misunderstanding, we aren't staying around to risk you being in danger again," Ravik explained evenly. "We knew we'd face issues in some territories. Just didn't expect it to be this one."

"I'll have Banthor grab us a car from the garage. He'll have to hot-wire one," Thornar added.

"To get to the plane?" I frowned.

"No. Can't risk going to the same airfield. We'll have the pilot meet us at a different airport," Basir said.

I nodded in understanding. This territory wasn't safe anymore. They knew we were here, and they wanted us dead.

"We're leaving?" Banthor called from behind Ravik. His eyes dropped to the body, then lifted to Basir. His expression was almost thoughtful. "Clean one."

Then he was gone. Clearly, death didn't faze any of them. I could hear Elowen in the living room as lights flickered on, Ravik stepping back inside to relay instructions.

Looking up at Basir, I offered a small smile. "I'm so glad you're okay."

The look on his face wasn't one I could fully dissect—but Thornar seemed to. As he passed, he clapped Basir on the shoulder. "See? You were worried she'd think you're a monster. Our mate's stronger than that, Basir."

Hadn't I already told him that? Seeing death didn't shake me nearly as much as the thought of Basir being hurt.

"You were protecting us," I pointed out softly, hoping to remind him of the conversation we had on the jet.

Basir pressed his lips to the top of my head but he didn't say a word. When he lifted me over the body and carried me back into the hotel room, I rested my head against his shoulder.

His silence wasn't distance; it was him pulling me behind his walls. He wasn't ready to talk, but he also wasn't letting me go.

When he did place me down, I focused on what we could control. I moved quickly, packing my things, disposing of my socks, and helping Elowen gather her books and documents. Within thirty minutes, the hotel was fading fast behind us as the dark SUV Banthor had stolen from the parking garage cut through the desert night.

It was nearly ten, and the car was filled with a soft string of music playing through the speakers. And while we were putting distance between us and the city, it didn't feel like we were safe yet. I didn't think my mates would feel at ease until we were out of the territory entirely.

I sat between Ravik and Thornar, with Basir up front beside Banthor to navigate. Elowen rested in the back. I didn't hesitate to do the same, though I found myself wanting to stretch out against one of my mates in a bed instead of a car. My cheeks warmed at the thought.

"Get some rest, *lux mea*," Ravik murmured. "We'll wake you when we make our next stop."

I looked up into his golden gaze and nodded, taking his advice as I settled between them. My eyes grew heavy almost immediately, the darkness settling around me like a comforting blanket.

"*THIS IS* the closest place to stay near the airfield?" Elowen scrunched her nose as she eyed the motel that was attached to the gas station we had just pulled into.

It was late—or really early—and the star-filled sky above us did very little to shed light on the long row of worn doors.

"Yes. You'll be fine," Thornar said before glancing at me. "That being said, if *you* want to sleep in the car, Gracie, I'll happily stay awake so you can."

I smiled at him before shaking my head, nodding toward the motel. "I think this looks great. A place to rest your head is as good as any."

Elowen grumbled something but my attention shifted to Ravik as he stepped out of the store, tossing room keys to Basir and Banthor. They immediately split off, each taking a door and sweeping the space before letting anyone else in.

"The jet will land at two in the afternoon," Basir said. "It isn't taking off until well into the morning—we want them to assume we're still within city limits. We've driven as far as we can from it. Until then, we need to lay low and probably stay in our rooms."

"Not an issue!" Banthor called out, sweeping Elowen up and carrying her away. She didn't even argue or throw out a comeback because she was already half-asleep in his arms.

I walked toward the door Basir stood in front of and rested my hand against his muscular chest. "You should get some rest."

His eyes darkened slightly as he nodded. "I'll try, glow."

I wasn't sure I completely believed him. "Seriously," I said. "I want you to rest."

With that, he followed me into the room. I slid off my shoes and crawled onto one of the two beds, patting the mattress. In a surprisingly fast move, Basir was beside me, his legs stretched out and his back against the headboard. It wasn't exactly the restful position I'd envisioned, but it was a start.

"I'm going to shower really quick," Ravik said in the quiet of the room, the door shutting behind him. Thornar sat on the edge of the bed across from us.

"How are you feeling, little flame?"

Despite his light tone, I could hear the concern in his voice. I offered him a small smile, because what he was really asking—his expression open, easy for me to read—was whether I was okay after seeing a body.

And I was. Truly.

"A little tired," I admitted. "Although I feel like I'm getting more sleep than any of you..."

A shift in weight had me glancing over, my words trailing off as relief loosened something in my chest. Basir's eyes were closed, his breathing already even. I was so thankful he was resting.

When I looked back at Thornar, he was watching me with a warmth that had my cheeks heating.

"What?" I asked softly.

"You convinced him to sleep. That's a skill."

"He's been through a lot tonight. He was really upset earlier. I can't imagine taking a life, but—"

"That wasn't why he was upset."

I frowned. "What do you mean?"

"Basir has killed before," he said plainly. "He was upset with how close it came to you and that you saw him like that. He's been trying to hide that side of himself."

Oh. That made sense, especially considering how hard he fought to keep himself contained.

"Why?" I asked. "Why is he trying to hide part of who he is?" I couldn't hide anything from these men.

Thornar leaned forward, bracing his elbows on his knees. "Little flame, he slit someone's throat without hesitation. Do you think most people would take that in stride? Most people would run from it. You didn't even blink."

My brow furrowed. "I didn't really think about it like that. But protecting the people you care about—even if it's violent—doesn't make you a bad person. When I think about the people who fought back against Ivan...they're not bad."

"I agree," he said. "It's probably better you see it that way, little flame. After all...it's not just his darkness you're stepping into."

*What? What darkness did he mean?*

Before I could press further, he continued, "That being said, if it bothered you, we could do our best to keep it from you."

"No," I said softly but with urgency. "I don't want anything hidden. Even that."

Thornar gave me a slow, approving smile, but before I could ask him what he meant about the darkness, the bathroom door opened and Ravik stepped out.

"Get some sleep, Gracie." Thornar's suggestion had me nodding but I wasn't sure I could. His words echoed in my head.

Did Thornar mean *his* darkness?

# CHAPTER 12
# GRACIE

THE FOGGY MIRROR slowly cleared as I brushed out my hair, the yellow lighting of the motel bathroom making my skin look paler than usual. Or maybe it was just the restless, dream-filled sleep.

Either way, I felt a little shaky, and I was grateful my mates had packed so many comfortable options for me. I slipped into a cotton striped sundress and sneakers before leaving the bathroom, my toothbrush still in hand.

In the light of day, the motel room felt cozy. I knew my mates weren't particularly fond of it, mostly because of the dust, but the thin curtains let in the morning light in a way that brought the space to life. Even the faded pictures on the far left wall stood out to me, a bustling city I'd never seen before shown in black-and-white.

"Feeling a bit better?" Thornar asked. He and Basir were sitting on one of the beds, papers and a tablet spread between them on the quilted duvet cover.

"Yes?" I said, not entirely sure. "I'm a bit hungry though."

"We're going to grab breakfast," Ravik said, standing in the doorway of the room, the morning heat slipping past him. "They have a restaurant in the gas station."

"Are you two hungry?" I looked over at Thornar and Basir. I was worried they weren't taking care of themselves with all of our traveling.

Basir's gaze held mine for only a second before returning to the papers. "Do you want us to come with you, glow?"

"I mean, I always want you two to come."

Thornar chuckled, but the way he did—the heat in his gaze—made my cheeks warm. Obviously I knew why he was laughing—I'd heard many jokes along the same thread in the Cold Moon Pack. So why didn't it bother me when Thornar did it? Why did I like it so much?

Basir shot him a look before he exhaled. "Maybe it's better we finish our work here."

I hesitated for half a second, worried he was still caught on the events of last night, but Thornar didn't linger. He was already moving things along.

"That's the spirit." Thornar flashed a smile to him

before looking over at me. "Thanks for thinking of us though, little flame."

"Come on." Ravik smoothed a hand over my back as I turned toward him. He looked particularly handsome today. The tight short sleeve shirt he wore was more casual than normal, and it also showed off so *many* of his muscles.

I wasn't entirely sure how it was fair for one person to have that many.

When we stepped into the sunlight, I lifted a hand to shield my eyes. Ravik grumbled before tucking me into his side, shielding me in his shadow as he guided us forward. I found a laugh slipping from my lips, and he paused to look at me while arching a brow.

"It's just sunlight," I teased. "I promise I'm fine."

"If it's hurting you, I'm not a fan," Ravik said, pressing a finger under my chin. "But I love seeing you smile, *lux mea*. I need to see it more."

"I feel like I'm finally getting the chance to," I admitted. "Mostly because of the three of you."

Was that too blunt? Maybe, but the way his eyes warmed made it worth it.

"Its also because of us that you didn't sleep well last night," he murmured, drawing me to his side again as we continued toward the gas station restaurant.

"Maybe because of our *bond*," I admitted. "But that was all Nyxarra...and the other gods."

I didn't say either of their names. My dreams last night had featured them, and though I didn't have a visual, both Nyxarra and their power had grown to feel so much more solid and real. As if giving them names and a history had made my connection to them feel that much more tangible.

At some point in the night, a painful pulse had torn through my chest, like something had grabbed hold of our mate bond and yanked. I shot up in bed, the movement echoed by my mates.

Ravik had already been sitting up, his knuckles white where he gripped the bed frame. Thornar had sworn under his breath, scanning the room, while Basir had gone completely still and alert in a way that felt almost eerie.

Even though I'd managed to fall back asleep at some point, my dreams had been filled with fragmented visions of Nyxarra trying to speak to me. In between dreams, I'd heard my mates say the pull on our bond had to be connected to the god scar. Either Nyxarra or one of the other gods had been trying to use it to communicate with us.

So sleep had been limited, to say the least.

"I know it may be a lot to ask," Ravik said in a low tone, "but another one of those conversations would be appreciated."

"One where Nyxarra explains a bunch of stuff?" I teased as he grunted in acknowledgment.

I didn't disagree. More answers would be really nice. But I also knew, considering I'd lived for so long without answers to *anything*, that I couldn't expect that. Thinking like that—always looking for a reason for something that happened in the past—made it hard to stay in the present. And truthfully, I didn't want to waste a moment with my mates.

Or appreciating this beautiful landscape.

"My wolf may hate this heat," I told Ravik as we turned the corner of the motel block. "She wouldn't shift even if I begged...but it is beautiful. In a different way."

Very different from anywhere that I'd lived or visited before.

The motel almost blended into the desert, covered in dust and more than a little sun-bleached, but the flashing neon signs posted outside stood out even from the highway. Maybe because it was such a bright signal against the endless stretch of brown. I didn't know how close the nearest town was, but I couldn't see anything except open, heat-soaked land in every direction.

"This type of heat is dangerous," Ravik said. "At least for wolves like us with thick fur adapted for living in a colder climate. I wouldn't mind it in the dead of winter though."

I tilted my head in thought as we entered the

restaurant, a chime sounding above. "What is it like in Ironsun territory during the winter?"

"We're fairly high in the mountains, so it's cold, but depending on where you are in the territory, it can vary. The west side is a lot warmer compared to the capital city." Ravik paused, worry filling our bond. "If you don't end up loving the cold, we can always find places to visit during that time of year."

"I actually don't mind the cold if I have somewhere warm to be inside, but I would love to see more of the territory before it gets too icy or snowy to travel. Especially some of the land we flew over on the way to Nightstar Flight territory."

"We'll do that before the weather gets too intense," he agreed, squeezing my waist. Then he addressed the restaurant staff waiting at a small podium near the front. "Just a table for the two of us."

It felt like a new world, simply going into a restaurant, so everything from the plastic-looking yellow booths to the scent of overcooked food in the air caught my attention. The place was nearly empty, but the man happily led us to a small corner booth where I could sit next to Ravik, two plastic-covered menus with bright pictures set in front of us. The sunny, worn-down restaurant felt simple compared to the chaos of the past few days, and I felt my chest loosen, some of the tension from last night's dreams finally easing.

"What are you getting?" I asked Ravik, looking up to find his gaze already on me.

"A skillet," he answered. "You should make sure to eat a lot—I have no idea what today will bring."

"What territory is next?"

"Bloodrose Sloth territory—Alpha Lacey Harrison has responded already, welcoming us..." Ravik sighed. "Somewhat."

"She doesn't like us?"

"Not exactly. She just hates Alpha Kaliyah Greene, so she'll probably try to convince us not to go there and make her help contingent on that point. Anything to get one up on her."

"Couldn't we use that against her?"

Ravik tilted his head curiously, and I continued. "If she doesn't like her and always wants to get one up on her, she may be more willing to help...if she thinks Alpha Kaliyah already is."

My mate's smile was gorgeous as he surprised me, tilting my chin up and pressing a kiss to my lips. When I pulled back, my eyes went wide. "What was that for?"

"I'd never ask you to be interested in politics. Most don't like it," Ravik said, smoothing his finger over my lips. "But seeing you step into that role, especially as my mate..."

*Oh.*

I spoke honestly, despite feeling a hint of nerves. "I

want to try to help. It's a lot of...new experiences for me, but this sort of *started* with me. I don't want to ignore the problem or avoid the best solution, even if it's a big change."

Ravik let out a hum of understanding. "Not just a big change, but a dangerous one. How do you feel about last night?"

I wasn't surprised he was asking, and I wasn't surprised he'd waited until we were alone. Ravik had a sharp instinct for how his words would affect the people around him. Like Basir and the guilt he carried over exposing me to violence.

Still, I hesitated. "Honestly?"

"Always."

*Right.*

"I don't feel anything but relief. I don't think Basir did anything wrong...and there is *relief* in being protected like that."

Ravik was quiet as I stared at the scratched table under my menu, finally asking, "Is that bad? Does that make me a bad person?"

It was a raw but simple question.

"No."

His surety was a balm to the lingering sliver of doubt. His words were clear as he held my gaze, offering steady reassurance. "Wanting protection, wanting to survive—in whatever form that takes—is never wrong, and it's never a weakness. Our bond exists for a reason, *lux mea*, and one of them is for you to trust us to take care of you. For you to feel safe with us."

"I do. I really do," I said softly.

"Hi there!" A middle-aged woman approached us with a bright smile. "My name is Jessica, and I'll be taking care of you today. What can I get you two?"

"Sausage skillet. Three of them, two to go," Ravik said, then looked to me.

My eyes widened as they darted down to the menu, picking out the first thing I saw. "Blueberry pancakes would be amazing, thank you."

"Coming right up." Jessica's gaze was warm, and she disappeared as quickly as she had arrived. I melted into Ravik's side as he brushed his lips over the top of my head. The peaceful morning was exactly what I needed, especially knowing that all too soon we would be moving forward on our journey.

Ravik wasn't wrong. There was danger ahead. But I'd survived worse alone, for nearly a decade. Now I had *them*.

And I wasn't letting that go.

# CHAPTER 13

# GRACIE

"Are you sure you won't come with us?" I asked Elowen. We stood at the bottom of the jet's staircase. Banthor was leaning against the car talking to Ravik, while Thornar and Basir focused on getting us settled and ready to go.

"I promise we'll be back on the road soon." She reached forward and squeezed my hand. "I already packed up any books I felt like you needed, and I'll work on transcribing the other information before returning the rest to the archives. Banthor and I have a few things that we want to handle here, especially considering the turn everything took."

*As in the Alpha of the territory refusing to even acknowledge us.*

A small knot formed in my chest at the thought of them staying behind. Things hadn't exactly gone smoothly here, and the idea of splitting up—even temporarily—sat uneasily with me.

"Alright, please stay safe," I said, hoping they didn't plan on doing anything dangerous, as she pulled me into a tight hug and turned on her way. She shouted something to Thornar in passing, already halfway back to the car.

My mate passed her and picked me up in a single arm scoop while carrying me up the stairs. I let out a small giggle of surprise before melting against him.

"Ready for another flight?" he asked, setting me down in one of the large leather chairs. "It won't be a super long one, but I'm hoping you'll get some rest in."

I was hoping to as well. I'd thought the heaviness in my body had been due to lack of sleep, but the longer the day went on, the more *off* I began to feel—not just tired.

"I could use a nap," I admitted, happily taking the blanket he offered and tucking it around me. Thornar sat beside me after a few minutes of talking to the pilot, my eyes already growing heavy as I heard something about getting ready for takeoff.

It wasn't until we were high in the air, as I fluttered between consciousness and sleep, that I realized something was in fact wrong. My throat felt tight, and the back of my head ached. The longer I sat under the blanket, the colder I felt, even as I twisted and adjusted myself to be comfortable.

"Little flame?" Thornar's voice was warm against my ear as I let out a sound of frustration, although it wasn't toward him. When I felt his massive hand press against my forehead, I was surprised by the curse that left his mouth.

"What?" Ravik demanded as my eyes opened, barely, finding that both he and Basir had leaned forward, looking at me in concern.

"She has a fever."

Thornar's voice held a seriousness I instantly disliked, but the dizziness creeping in, paired with the cold chill, made it hard to even lift a hand to touch his face.

*A fever.* That...that was such an odd concept. I'd felt somewhat miserable my entire time in the Cold Moon Pack, but actually being sick? Having a fever or a sore throat, sneezing or coughing? If I had any of those, I couldn't remember it. So why now?

"Gracie, how are you feeling?" Basir asked.

I found the strength to reach out and squeeze his hand before saying, "Exhausted, and honestly, I haven't felt this sick in...years. I don't remember the last time I had a fever."

"I'm telling them to land." Ravik's tone brooked no argument, and I didn't have the will to stop him. I didn't understand why we needed to land, though.

"We can at least get her some medicine," Thornar agreed.

"We should have thought to be prepared for this. I don't think we have anything on the plane beyond basic first aid. Maybe some pain relievers." Basir sounded frustrated.

"I'm sure I just need sleep," I murmured.

"It's probably because she's been meeting so many people and traveling so much," Thornar pointed out. I didn't think they were purposefully ignoring me, but I also wasn't sure I was speaking loud enough for them to hear me.

Basir's rough hand brushed across my forehead and then cupped my cheek. His words were heavy. "The sooner we land, the better."

"We're making an emergency landing in twenty."

That was one of the last things I heard from Ravik before darkness crept in at the edges of my vision, slow at first, then all at once—like my body had simply decided it was done.

Had sickness always come on this fast? I'd heard shifters in particular experienced it more intensely but that it also passed faster. Either way, it was horrible, and I couldn't muster the energy to do anything but lie there, feeling pathetic.

"I'll be back with medicine, glow." Basir's voice was soft in my ear before Ravik leaned down to press a kiss to the top of my head. Then they were both gone, our bond stretching farther and farther. When my body was suddenly jostled, my eyes opened to see the cabin shifting around me.

"If you can flatten those, that would be great—thanks, Stephen." Thornar's voice carried a quiet command, and while he was clearly speaking to the pilot or a crew member, I couldn't focus on anything but him as he gently lowered my body onto the cool leather of the now-flat chair. A heavier blanket settled over me as he carefully removed my shoes. I watched him kneel beside me, his fingers slipping between mine.

Reality flickered out again, only pulling back into focus when Thornar coaxed me into drinking some water, the cool liquid easing my throat. I tightened the blanket around me and fell right back asleep. Unlike most of my nights, these stretches of sleep were empty. No visions. No gods. Just a heavy, blanketed darkness.

I was almost frustrated when it was interrupted by familiar voices.

"Let's give her the medicine when she wakes up," Thornar suggested. "She finally got comfortable."

"We've got to get that fever down—103 isn't something we can wait on," Basir argued. "She is shaking. Literally fucking shaking."

Was I? My body did feel like it was uncontrollably trembling. I was just so damn cold.

"Once we're cleared to take off, we'll wake her up

to take it. The flight is going to be a few more hours than expected because we have to detour. The weather is bad in the mountains, but she'll have more time to rest," Ravik explained.

"Glad we made a stop, then. Wouldn't want to be caught in that shit," Thornar agreed.

For a long moment, there was quiet before Basir spoke again. "Why now? I don't like that we just left that territory. She hasn't been sick in a decade, and now she's come down with something."

"I think it's simpler than that," Ravik said. "Gracie has been in survival mode for ten years. Now that she isn't, her body may finally be allowing itself to be vulnerable."

I didn't know if there was any science behind Ravik's theory, but it made sense. I was sure there had been times I'd been sick in the past ten years that just didn't come to mind because I'd been too focused on avoiding Ivan and the other predators in the Cold Moon Pack.

"Still don't fucking like it," Thornar muttered, brushing some of my hair back. My eyes slowly managed to open, finding him looking down at me.

"Ready to take some medicine, *lux mea*?" Ravik asked. "We're taking off soon."

Nodding slowly, my brain feeling like it was bouncing around in my head, I tried to sit up. I made it to my elbows before Basir stepped in to help, Thornar handing me a bottle of water to go with the medicine Ravik offered. I couldn't remember the last time I'd taken anything like it.

I swallowed the two pills quickly, trying to steady my hand enough to drink the water, before curling back up under the blanket.

"Thank you," I whispered to the three of them.

My body gave in fully then, exhaustion hitting hard and fast. I fell into a heavy, uninterrupted sleep, knowing Ravik was right.

*I was safe with them.*

# CHAPTER 14

# THORNAR

TONIGHT HAD TURNED into a chaotic clusterfuck, and I was about two seconds from losing my patience with it.

We'd left the Blazefur Pride territory early afternoon, made a quick landing for medicine not long after, and should've been back in the air within the hour. But every flight in the mountain region had been grounded due to weather, leaving us stuck for hours at the edge of the territory we needed to cross.

Now we were finally approaching our destination, the midnight hour closing in fast.

The only positive—the *only* fucking one—was that Gracie had slept the whole time. Her medicine had kicked in, her fever cooled, and while I didn't like how flushed her cheeks still were, it was better than their chalky appearance from this morning.

"We're going to have to grab a hotel for the night. There's no way we're making it into the city," I said, smoothing my hand over Gracie's head. I was sitting on the floor near her, and the other two were seated as close as possible, positioned on leather chairs and leaning forward.

"Already found an Inn," Basir said, allowing me to relax a bit. Normally I wouldn't have thought anything of driving at night, but it was better not to risk it.

Especially in Bloodrose Sloth territory, which was kept purposefully undeveloped and integrated with nature. There were no bright highway lights—hell, there weren't any highways at all, at least the last time I'd visited.

"I informed Alpha Lacey of the delay," Ravik said.

"I would have suspected her to be more of a problem than Alpha Chace," I admitted.

"Chace does surprise me, but maybe it shouldn't." Ravik sighed. "I am regretfully in the dark about his motives or plans in general."

"And even at the TTC, in my time observing him, I didn't notice anything out of the ordinary," Basir agreed.

"We're definitely missing something when it comes to him." The other two nodded at my assessment as I continued. "Lacey, in my mind, while unpredictable in what she will decide, is a bit easier to decipher."

"Gracie thinks we should play into her competitive side with Alpha Kaliyah," Ravik said, drawing a smile to my lips. I loved that my little flame was thinking like that. I didn't like this political bullshit, but it was part of our lives, and I wanted nothing more than for her to be part of *all* of it.

"If she does decide to help, there will be conditions. She won't be as free-wheeling with it as Alpha Haiden," Basir agreed. Gracie suddenly shifted, momentarily drawing our attention away from the conversation.

"I did receive intel about her brother," Ravik said quietly.

I shot Ravik a questioning look. I knew how important it was to Gracie that we find her brother. Elowen, despite being annoying—*often*—had been by my side every step of the way. Which was why I'd given Banthor a fuck ton of warnings about how to treat her.

Though, after traveling with them, it was pretty clear that wasn't an issue.

"What did you find?" Basir asked.

"His name was found on a registry for citizenship in the Bloodrose Sloth territory, alongside another name," he explained, flipping open a folder of papers. "A Nori Holloway."

"So he's married. That will be interesting."

"I think locating him and getting more information is important before we tell Gracie," Basir said evenly. "I don't think he's dangerous, but..."

"Better to be safe," I agreed.

A few minutes later, Gracie shifted, trying to sit up as the soft chime in the jet alerted us that it was nearly time to land. I helped right her seat, adjusting the blanket, her gaze still a bit hazy. When she curled up against me, her head resting on my shoulder, I didn't try to keep her up. I'd carry her straight to the inn so she could rest.

"How far is the inn?" I asked as we landed, the jet gliding smoothly down on the runway. Despite the delay overall, I was thankful our patience meant we didn't have turbulence, ensuring Gracie could rest easily.

"Only a short drive," Ravik assured me as we made our way to a bright red truck sitting in an otherwise empty parking lot. Luckily, even though this wasn't our territory, we had enough pull to arrange things like transport.

I kept Gracie tucked against me, buckling the seatbelt haphazardly around us. Even with how much I hated that she was sick, I still found myself savoring the chance to hold her, especially with how busy we'd been.

I needed more time with her. Another date, at least.

When we reached the inn, a small, cottage-like

building on the edge of an isolated road, I considered that it may not be open at such a late hour. But the warm light spilling over the stone and the low buzz of music from inside told me we'd most likely be fine. The air was damp and cool, a breeze brushing over us as Gracie shivered against me. The storm was fading, but with it, the sharp drop in temperature compared to the southern territory probably wasn't helping her.

I'd need to grab her jacket.

"Hi there!" a man greeted from the front counter. As Ravik moved ahead to speak with him, my gaze swept the room, taking in the stone floors and walls, the handmade quilts, the mismatched wood furniture gathered around a living space with a low, steady hearth. There was a bar, too, and a sitting area that could fit at least twelve, but beyond that, the inn felt more like a home than anything else.

"How many rooms?" the man at the desk asked. I smirked, wondering if he'd be surprised by the answer of *one*. But he didn't question it, simply gave us a quick tour and told us breakfast would be ready in the morning at eight, then showed us to our room.

I laid Gracie down on the larger bed while keeping the blankets tucked around her. The older man lingered in the doorway, concern written across his face.

"Sick. Just feeling under the weather," I explained as he frowned.

"I'll have Margot make something for her in the morning. Please let us know if you need anything at all." Then he was gone, Basir closing the door.

I glanced back at him and Ravik. "I shouldn't be surprised they're so friendly, but after the last territory..." I trailed off, sitting to pull off my shoes.

"It's different," Basir agreed.

I didn't plan on sleeping much tonight, so once Gracie was settled, I made sure to start a fire before dropping into a large armchair. Once her fever broke, I'd feel a lot better about resting.

"THEY WERE SO SWEET," Gracie said, her voice still a little hazy as the innkeeper's wife, Margot, headed back inside. They'd packed the car with a full spread of breakfast, all of it clearly meant to help us take care of our mate. Leo, her husband, had nearly refused our money, but after some convincing—and letting him "treat" us to the food and settle everything into the car —he'd finally accepted payment. I watched Ravik shake his hand before circling the car.

"They are," I agreed. "This whole place is a welcome change."

I had to hope the change would continue.

Outside the car the land stretched wide, fields rolling beneath an open sky that felt cooler, almost washed clean after the storm. It was a quiet and calm territory, showing off the kind of deep green I'd only ever seen as a child in the thickest forests of Silverpine or when we'd traveled overseas.

"Maybe we could come back at some point," Gracie suggested as she started on the food they'd packed. I looked her over once more before nodding, even more willing than usual to give her anything she wanted. Anything to help her feel more like herself.

She said she was feeling better, and I believed her since the fever was gone, but I still wasn't happy with how she looked. The sweater—one of mine—was practically swallowing her whole, even as it kept her warm against the lingering chill. And while her face was flushed from the shower this morning, she still looked sick.

I wanted her to see a medical team as soon as possible, even if it wasn't one of Ironsun's healers.

"Everyone good to go?" Ravik asked. I nodded, settling back into the seat while Basir took the passenger side. As we started driving, I noticed the road was rougher than I remembered—nothing like the smooth highways in the other territories. I did appreciate the lack of people, though. In cities, I always felt like I had to stay on high alert.

"How long of a drive do we have?" Gracie asked.

"Until the central settlement? Maybe thirty or forty minutes," I offered.

"Settlement?" she asked, a hint of doubt in her voice. "Like the compounds?"

"No," Basir answered. "It's more like a town; not large enough to be a city. Everyone in this territory is more spread out. They don't have the same kind of localized power."

I couldn't fully remember what it had been like the last time I'd visited, but it had left an impression. And as we approached the spread of stone and wood clustered together in the distance, more of it started to come back. Everything was connected by stone paths, and while waterways wove through the town, most people walked everywhere rather than using boats or cars.

I didn't fully understand the competition Alpha Lacey had with the other sloth territory, especially when it came to success and prosperity. The way this place would measure was completely different from Scarlet. It was just a different kind of territory.

"This is so cozy," Gracie murmured, looking up at me to gauge my reaction. I'd stretched an arm across her shoulders, my fingers playing with the ends of her hair.

"Lacey's estate is just ahead," I said, having already memorized the map of our route last night. Unlike the other cities, the drive from the edge of town to the Alpha's estate was quick, and I could see Gracie taking in the way it sprawled—several cottages built out in pieces until it almost formed a manor.

"I'll be damned." Ravik's voice had me leaning forward, brow lifting in surprise.

"Did he give you a heads up?" I asked.

"Not at all."

"Is that Siguun and Zia?" Gracie asked. I gave a slow nod, curiosity sparking at the sight of Ravik's youngest brother and his friend waiting out front.

"Doesn't Zia know Alpha Lacey?" Basir mused. "I think Siguun mentioned that."

"Could bode well," Ravik murmured. "Now that you mention it, I think she may be related to her—or a family friend."

Either way, the familiar faces were welcome, giving me a cautious optimism as the car came to a stop.

"Siguun!" I called as I stepped out of the car. "We didn't know you were meeting us."

Ravik's younger brother was more soft-spoken than Banthor, but he responded in an upbeat tone. "Zia thought that if we came by before all of you, it would make it a bit easier."

I offered his friend a nod of thanks while helping Gracie out of the car. She gave a small wave, and I immediately saw both of them—Zia especially—clock her state. I almost stepped back as Zia moved in front of us, concern filling her gaze. I knew Zia wasn't a threat, but I did have to fight the urge to pull Gracie behind me on principle.

"You're sick." Zia lifted her hand toward her forehead. "May I?"

I assumed Zia planned to check Gracie's fever, but instead she closed her eyes, pressing a single finger to Gracie's forehead. I didn't like the idea of not knowing what she was doing to my mate.

Siguun made his way over, greeting Ravik and Basir, who were also focused on what was happening. "Zia is a healer."

Zia offered Siguun a soft look. "Healer in training. Gracie should see a real healer. I'm worried about how fast this came on."

How did she even know that?

"And I can tell you're exhausted just from looking at you. Let's get you all inside and settled."

"Where is—"

"I'm here."

My question was cut off as we all turned toward the doors, where Alpha Lacey Harrison waited. The usually serious woman seemed relaxed despite her usual formality. "I'm glad all of you made it safely... although not well, clearly."

"I'm just sick, it's nothing to worry about," Gracie said. "It's good to see you again."

Lacey let out a quiet, noncommittal hum. When she did speak, it was measured. "I think it would be wise for you to see a healer. We have plenty of them here."

"We appreciate that," Ravik said.

Lacey's gaze flicked briefly to Zia before returning to him. "As for the rest...we'll have dinner tonight. I want to think over a few things Zia has recently explained to me."

Not a refusal. Not agreement either.

"Then we'll talk."

# CHAPTER 15

# GRACIE

"GRACIE HOLLOWAY?"

My eyes lifted to a woman slipping into the room through a series of thick curtains, closing them behind her to create a private space for Ravik and me. I hadn't been to a healer—hadn't been allowed any kind of medical care—in over a decade, so naturally I was a little uneasy.

It helped knowing Basir and Thornar were just outside, too. The facility had allowed only one extra person to come with me, and my mates had decided on Ravik. The room was too small to fit any more.

Even though I was nervous, I was grateful Zia had pushed me to come. I wouldn't have done it myself, and with how awful I still felt, it was probably necessary.

"Yes. Hi," I said, sitting up a little straighter as

the healer took the chair across from us. I was perched on a medical table that felt more like a bed, with Ravik seated beside me, our fingers intertwined.

Her gaze shifted to him, offering a small nod. "Ravik Gentry, we're honored to have your family here. For transparency, I'm Alpha Lacey's sister, Starr. Lead healer of this territory."

She paused, no doubt noticing the way Ravik straightened at that piece of information, before addressing her next comment directly to me. "If you're not comfortable with me conducting your exam, I can have one of my assistants step in. I will, however, have to review your information to ensure that they are correct in their conclusions."

"I'm okay with it," I said honestly, clearing my throat and wincing at the pain. "I haven't had any kind of medical exam in years."

Starr jotted something down, offering me a curious look. "When was the last time you saw a healer? Do you remember?"

"I think it was right around my eleventh birthday, about ten years ago," I explained. "I've lived in the Cold Moon Pack territory until recently."

"A decade? That would make you twenty-one?" Starr barely masked her surprise, her gaze darting to Ravik whose hand was tightening in mine. I knew that none of this made him happy to hear, but it was also unavoidable. I couldn't change what nearly half of my life had included.

"Yes."

Starr's aura was grounded and calm. It reminded me of Zia, and the way she nodded thoughtfully and moved toward a sink to wash her hands made me want to know what she was thinking. I also appreciated that her pace wasn't rushed. The confidence and certainty of it lessened my anxiety.

"And we aren't just in here for a normal physical, I'm assuming?" she asked, turning toward me. "I haven't read the full brief you provided, but I can tell that you're running a temperature and have a sore throat. Anything else I'm missing?"

It was almost unsettling how much she had gleaned during the couple of minutes she'd been in the room with me.

"I'm also very tired," I admitted.

She nodded and approached, lifting her hand. "May I?"

"Of course."

Ravik didn't let go of my hand as Starr began her exam. I wasn't sure if it was because I hadn't been around a healer in so long, but much like the priestess magic, this felt like such a different thread of power than my own. Everywhere she touched, from my pulse, to my head, to the center of my chest—even as she listened to my heart with a thin metal device—

carried a pulse of warmth that felt like golden sunlight moving across my skin.

She wasn't healing yet, just observing.

Her frown was slight but noticeable enough for Ravik to sit up straight. His question was unspoken, but she answered it. "You've been running on very little for a very long time, Gracie. Every power reserve you have, every physical reserve you have is almost empty."

*That wasn't good.* The muscle in Ravik's jaw jumped once before he went completely still beside me.

"With that being said," she continued, her finger moving to my temple, eyes closing. "I can tell that the little amount of energy you have left is new and seems to be fueled in part by your mates."

She pulled back and tilted her head. "Your health needs to become a priority—you'll need to repair it slowly and steadily rather than all at once. We have a tonic that will help with that. I'll be sure to have a supply sent with you."

"What does it do?" Ravik asked.

"Think of it as a vitamin of sorts. It fixes nutritional deficiencies," Starr said. Then her expression sobered. "With that being said, it will not fix all damage.

"I know very little about your life, Gracie, but I can tell that your body has been worn down by stress. That you haven't been able to rest." She paused, her tone quieter now. "I would highly suggest seeing a healer regularly in the upcoming months, more than the normal prescribed amount, and a specialist who can help ground your magic and energy. The toll this has taken on your body is significant."

I could hear that she was really trying to convey how serious this was.

Ravik squeezed my hand as I nodded in under-standing. It shouldn't have surprised me that my time in the Cold Moon Pack had left such a mark, but at the same time it was almost embarrassing that she could tell.

As Starr went to sit and jot a few things down, she spoke more openly. "What you have now is a simple cold, but naturally it feels worse than that. Oftentimes when the body is placed under prolonged stress, it will have a delayed illness response—the body waits until it feels safe enough to be vulnerable. I believe that is exactly what is happening here."

Which was exactly what Ravik had said on the plane, the conversation I'd overheard in the throes of my fever drifting back to me now.

"Beyond the tonics," she said, jotting a few more words, "I will give you medicine to bring down the fever and relieve the soreness. If you get sick again, it shouldn't feel as extreme. Your body simply knows it can afford to be now."

"Thank you," I said softly. "I was nervous coming in here. I didn't know what to expect."

Starr put down her pen and looked at me for a long moment before her gaze shifted to Ravik. When she spoke again, her tone was matter-of-fact.

"Considering everything you've shared and the deficiencies I'm sensing, there are a few other things I'd like to check. When was the first day of your last period?"

Oh.

My eyes widened as I tried my best to recall. "Maybe a year ago? I have never had a consistent period. In fact, I would go months without one."

In a way it had been a blessing, given the circumstances, but now a sliver of doubt wormed its way in.

"Irregular cycles are a natural consequence of prolonged stress and poor nutrition. It doesn't surprise me, but it is something to be mindful of going forward. Now that your body has what it needs, things should regulate on their own within a few months. If they don't, we can look further into it."

The words slipped out before I could stop them. "Will that affect my body long term?"

"In terms of reproduction, no. It shouldn't, unless there are underlying conditions. Most likely your body was protecting itself, preserving energy the only way it knew how."

"Okay, thank you. And thank you for doing this

exam. I know you aren't the healer I would normally see, but having answers makes me feel a lot better, even if the rest of me doesn't quite feel it yet."

"Of course. That's what healers are for." She stood, tucking her notes under her arm. "My assistants will gather everything you need. In the meantime, I'd suggest rest and a stop at one of the local apothecaries. There's one in town that makes lemon and honey cough drops that work wonders."

As Starr closed the curtains behind her, my body slumped. Ravik let out a low rumble. "You okay, *lux mea?*"

"Yeah." I sighed. "I was so relieved to finally be *living* again that I didn't stop to consider the rest of it."

Ravik didn't answer right away. Instead he lifted me onto his lap in one easy move, his lips pressing to the top of my head as I let out a slow breath against him.

"Empty." His arms tightened around me. "She said you were running on empty, Gracie.

"That will never happen again."

THE FRESH AIR hit me the moment we stepped outside, cool and damp against my skin, refreshing after the stillness of the healer's wing. I hadn't realized how much I needed it until I was breathing easier, the stone path beneath my feet soft with moss.

"Zia kept talking about you the entire time," Thornar said after a moment, falling into step beside me. "How worried she was."

*That was so nice of her.* Though we'd only had short interactions, I really liked Zia, and I was already looking forward to more time with her. At least once I was feeling better.

But for now, the fresh air and the quiet rhythm of this place were doing more for me than any medicine, and we still had the apothecary ahead.

My mates broke into quiet conversation as we took the path from Alpha Lacey's home into town. The sound of a nearby creek caught my attention, and the damp breeze seemed to lull everything into a slow, gentle rhythm. The cottages we passed were spaced unevenly, built around the natural waterways, with people moving at an unhurried pace that felt...good. Really good.

Thornar stayed close by my side as we walked, his hand brushing mine while Basir and Ravik flanked us. By the time the apothecary came into view, tucked between two low buildings with herbs hanging in the windows, I realized my heart had slowed, my body finally starting to relax.

Unintentionally, this place was exactly what I needed right now.

A series of soft bells chimed as I pushed open the lavender-painted wooden door, the sound light and beautiful. Almost like the jet's chime, but more cheery.

Warm air wrapped around me the moment we stepped inside, thick with the scent of herbs, oils, and something faintly sweet. Bundles of drying plants hung from the ceiling in clustered rows and shelves lined the walls, crowded with tins and dark bottles.

Everything felt carefully placed but well-used, the shop busy with at least six different people milling about. Several of them already had items gathered in their hands, moving through the shelves with quiet familiarity, like this wasn't their first time here.

We turned down the third aisle, making our way toward a section marked *mend* on a cast-iron sign hanging from the ceiling. Two people stood at the end of the aisle, a man and a woman speaking in low, worried tones.

Keeping my gaze on the shelves, I started searching for cough drops, knowing my mates were close behind me.

"Gracie?"

I froze. That voice was very familiar, plucked straight from my childhood memories. *Nori.* I turned right away, taking in the woman who looked both exactly like the Nori I knew and someone much older.

That wasn't what made my heart stutter, though. That was the result of the man who stood next to her.

"Owen?"

# CHAPTER 16

# GRACIE

I COULDN'T BELIEVE I was sitting across from Owen.

On the jet, half-conscious, I had heard my mates say his name—had heard them talk about finding him here. It had felt like a dream then, and it still felt like one now. I couldn't stop staring at him.

Both Owen and Nori looked exactly as I remembered, just older. My brother was much larger than he'd been at fourteen, and his once neat black hair now sat on top of his head in messy waves. His green gaze was the same, reminding me so much of my mom's, but now there was a scar through his left eye. His hand rested protectively around Nori's shoulder as she leaned into him. I could tell she was examining the four of us in the same way I was looking at them.

Nori's hair, once filled with leaves from playing outside, was now a silky straight veil of blonde. She was even more beautiful than when we were younger. And seeing them together? I suddenly understood why my mom had always hoped they would end up being mates. They fit each other perfectly. I wished she had lived to see it.

"I don't know what to say." My voice was a hoarse whisper, my eyes burning. "I can't believe I'm sitting across from either of you."

Truthfully, I wasn't sure I would have made it out of the apothecary at all if it hadn't been for my mates. Ravik's hand was warm and steady on my shoulder, and I was acutely aware of Thornar and Basir on either side, grounding me. It had been their quiet suggestion that moved our reunion three doors down to this cottage, because I had been *entirely* incapable of doing anything but staring.

My hands were folded tightly in my lap, and I hadn't released them since we sat down.

"You escaped." Owen's voice was rough with grief and guilt. "You escaped that bastard's territory."

"Yes. But I wouldn't have been able to without my mates." I gestured between them. "Ravik, Thornar, and Basir." I didn't tell my brother yet that escaping Ivan had become the least of our worries.

"Ravik Gentry." Owen's gaze moved over my mates, something cautious shifting in his expression. "Future Alpha of Ironsun territory. We heard you'd come into town."

"Word travels fast," Thornar mused.

I watched Owen take them in—*really* take them in—and felt a strange nervous jitter invade my system. Whatever he saw, I hoped it was what I knew and saw in these men. I had learned not to care for the opinions of others, but this was my brother.

"We've been searching for you since Gracie told us you'd been separated since that night," Ravik said. Owen's face fell, his gaze shifting back to me.

"I assumed..." Owen looked down at Nori for a long second, something passing between them that felt private, before he seemed to bolster himself. "I never thought I would see you again, Gracie. I didn't want to consider..."

"That you and your parents had passed away," Nori finished softly. She reached across the table and briefly touched my hand. "Gracie, I am so glad you're here. I thought I was seeing a ghost at first."

Hadn't there been a time in the Cold Moon Pack when I had looked at my own reflection and felt the same? So much had changed since then.

"I'm so happy to see both of you safe." I let out a small exhale. "But you aren't wrong about Mom and Dad."

My words constricted the air around us. Owen's jaw tightened and his eyes closed, and I could feel the pain radiating off of him. Nori immediately moved closer, her hand finding his without looking.

Guilt flooded me. I'd had years to deal with this—years to grieve, to adjust, to *survive*. He was hearing it for the first time. Should I have softened it? Hidden it longer?

Basir's hand settled on my leg and I felt reassurance pushing through the bond from all three of my mates, quiet and constant. It kept from unraveling entirely.

"When?" Owen asked, his eyes still closed. "From the start?"

"Dad, yes," I whispered. "Mom was with me for a few years."

Owen's eyes opened, bright with unshed tears, as he leaned forward and crossed his arms on the worn wooden table. "I should have done more. I should have tried to break back in. Done *something*."

"What exactly happened that night?" Thornar asked him the question I couldn't manage myself. I glanced at him, grateful for his ability to step in when it was needed most. It also allowed me to find my voice.

"You two escaped together, I assume?" My question was steadier than I expected. "How did that happen? Have you been here the entire time?"

The two of them exchanged a look before Nori began. "We were together the night of the attack. Back then, we used to sneak out to the creek to talk and just...be." A faint smile crossed her face at the memory, but it faded quickly. "We could see the village from where we were. We saw the trucks approaching."

"We saw the flames," Owen continued, his voice tight. "I saw how many soldiers there were. I heard the guns. I saw our house burning." He paused, his face contorting in pain. "I tried to convince Nori to run—that I would catch up with her."

"I wouldn't let him." Nori's eyes closed briefly. "I wasn't being brave. I was selfish. I knew if he went back home, he wouldn't come back to me."

A sensation moved through me that I didn't have a good name for. Relief, maybe. Gratitude that Nori had held on to him when he was willing to throw himself into harm's way.

But underneath that, quieter and less comfortable, the awareness that while I had been in that compound, Owen had been *living*. Building this life of freedom with someone he loved. I kept my face expressionless, although it was difficult.

Through the bond I could feel my mates' reactions to not only the recounting of what happened but also the wave of feeling it inspired in me. A low, controlled fury from Ravik. Something darker and silent from Basir. And from Thornar, something more raw, closer to the surface and volatile.

I took a moment to sit with it all, then to let it go so I could truly mean what I said next.

"I'm glad she didn't let you," I said softly. "I'm glad you ran."

"I should have come back," Owen said. "Should have gotten help, called on others—"

"You were fourteen," I interrupted gently. "You're *alive* because you ran, Owen."

"Maybe." He dragged a hand through his hair and looked away. The word sat in the air between us, and I didn't try to fill the space. The guilt wasn't mine to take from him, no matter how much I wanted to.

"What happened after that?" Thornar prompted.

"The night we left, we had nothing. We had to travel town by town for a while, slowly moving toward Scarlet Sloth territory. We didn't risk crossing any borders until we had to—it felt like we were constantly a town or two away from Ivan's reach through the territory," Nori said, a slight shiver running through her. "It took months, going through the mountains and near the waterfront."

"Hardest path you could have taken, but probably the best to stay undetected," Basir noted quietly.

Pain lanced through me imagining it. Two teenagers, no money, no pack, no one to call on. *They must have been so scared.*

"We reached Scarlet Sloth territory after a year of traveling, staying in places as long as we could and working small jobs," Owen explained.

"But we didn't last more than two years there,"

Nori added. "The number of diplomats coming and going made us nervous we'd be caught. Ridiculous, in retrospect. They weren't looking for us, but at the time...we were young."

I thought of myself at seventeen. What I had been doing while they were deciding where to live. The comparison sat uncomfortably in my stomach before I pushed it aside.

"After that, we made our way into Bloodrose Sloth territory," Owen continued. "The quiet was nice after everything we'd been through."

"And they didn't question where we came from," Nori said. "They even let us purchase land and build a home."

My gaze moved around the cottage. Their home was comfortable and lived in, filled with hand carved wooden furniture, a glowing hearth, and quilts covering every surface. Three doors led deeper into the house from the main living area, and a humid breeze drifted in through the open window.

"So we've been here ever since," Owen said. "And by the time I worked up the courage to go back and find you, to find our parents..."

"I was pregnant," Nori said gently. "Five years after we escaped, we started a family. I didn't want him going anywhere." She paused, holding my gaze. "It was selfish."

The words landed differently than she meant them to. *Kids*. They had kids.

Owen had stayed because there were children here...children who needed their father. Suddenly, underneath the complicated tangle of everything I hadn't let myself feel, my chest loosened.

If he had gone back—if Nori had let him—he would have died. I knew that with certainty. Whatever I had lost in those years, I hadn't lost him. He was here. He was safe. That was enough.

"Kids?"

"Yes," Nori said, unable to help the smile that pulled at her lips. "Two of them. They should be back soon—they're part of a small school collective that takes them out during the day."

"You're an aunt," Owen added, pride slipping into his voice.

The words didn't make sense at first. I turned them over in my mind, waiting for them to land.

An aunt. *I was an aunt.*

I blinked as tears filled my eyes. I'd thought I'd lost all of my family, and now I found that Owen and Nori were alive and that there were two small people in the world who were so incredibly important to me, who already mattered more than they could possibly know.

My wolf stirred inside me, something instinctive and protective moving through her at the idea of our *pack.* I hadn't felt that pull in so long that the force of it nearly stole my breath. I pressed a hand to my sternum just to steady myself.

"What are their names?"

"Jackie is our oldest. She's a little wildfire," Nori said fondly. "And Ever just turned two. He's quieter, but completely attached to his sister."

Through the bond I could feel the quiet and contained surprise moving through Ravik. I watched Basir's gaze travel quietly around the room, settling on the wooden toys scattered on the couch and the small brightly colored plates near the sink. And Thornar, without a word, intertwined his fingers with mine. I held on, using him as an anchor against the overwhelming wave of emotion pressing in at the edges..

"Please stay to meet them," Owen said, then looked to my mates. "All of you are welcome. If you've protected my sister, I trust you're good people."

"How did you even meet?" Nori asked, her gaze moving between me and my mates. "If you're from Ironsun territory?"

I froze. How did I answer a question that had so many dark layers to it? I didn't want to expose them to any of that—they had a happy and peaceful life here. My brother already felt guilty over everything that had happened, and I didn't want him to feel any more.

Thornar felt my panic through our bond and

answered for me. "Gracie was brought to the Thornfell Trade Conference. We met her there and got her out of Cold Moon territory shortly after."

The room went silent as Owen's eyes cut to me. I held his gaze while managing to keep my expression calm. I could see him working through what 'brought to the Thornfell Trade Conference' actually meant. I gave the slightest shake of my head, not wanting to delve into it. His brows furrowed, but he didn't push for more information.

The silence sat for a moment before Nori spoke again, softer this time. "Why are you here, though? In Bloodrose territory?"

How did I explain the war coming? The politics? Everything here felt so simple and safe.

"We have a meeting with Alpha Lacey," Ravik answered.

"Mom! Dad!"

A high-pitched squeal filled the air as the door was thrown open and two small balls of chaos barreled in. My eyes briefly tracked an older woman waving goodbye from the road with a few other children, but then my attention was fully on my niece and nephew.

*My niece and nephew.* That was insane.

The cottage felt smaller and more alive all at once. Jackie launched into an excited story, her words tumbling over each other as she pulled at Nori's sleeve, demanding attention. Even Ever was in motion, sending a paper airplane through the air toward Owen, demonstrating how it would float for full seconds before dipping.

Neither of them had noticed us yet, completely absorbed in their own worlds as children so often were. Even those at the Cold Moon Pack, alone in their bunkers, had been able to escape in their own imaginative play and daydreams.

"Okay, okay!" Owen raised his voice over the noise. "You both clearly had a good day, but before we hear all about it, I have someone I want you to meet."

Jackie snapped her head toward us, and static rang in my ears while shock radiated through me. *She had my mom's face.* Different, almost strawberry blonde hair, but the same face shape and the same eyes in a startling shade of green. Her smile was instantaneous and contagious as she threw up a big wave.

"I'm Jackie!" she announced. "This is our house."

Nori shook her head with the patience of someone very used to this, letting Jackie take the lead. "And this is my brother," Jackie said, gesturing at Ever with great importance. "But he doesn't talk yet."

Ever looked over then. His brown eyes, so much like Nori's, found mine first and held them for a prolonged second before sliding to my mates. Then he stumbled back and burst into tears.

*Oh no.* My heart clenched. I stayed seated, but every instinct pulled me toward him. I wanted to comfort him but had no idea if moving closer would only make it worse.

"He's just surprised," Owen assured us quickly, but it was Jackie who leaned toward us and lowered her voice to a loud whisper.

"He cries a lot. It's because you're all bigger than him."

She wasn't wrong. My mates were *much* bigger than both of them.

I glanced up at Ravik. "Maybe sit down? You're pretty tall; it might help."

Ravik's mouth curved, and he reached for a chair from the corner without a word, folding himself into it. Owen motioned me over and I stood carefully, rounding the table.

"Come say hi. He'll calm down," Owen promised. Already Jackie was straining against Nori's hold, excited to join us. When I came face to face with Ever, he sniffled and watched me with cautious brown eyes. I did my best to block my mates from his view.

"Hi Ever, I'm Gracie." I kept my voice soft, falling back into the gentle tone I had learned to use with the children in the Cold Moon Pack. "I heard you had a fun day at school."

"So fun!" Jackie called out from behind us.

Ever considered me for a long moment before

slowly raising his paper airplane toward me. My throat tightened at the small show of trust. I took it gently and turned it over in my hands.

"This is very neat. Did you make it?"

"The teacher—" Jackie's words dissolved into muffled giggles as Nori intervened. It was hard to not crack a smile at the girl's enthusiasm.

Ever glanced at his sister, then back at me. "Yes."

The word was so clear and certain that Owen went still beside him, staring at his son. "Did he just—"

"Talk!" Jackie tackled me, cutting off Nori's question as a giggle escaped me. I caught her easily and turned to face her with a bright smile.

"Jackie, I'm so happy to meet you."

"Thank you." She beamed. "How did you make Ever talk? He can't talk, not usually." She said it simply, the way children say things that adults would soften or avoid altogether. "He's sick."

I looked to Owen and then Nori. They were exchanging a quiet look that had me straightening to stand. Through the bond I felt my mates clock her words, creating a subtle shift in the room's energy. My wolf went still beneath my skin, our attention sharpening on Ever.

He looked perfectly healthy to my eyes—rosy cheeked and bright eyed. But Jackie didn't strike me as the kind of child who fibbed, and those were the words of a child who didn't understand the full picture.

Nori ran her hands through Jackie's hair before encouraging her to sit. Her voice dropped quiet. "Ever is sick. We don't know exactly what it is, but his wolf isn't settling the way it should."

"The healer here has done what she can," Owen continued, "but the help he needs is beyond what's available in Bloodrose territory. He needs someone who can discover what's actually wrong, not just manage it day to day."

Ravik shifted in his seat. "What exactly is happening with him?"

"His wolf and his human side are so interconnected that there's almost no separation between them," Nori said in a way that told me she'd explained this many times before. "It's been affecting his development. His speech. He needs to learn to ground his power, but we don't know if that's even possible at his age."

My brows furrowed as I looked at Ever, letting my wolf reach out to greet his magic. Right away I could feel it, the sheer weight of it.

"It may be because he's powerful," I suggested. "I can feel it even now."

Ever tugged on a strand of my hair, unbothered, as if we'd known each other every day of his two years rather than only the last ten minutes.

"I've seen that before," Basir said, drawing the room's attention.

"You have?" Owen's voice pitched with hope and emotion.

"*Experienced* something similar," Basir corrected, his voice measured. "I didn't come from a family line with a power hierarchy like Ravik and Thornar, but when I was born it was clear I was an Alpha. I had power that couldn't be balanced until I was older and had proper training. My wolf had overtaken much of who I was as a child."

My eyes widened, and Ravik and Thornar exchanged equally surprised looks. I hadn't known that about Basir—nor had my mates—and I couldn't stand the quiet sadness that crossed his face. That also meant, though...

"Do you mind if I come closer to him?" Ravik asked Owen, already rising.

"Careful," Thornar warned.

Ravik nodded and approached slowly. I stayed close to Ever, whose tears had dried, his eyes now narrowed on my mate with open suspicion. Nori made a soft, surprised noise at the tiny rumbling sound coming from Ever's chest.

My mate extended his hand. Ever eyed it from the safety of his father's arms for nearly a minute before hesitantly placing his small hand in Ravik's.

*The room shifted.*

A phantom wind moved through the cottage, stronger than the breeze wafting through the window, and Jackie screeched with delight as the paper airplane lifted off the table and went sailing. Through the bond I felt the power I'd sensed in Ever now rising to meet Ravik.

Then Ravik stepped back, the paper airplane gliding to the ground as the wind receded. "Basir is right. That is exactly what is going on. Normally, when you're born with Alpha power you're raised from an early age to handle it. It's made a lot easier by being around other Alphas, usually your family."

"But he doesn't have that," Owen said.

"So what do we do?" Nori asked.

"Come to Ironsun. We have teachers who understand this exact issue and Alphas who can help him learn to ground his power, especially with how close we are to the university. The environment alone would make a difference."

"You're asking us to leave our home," Nori said quietly.

"I'm offering you a choice," Ravik countered. "You can stay here, but he will struggle—Basir can attest to that. Ironsun would be a change, but he would have what he needs."

I could see how the picture he painted affected both of them.

"Basir would be able to work with him directly once we're done traveling," Thornar added. "We'd make sure you had everything you needed, including movers."

I couldn't help but feel an overwhelming amount of gratitude for my mates at this moment. Without hesitation, without being asked, my mates had stepped up for my family as if they were already their own.

The silence that followed was heavy. I watched Owen and Nori look at each other before Nori's gaze dropped to Jackie in thought. Owen looked at his son, still tucked in the crook of his arm, clearly no longer bothered by my mates' presence.

"We'll think about it," Owen said finally.

"I'm hungry!" Jackie announced, heading toward the kitchen and breaking the tense silence as if the matter was settled. "You should eat with us."

I smiled at her thinly disguised order. "We would love to."

So we stayed for lunch. Jackie took over the conversation, moving from topic to topic with breathless energy while Ever sat pressed against my side, occasionally offering me bites of his food.

I watched Owen and Nori move around each other in their small kitchen, easy and practiced, while trying to memorize all of it. The way the light came through the window. The sound of my family's laughter. Even how my mates settled into the space.

I hadn't expected to find my brother today. I

hadn't known he would have a family and a home worth protecting. Asking him to leave it, to step into something he knew nothing about, was a decision that couldn't be made lightly.

Selfishly, I wanted them in the safety of Ironsun territory if war broke out. But they didn't need to know about that yet.

# CHAPTER 17

# GRACIE

AN HOUR AND A HALF LATER, with the promise to speak to my brother tomorrow about their decision, I stared at the tonic sitting on the vanity of our guest suite. It was a cozy and warm space—a living room in the center with two bedrooms on either end. Would the same feeling of comfort translate into dinner tonight with Alpha Lacey?

Each of our experiences in the other territories had been so vastly different from this.

My mates had claimed the smaller bedroom to get ready for the evening, leaving me to the larger one with the promise of a bath and an hour of quiet before we needed to leave. I had taken them up on it immediately.

Picking up the tonic, I read the note attached. *This*

*dose should be good for twenty-four hours. Make sure to continue to take it daily. - Starr*

I was so thankful for her. My anxiety about my own medical care had reduced drastically since our appointment today, and with the medicine from the jet, I was still feeling far better than I had hours ago. As I opened the tonic bottle, the scent of oranges bloomed through the air. I brought it to my lips—

*The bottle was plucked right out of my fingers.*

My eyes widened as I looked up to find Thornar leaning against the bathroom vanity, holding the open bottle balanced on his palm and offering me an affectionate look. I tilted my head, noticing something behind his usual warmth that I couldn't quite name.

"Little flame, we don't drink things without checking they aren't poison first."

My brow furrowed. "She's a healer though."

"Doesn't matter." He flashed me a smile that absolutely didn't match his tone.

"Okay so how do we even—*Thornar!*"

He drank it. He actually drank it. Not all of it, but a full sip—before capping the bottle and setting it back on the vanity like he hadn't just done something insane.

"What?" I stared at him, mouth agape. "What was that?"

"Now we wait and see." He winked. "I'm sure it's

fine. Like you said, she's a *healer*." And then he was walking away.

I moved before I could think, nearly tackling him from behind. Thornar caught me instantly, chuckling as he pulled me up his massive body and walked backwards until he could lift me onto the counter. I gripped his shirt as he stepped between my legs and raised a single curious brow.

"Yes, Gracie?"

"If it's poison you could *die*," I hissed.

My throat felt tight as anxiety flooded my body. I hadn't considered that it could be dangerous, it was medicine! Now I had to sit with the possibility that my mate could get hurt because of me.

"But then you won't," he mused, like it was the simplest solution in the world.

Everything slowed down for a second. I tilted my head, examining the lightness of his expression that sat so differently from the look in his eyes.

Thornar had just drank potentially poisoned medicine to make sure it was safe for me.

"Why?" I whispered. "Why would you do that?"

Thornar's expression shifted, the lightness disappearing as his jaw tightened. He usually always had an answer, but this time he said nothing at first. He just looked at me before bringing his hand up to cradle my face, his thumb brushing my cheekbone.

"Thornar?" I asked again, my voice softer than I

intended. His scent was surrounding me, brown sugar and bourbon, and the way he wrapped me in his shadow had my thoughts scattering and cheeks warming.

"Gracie," he said simply. It didn't escape my notice that he still hadn't answered.

Thornar's gaze dropped, tracing the line of my neck down to where my plush robe had loosened. His other hand tightened on my waist, pulling me closer until I was pressed tight against his frame. His mouth found my collarbone, my throat, the curve of my shoulder. His pace was hot and unhurried, like he had all the time in the world and intended to use it.

My skin broke into a heated flush. I was acutely aware of how little the robe covered and even more aware that he knew it. The fabric slipped from my shoulder as he continued, and I found myself wanting him to keep going but also desperately needing him to kiss me.

As he trailed back up my throat and jaw, I realized he was purposefully avoiding my lips.

"Thornar." My fingers tightened in his shirt, my voice coming out in a plea. "Kiss me?"

Thornar pulled back just slightly, apology and heat fused in his gaze, before dipping his head to brush his nose against mine. "Not until we know it's safe, little flame."

My heart broke open at his reason.

"Don't be disappointed. I'll make you forget about it." His promise was followed by his fingers finding the tie of my robe, pulling it loose slowly.

The material fell away, pooling around my elbows, my chest bare to him. My nipples were already pebbled, and he let out a low, pained rumble as he took me in.

"So fucking beautiful," he murmured. The words were so raw and simple that my entire body shifted forward, just to be as close as possible to him.

Thornar stilled me immediately, his natural dominance coating the bond between us as he offered me a wicked grin.

His lips found my collarbone again, then moved lower—a trail of hot, open-mouthed kisses setting my skin on fire. When he reached my breast his mouth closed over the sensitive peak and pulled a moan from my lips. The warmth of his tongue teasing, circling, flicking was enough to have me shifting against the counter, desperate for any kind of friction. He lifted a hand to cup my other breast, his thumb brushing the peak in that same devastatingly perfect rhythm.

"Thornar." My whispered moan was honest and full of need. *More. Please, more.*

He wasn't rushed, though, despite the need pulsing through our bond. Instead he lavished attention on one side then switched to the other, his movements entirely focused on slowly unraveling me. I could feel how wet I was, embarrassingly so, with nothing but the cold counter beneath me and the robe twisted around my body, trapping me so I could barely move.

I tangled my hands in his dark coiled hair, holding him to me, feeling the scrape of his teeth and then the soothing lap of his tongue afterward. *I needed more.* I had a feeling he knew that but had absolutely no intention of giving it to me yet.

My desire left me feeling emboldened, and my hands slipped down from his hair to slide against his hard length through his pants. My touch instantly had him biting down in a slightly punishing way that drew a whimper from my lips. I didn't stop though, feeling how massive he was and fighting the urge to rush my exploration.

Thornar pulled back, his eyes darker than I had ever seen them, a shift in his expression making my breath catch. His voice dropped to a deep warning.

"Gracie." Just my name, but the way he said it this time was different from before. "If you keep touching me like that..."

The smart thing would have been to stop.

Before he could finish, and before I could lose my nerve, I slid off the counter. My robe fell completely as I sank to my knees.

I felt a pure wave of possession surge through our

bond, and the moment my eyes met his, his hand caught my chin, tilting my face up.

"I don't know what to do," I admitted breathlessly. "I've never...I've never done this."

Thornar's eyes closed, his jaw tight like he was summoning every ounce of control he had left. But I was completely mesmerized by the power of his body, the barely contained tension running through him. My hands found the button of his pants, undoing it quickly before I lost my nerve entirely.

His eyes snapped open the moment I did. His fingers tightened on my chin.

"You want this?" Thornar's voice was rough, the question genuine. "Are you sure?"

I took a moment to consider it.

"I want you."

I tugged down on his pants over his hard length, emphasizing my point, and let my eyes roam over the hard planes of his abs and hips as he pulled his shirt up and over his head. A sharp breath left me when I saw his size, and I tugged his boxers down so that he was completely bare to me.

I couldn't help but stare. I mean—he was magnificent. I knew my mates were large, but experiencing it in this way had my body lighting up in a way that was overwhelming. I lifted my fingers to wrap around him as best I could, and I watched his abs tighten in response, his hand rising to hover near my head. Not touching, just there.

I was nervous about not knowing what to do, but the heat of him beneath my fingers was so intoxicating I couldn't stop myself from running my hand slowly along his rigid length.

Despite having no experience of my own, I had heard enough talk in the barracks to know what women did in this moment, and I found myself wanting to try. *So I kissed him,* a soft press of my lips against the head. He hissed, a sharp intake of breath, his hips jerking before he caught himself.

My stomach fluttered at the rawness of his reaction. My confidence, fragile as it was, unfurled a little. I did it again, then let my tongue venture out, a slow stroke around the crown before I tried to take him deeper. The salty taste of him bloomed against my tongue, and the gentle brush of his fingers against my hair had my head swimming.

"Little flame..." Thornar's groan was low and appreciative.

I took him into my mouth, slowly but deeper this time, trying to memorize every reaction—the way he seemed perilously close to snapping despite the iron grip he kept.

I craved his reactions though. They were my anchor. The low rumble when I tried to take him as deep as possible, pushing myself until my eyes watered. The way his length pulsed when I brought my hand up to work together with my mouth. Every sound he made was another bolster to my confidence, pushing me forward.

It wasn't until I held him as deep as I could for as *long* as I could that the control he'd been clinging to finally snapped. His fingers tightened in my hair, holding me there, and when I looked up at him through watering eyes he let out a *fuck,* his cock pulsing hot against my tongue.

"Such a pretty fucking mouth," he growled, the words sending a pulse of heat straight through me. "Stand up, little flame."

The command had me gasping as he pulled out of my mouth. I stumbled to standing on shaky legs, barely catching myself before his hands were on me.

"What are you—"

He lifted me onto the sink in one motion, spreading my thighs as he gripped his length and slid it through my wet center. The moan that left me was embarrassingly loud. My arms shook as I gripped the counter, my head falling back as he dragged himself slowly against my clit, the sensation so extremely intense.

With his free hand he gripped my chin, forcing my gaze to his. "I can't come down your pretty throat. Not for the first time. I want to mark up this perfect body and leave my cum exactly where it belongs."

*The Eight.* My body felt like it was about to combust, and when I felt him press against my entrance, a whimper broke free before I could stop it.

"Please," I whispered.

"Please what?" Thornar demanded. "Say it."

"I need to come." The words came out breathless and brazen all at once.

Thornar rumbled his approval, but I watched something shift in him as his gaze dropped to my throat. His words were a dangerous murmur against my skin. "Have to mark you, Gracie. I have no choice."

There was no warning. His thumb moved to swirl over my clit as he pressed against my entrance, and instead of kissing me—

*Thornar bit.*

Not a playful nip. Not a love bite. A true claiming bite, his teeth sinking into the curve of my throat. The pain was immediate, followed by a bright flash of white that dissolved into a wave of climax so intense his name tore from my lips in a scream.

An explosion of power burst between us as the mate bond solidified completely, not slowly but all at once. A bolt of lightning turned molten before hardening into a permanent pathway, no longer just between our wolves but now between souls. The room shifted and the air vibrated. I felt his release spill between my thighs, the sensation sending another wave of pleasure rolling through me.

Thornar released the bite, his lips coming away with a tiny bead of my blood. He licked it away, his gaze holding mine, filled with unshakable certainty.

"Mine." He breathed the word into existence.

Everything melted into a hazy warmth after that. I was lifted and carried to the shower as Thornar took care of me, his hands soft and deliberate. It was so different from everything that had just happened that it made my heart ache in the best possible way.

It wasn't until we had been standing there a long time, my eyes closed, that I felt the others' emotions stir in the bond.

"Hey Thornar..." I whispered.

His arm tightened around me as he pressed his lips to my neck again. I could feel his smile there.

"Oh, I know, little flame." He paused. "They can deal with it."

I tilted my head up and he gave me a slow, beautiful smile before dipping down to finally press his lips to mine.

"And now I can kiss you," he murmured against my mouth.

*Because it wasn't poison.*

# CHAPTER 18
# RAVIK

IF I HAD THOUGHT HEARING Gracie moan from the other room was a test of my patience, it was absolutely nothing compared to feeling her mate bond solidify with someone who wasn't me. I stood at the window of the guest suite, dressed for dinner, and barely contained the urge to go to her.

It hadn't been a painful sensation, but an intense one. It felt like something between the four of us had been rewired, and there was a buzzing under my skin, courtesy of my wolf who was howling at the idea of someone marking Gracie before us. Putting a permanent mark on *our* mate.

I knew I couldn't afford to think that way. I wasn't angry at Thornar; my mindset simply required an adjustment, and I was trying my fucking best to steady myself. My teeth practically ached with the need to mark Gracie so deeply it would never be questioned. Not just with a mating mark, either.

Next time, I wouldn't hold back. I wouldn't be able to.

The door to the living area opened as Basir walked back in, seeming shaken as he offered me a wild-eyed look. He had left because of her perfect moans, and I was sure the sensation of the bond snapping into place hadn't done anything for his delicate control.

"She's going to think you're angry at her if you leave again," I warned him.

"I know," he hissed, sitting down and running a hand through his hair. He stayed silent after that.

Minutes later, Thornar walked out, adjusting his suit jacket and offering me a momentary glance that said absolutely everything.

*Gracie was okay.* Good. That was all that mattered to me.

Except when he offered a cheery smile to both of us and went to grab his shoes from across the room, I could feel Basir bristle. I sighed inwardly. I could already tell exactly where this was going.

Basir would take extreme issue with Thornar's lack of control. I didn't see it that way, but compared to Basir's level of mastery over himself, I suppose it was accurate. And I had known him long enough to know that he wouldn't let it go.

"Why the hell would you put her through the power expenditure of making the bond permanent?"

*There it was.*

Thornar tensed as he finished lacing up his boots.

He stood and turned around as Basir pushed. "Seriously, Thornar, the healer said she's running on empty."

I knew what the bastard was going to say before he did.

"And now she's *not* empty. See, I'm—fuck." Thornar groaned as Basir appeared across the room, slamming him into the wall with a shoulder and a hit to the stomach...before disappearing again.

I sighed as Thornar flashed a dangerous smile and shook himself out. *This was unfortunately far from over.* We may have been brothers, but when you had three alphas in constant proximity to one another, shit boiled over.

"Don't be too worried, buddy—she feels much better now," Thornar jabbed before his face slipped into a more serious expression. "But if you come at me again tonight, you won't be."

Basir let out a low rumble as he paced across the room. I offered Thornar a look but he ignored me as Basir turned sharply toward him.

"Did she even get a chance to take her fucking tonic yet? Or was she too distracted?"

"I actually stopped her from taking it to make sure it wasn't poisonous. Had to test it."

Basir narrowed his eyes. "And how did you do that?"

Thornar offered him a mock confused look. "*Obviously* I drank it."

"Thornar," I grunted, knowing Basir was going to lose his fucking mind.

Thornar's voice lost all humor as he continued. "Gracie is perfectly fine. The tonic wasn't poisonous. We're all good. I knew exactly what I was doing, Basir."

I believed that, but his tone was absolutely layered. I had no idea if he and Gracie had slept together—it was entirely possible they had—but it didn't matter, because the bond was made and there was nothing more permanent than that.

Before Basir could explode, Gracie walked out. Although *floated* may have been a more apt description.

Her hair was damp, curling around her delicate shoulders, and she was dressed in a soft blue cocktail dress that wrapped around her. She offered all of us a shy look, her cheeks pink, as she slid on her shoes.

"Everything okay?" she asked, noticing the tension.

"Perfect, little flame," Thornar promised. "Basir is just worried you're too tired for dinner."

Which was both bullshit and accurate.

Moving across the room, she went to Basir and slipped her hand onto his chest before looking up at him. "I feel great. It's been a very long day, but I have a good feeling about this dinner."

Basir looked her over, nodding once and dropping a kiss to her lips. Then he was leading her toward the door. I stood and shot Thornar a look, but he just shrugged as we flanked them.

"He's not actually mad," I told him.

"I know." Thornar sighed. "But the bastard needs to chill out."

I smirked. "I mean, you did drink potential poison."

He chuckled. "Except his concern wasn't about that. Although you're right—I know he does worry about us." Basir probably worried about everyone far too much for his own good.

"We do need to be careful, specifically with shit like this. Especially after what Starr said about her reserves." I paused while keeping my voice low. "She also isn't on any kind of birth control. That tonic is the first medication she's had access to in years."

Thornar went quiet for a beat. When he spoke again, any humor was gone. "I know."

"Do you have a problem with that?" I asked.

He looked at me sideways. "Do you?"

I didn't answer. But that was answer enough for Thornar, who nodded in understanding.

"I just want to focus on her resting and feeling good," Thornar said quietly. "Anything else that comes, we can handle."

And we would. I wasn't afraid to admit that I wanted everything with Gracie, but I also understood that she needed to take the lead when it came to decisions like that. She was the one who had gone without freedom for a decade. That mattered.

"Basir—buddy—I want to talk to you!" Thornar suddenly called out as he strode forward and threw his arm around Basir.

I watched my Enforcer shake his head before smiling, Thornar's gesture having mended the trouble between them. Gracie waited for me to catch up, and I pulled her into my side while looking her over.

"Shouldn't they be more nervous going into this meeting right now? I'm a little nervous," Gracie admitted as I hummed in understanding.

"I think Thornar is a bit too distracted for that," I said, my voice neutral as my gaze dropped to her bare throat. A bite mark that would eventually turn gold sat at the curve of her neck, and my wolf nearly let loose a deep growl at the sight of it.

Though I'd managed to keep my emotions outwardly contained, Gracie must have felt it through the bond because she stumbled slightly in surprise. I caught her against me, keeping her close as we continued to walk.

"Ravik?" She searched my face with concern.

"Just trying to keep my wolf in check," I said evenly.

"What do you mean? Is your wolf upset about the mate bond?"

It was so damn refreshing how unintentionally straightforward Gracie was. There were things she still hesitated with, but for the most part she said exactly what she was thinking, especially as she grew more comfortable around us.

"A little," I said. "But *my* reaction is probably more concerning."

"Your reaction?"

"Of course. I'm imagining exactly where I want to place my own bite."

Gracie inhaled sharply, her eyes lighting up with interest, but before she could say a word we turned down the hall toward a set of wide open double doors. I didn't feel bad about letting her sit on my statement. In fact, I was entirely satisfied with the color it put in her cheeks.

Unfortunately, I had exactly three seconds between that and the doors of our destination to put those thoughts somewhere they couldn't distract me.

I wasn't exactly sure what to expect from Lacey Harrison. Unlike Alpha Haiden, I had never taken her particularly seriously—not because of her territory or her rule but because of her tendency to take offense in the inconsequential.

What I hadn't accounted for was the tone of the room when we walked in. She was taking this meeting very seriously—seriously enough to be petty about it —placing a familiar face on the opposite side of the table. A power move dressed as hospitality.

Singuun sat across from our place settings, Zia beside him, and gave me a shit-eating grin the moment our eyes met. *Ridiculous.* I ignored my brother.

"Alpha Lacey Harrison." I greeted her as she rose from the head of the table, smoothing her elegant robes before motioning to the four place settings.

"Ravik, Gracie, Thornar, Basir—I'm glad you could join us." Her voice was cool and measured as she waited for us to sit before taking her own seat. "I heard you had a rather eventful day after the healer."

Gracie spoke up, seeming more at ease here than she had been with Haiden. "Yes—Starr was incredibly helpful. But we ran into someone we didn't expect to."

"Oh? Who?" Lacey asked point blank as kitchen staff began to fill the warmly lit room. I was relieved she didn't press for medical details, but Thornar made an amused sound beside me, piecing something together I hadn't yet.

Gracie offered him a "go ahead" look, and he leaned forward with a surprised expression. "It was a bit crazy, to be honest, Lacey. We were heading to the apothecary to pick up medicine when it happened."

Lacey was fully listening now. The story had her attention.

"Remember, Gracie hasn't been outside of Cold Moon Pack territory in a decade," Thornar added as Gracie nodded in agreement. "So to run into someone she thought was lost to her…"

"In my territory?" Lacey clasped her hands, eyes wide. "You have to tell me who it was."

"My brother," Gracie answered. "I thought I'd lost him ten years ago. But he's been living here. He has an entire family here."

Lacey made a surprised sound and sat back. "So he married one of our own. When did he arrive? What's his name?"

"He actually married a girl from their home village," I said. "They were on the run for years and eventually settled here."

"Where they felt safe," Basir said.

Pride filled Lacey's expression. "*Well.* I would never have expected that." She took a long sip of her wine as the food was placed on the table and we began to eat.

This was a perfect example of why I didn't hold Lacey in the highest esteem. She traded in gossip, even in the most serious of situations. That wasn't necessarily a bad thing, it just simply wasn't how I operated.

"What's his name?" she asked.

"Owen Holloway," Gracie answered. Lacey's face softened, and she began nodding.

"Nori and Owen, yes. He's a carpenter, your brother. Made this very table." My gaze moved over the craftwork with curiosity. The dark wood had a carved design on the skirt, and it was covered in a coating meant to preserve it. I would have to make note of that for his job placement in Ironsun.

"I just feel horrible for their little boy—did they tell you he's sick?" she asked plainly, no softening around it.

I felt the sadness move through my bond with Gracie before I spoke. "Yes. We determined it's because he was born with Alpha power and has no way to channel it. We've offered them a place in Ironsun territory where he'd have access to resources for that."

"You did that?" Lacey offered me a questioning look. "You don't even know them, even if they are your mate's family. And from the sound of it, Gracie barely knows them herself."

"They're still family." Gracie's voice was filled with a cemented strength that I could see was interesting to Lacey.

"We can get to know them." Thornar shrugged. "Besides, we're trying to *hoard* all the powerful shifters in our territory."

Lacey sat back in her chair, deadpan. I nearly sighed. But unfortunately for my sanity and fortunately for his ego, Thornar's charm worked and she broke into a smile followed by a genuine laugh.

The moment cracked the stiffness open, and from there the evening flowed considerably smoother. Casual conversation filled the table, my brother and Zia quiet but still good company, and it wasn't until the plates were being cleared that the tone shifted.

"So." Lacey offered us a shrewd look. "You need my help fighting a war against Ivan Rivers."

I almost bristled at her tone, but Gracie stepped in. "Yes, we are here to ask for help."

My jaw tightened. I sure as hell wouldn't have been able to phrase it that way to another Alpha, but Lacey's ego seemed satisfied as she nodded in thought.

"Zia"—she looked over at the woman—"already explained to me the threat he poses, and frankly, I don't need much of an excuse to move against him. The way he handles himself is disgraceful."

One word for it.

"More so," Lacey interjected with a surprising smile, "I like all of you, I've decided. You're welcome."

Thornar chuckled as Gracie breathed out a sigh of

relief. I offered a conciliatory nod, hoping she wouldn't notice Basir's lack of response. Politics were not his strong suit.

Lacey straightened, folding her hands in front of her. "With that being said, I have one demand that must be met in order to have full access to my units."

This would be interesting.

"We're all ears," Thornar said. My gaze met Sigu-un's from across the table, and his serious expression almost broke. I turned my attention back to Lacey, refusing to show that I found this posturing somewhat amusing.

"My troops must have preferred placement over Kaliyah's Scarlet Sloth territory." Lacey's chin tilted up as if we would argue. "Better spots in camp, choice in when we deploy, and all of that."

"I think we can figure that out." Thornar glanced at Gracie. "Do you think that's fair?"

Gracie looked at the three of us before smiling at Lacey. "Yes. We agree."

We didn't need to tell her Alpha Kaliyah hadn't decided to help us yet.

One more ally secured. Sixteen days remaining. We still had territories to cover, a war to build, and a connection to The Eight that none of us fully understood yet. No matter the moment or atmosphere, I couldn't forget everything to come.

Lacey let out a satisfied sigh and sat back. "Perfect.

Now that that's decided, we can have dessert. I wanted to make sure you deserved it."

Gracie let out a giggle that softened the room, and I felt a smile tugging at my lips. Lacey was a piece of work, but this atmosphere made Gracie happy. And that was more than enough for me to stop and enjoy it.

CHAPTER 19

# GRACIE

"Are you sure you're comfortable with this?" I asked Owen and Nori.

It was warmer today than I'd expected, the damp breeze of the Bloodrose Sloth territory pushing through the open platform train station. Jackie stood at my side, bouncing up and down, while Ever sat on Nori's hip staring at me with curiosity.

"We aren't making an official move—not yet," Owen explained. "But we're going to take an extended stay there. We have to at least try."

Nori spoke up. "And we want to be around you. If it means moving to Ironsun to keep our family together, then that is what we'll do." My throat was tight with emotion as I crouched down to be level with Jackie.

"When I get back to Ironsun territory, I want to

take you to a treat shop. Does that sound fun?" I asked her seriously.

"Can I?" She looked up at her parents in question, her eyes lighting up.

"Of course," Nori answered. Jackie squealed and threw her arms around me, and I closed my eyes, savoring the hug. The Bloodrose Sloth territory had been an unexpected reprieve, but all of us were aware of what would come next as we moved closer to Cold Moon Pack territory. Even our travel had been rearranged because of our increased caution.

"Train is here!" Thornar called. I stood and immediately moved Jackie back, my family shifting to a safe distance. In a rush of emotion, I gave Nori and Ever a hug before turning to my brother. I could see unshed tears in Owen's eyes, and I let out a small sound of relief as he hugged me tightly.

"I'm so grateful we found you." His words had me nodding as I pulled back, knowing my mates—who had already said their goodbyes—were waiting for me.

"We will be together again soon," I said. "Stay safe. Siguun and Zia will escort you personally."

And I absolutely trusted the two of them to do that. The care and consideration they'd taken so far, coming to their house this morning to explain all of their options, showed that to me.

Basir appeared by my side then and took my hand, leading me toward the train that had pulled up. Shiny black and red paint adorned every inch of it, the gleaming metal sparkling underneath the sunshine. This would take us right across the border into Scarlet Sloth territory.

I didn't mind the change in travel, but I knew it was to keep a low profile as we grew closer in proximity to Ivan's sphere of control.

"Welcome aboard!" A friendly voice had me looking away from my family on the platform as we entered a cabin that was completely private, with the exception of an attendant.

I had been on trains before, but never like this. The seats were expensive leather, and there were velvet curtains shielding every window's light while still offering a view.

"Thanks." Thornar offered a charming smile as Basir led me to sit down at a table between two rows of leather couches. The four of us got comfortable as the train began to move, creating a steady rumble underneath us.

"Coffee or tea?" the man asked. My gaze darted over his warm expression, his uniform impressively crisp. His name tag read *Noah*.

"Tea," I answered. My mates ordered as well before the man disappeared through a set of doors.

"How long is the ride?" I asked.

"Only two hours," Ravik assured me.

"And this ensures Ivan won't get wind of our jet

traveling through the area," Basir pointed out, visibly more at ease on the train compared to the jet.

"For someone who claims they hate the territory next door, Lacey goes to lengths to ensure they're interconnected. I mean, they have a shared rail system," Thornar pointed out, making me smile.

I had grown fond of Lacey in the short time we'd spent with her, and I looked forward to seeing her again. *Even if she did like a bit of gossip.*

His words triggered a thought though, making my eyes go wide. I'd been so distracted by my brother that I hadn't thought about how our train ride into Scarlet Sloth territory...would unintentionally reveal that we hadn't talked to Alpha Kaliyah yet.

"She knows we haven't talked to her yet," I mused.

Thornar's gaze lit up as he chuckled. "So all of that bravado yesterday was what?"

"A show of power," Ravik offered.

I had a feeling we were missing some piece of the story, but I also didn't think we would get an answer anytime soon.

As the train chugged along, I rested my head against Basir's chest, his body angled so I could watch the surrounding country landscape out the window. Thornar was resting as well, his eyes closed, and Ravik sorted through papers until Noah came back with a tray of tea and some pastries. I eagerly grabbed one, pleasantly surprised by the cherry taste.

"How are you feeling?" Basir asked a minute later, his fingers gently twirling a strand of my hair. I wasn't sure he even realized he was doing it, but I didn't want to risk him stopping.

"Good. The side effects of the tonic wore off pretty fast."

When I took it this morning, I had felt sick to my stomach for half an hour. With that being said, I'd woken up feeling much better than yesterday, after only one dose. We had a box of tonics with us and the rest were being shipped back to Ironsun territory along with notes Starr had written for the attending healer there.

Part of feeling better may also have had to do with the amazing orgasm and mating bite on my throat, though. One that Thornar made a show of looking at and kissing whenever he had a chance, to the point that my cheeks had been hot pink this morning in the suite while packing up. I didn't mind in the least. In fact, I loved it.

I was incredibly relieved neither of the other men seemed bothered by it, and the connection between all of us felt strengthened because of Thornar's actions.

"Been on a train before?" Basir asked, breaking the comfortable silence.

"Yes," I answered. "That was really the only way we traveled, although we didn't leave our village often. My parents loved our home too much."

The soft affection in my voice piqued Basir's interest. "What were they like?"

I considered his question for a long moment, knowing the other two were listening and hoping I could do them justice.

"My mom was amazing. She was always trying out new hobbies or learning new skills. I think she taught us more than any schooling did. Sometimes it would be hunting or gardening, but other times it would be creating entire pieces of furniture from wicker. It was really fun. She was always smiling and happy."

It had been that imagery I'd hung onto, even while in captivity with her.

"And your dad?" Basir asked.

"Funny," I said, looking up at him. "Really funny, and he loved cooking and baking. He was a farmer by trade, but he also did a bunch of random jobs around town. His favorite thing to do was build out the garden for my mom. They loved each other so much. I knew that even as a child."

I paused for a moment. "Until Ivan took over the territory, our lives were peaceful and happy. Almost perfect."

Of course there had been problems, but nothing that held a candle to what came after.

I looked at Basir and then the others. "I wish you could have met them. But I feel really thankful we found Owen and Nori. Especially since we could help them."

"Your nephew is going to be okay, glow. I didn't have any constructive influence around me until my early teenage years when I arrived in Ironsun. I didn't talk much until then either."

Gratitude hit differently in that moment as I realized Basir wasn't just reassuring me about Ever—he was addressing his own past. Something he rarely talked about. I knew it was hard for him, but this was his way of telling me that even with all of the pain he endured, he was here and in a position that was far different than he probably ever expected.

"And now he won't shut up," Thornar said, eyes still closed, pulling a sound of amusement from Basir and a chuckle from Ravik.

"He'll be okay," Basir assured me, his tone turning serious once more.

"I know," I said, looking back out at the shifting landscape. "Because of you three."

Following that, the compartment settled into a relaxed quiet for about fifteen minutes, Thornar's breathing slow and Ravik eventually standing to go find Noah about getting more tea. I tipped my head back against Basir's chest and spoke quietly enough that it was just for him—needing to express my gratitude.

"You didn't have to tell everyone at my brother's

house. About when you were young. You could have just told them you'd seen it before."

"I know," he said simply.

"But it helped." I paused. "And I'm glad you told me."

His arm tightened around me. Basir didn't say anything else and I snuggled against him, loving the security I found in his arms.

THE LANDSCAPE slowly changed as we watched the world pass by. The soft green rolling fields of Blood-rose territory had given way to something more built up and developed, and after a bit I sat up a little straighter to get a better view.

I recognized we were in Scarlet Sloth territory before it was confirmed by the large crest-covered signs that lined the flat, distinct roads leading into the city. My stomach clenched uneasily because despite its beauty, this place represented so much to me.

The last time I'd been here, my life had been so different—I hadn't experienced it like this. Not with warm arms around me and tea going cold on the table or the sound of Thornar breathing softly across the way. Last time I had been here, Ivan's hand had been at the back of my neck like a shackle and my eyes had been pointed at the ground, unable to even react to my surroundings.

But I remembered sneaking a look through the car windows. It had been the first time I'd seen beauty in over a decade.

When the train came to a stop and Noah wished us goodbye, a nervous sensation worked its way up my spine. Unlike the first time I visited, we weren't driving straight to the TTC's location. This time we arrived right in the center of the city, and the difference from the Bloodrose Sloth territory was unmissable.

Stepping out of the station onto a wide boulevard, I stayed close between Ravik and Basir while Thornar moved a half-step ahead, already scanning. I tried to do the same. I tried to stay watchful. But the city kept pulling at me.

The copper rooftops were even more striking at street level than they had been through a car window, their green finish catching the light of the sunshine. The terraced townhomes rose on either side, and the smell of bread and coffee drifted from open windows as we passed bustling cafes.

My mates moved us through the crowds, people adjusting and moving out of our way. I was thankful for it at the moment because it really allowed me to catch each detail of the cityscape. It was so different from previous territories, especially Ironsun, and perfectly unique.

When a temple rose ahead of us I found myself moving just a bit faster, feeling the pull to truly get eyes on it. It was enormous, the kind of building that made you feel like you could never grasp the actual scale of it. Limestone columns with carvings of female figures lined the entrance in perfect symmetry, and above it all a great dome of glass rose against the sky with a woman at its crown.

"The temple of Sylvaern," Ravik said. "It's their favored god."

*The mother of growth and root.* Were the women carved into the columns supposed to be her? I examined the tunic of the nearest figure, noticing the stone petals of greenery curling around the hem.

As we reached the front of the temple, the doors wide open, I couldn't push myself to walk past it. Even the scent drifting from inside—something mossy and natural—seemed to pull me forward.

"Can we go inside?"

My mates all nodded, and Ravik took my hand while the other two settled outside, placing our bags down and getting comfortable.

As we stepped into the warmly lit temple, my eyes moved to the fantastic displays of art. Mosaics of every color, and overgrown plants adorning sculptures—all centered around a gorgeous tree that reached toward the glass dome of the roof.

"Welcome to the Temple of Sylvaeren," said a soft-spoken woman with green hair intertwined with vines. Her power signature told me she was a shifter, but she looked as far from one as possible. She had an ethereal way about her, emphasized by her camel-colored robes decorated with real flowers.

"Thank you," I said before explaining, "we just wanted to look inside."

"Of course." She motioned to the gigantic room. "Take your time. We don't have any ceremonies going on, but if you would like a blessing, Chastidy is doing them near the tree.

"I'm Amber. If you have any questions, don't hesitate to ask."

Ravik offered her a nod of understanding before leading me toward the tree, which was the true showpiece of the room. Words were carved into the trunk, and the more I looked at it, the more I realized the leaves shifted and moved under our watch despite there being no breeze.

"A bit different," Ravik murmured, his voice cautious as he caught my arm before I could drift closer. The woman standing at the base of the tree was dressed in a simpler robe, her silver hair pulled back around her face, as she offered us an understanding smile.

"I promise it's not dangerous," she said. "At least not right now. When she was younger, possibly, but she's settled with age much like myself."

*There was so much to unpack there.* I tapped Ravik's hand, and he produced a low rumble before releasing me to walk forward. I decided to ask the most obvious question. "She?"

"Of course." She motioned to the tree. "Much like my own name—Chastidy—this tree also has a name and a distinct energy."

My eyes widened as I nodded, but I didn't ask for the tree's name. My instincts told me that doing so would lead to more questions than answers.

"She called you here, didn't she? These trees act as conduits for our goddess," Chastidy explained. "Would you like a blessing? You may hear what she has to say."

Ravik pressed a hand to my back, and I looked up at him. I could feel his worry through our bond and I completely understood it—after all, I was more than a bit sensitive to anything related to the gods.

The thought didn't make me feel uneasy, though. *Chastidy was right.* What I was sensing, the pull I had been feeling, was a call. I felt proud I'd recognized that and that I was starting to trust my instincts more with each passing day.

"What do I need to do?"

"Simply press your hand to the tree and I'll recite the blessing," Chastidy said, before glancing at Ravik. "You're welcome to remain by her."

"Be careful, *lux mea.*"

"I will," I told him, feeling at peace with the decision. I approached the tree, which was slowly shifting and creaking, the movement more obvious up close. Ravik was shadowing me, and the comfort of his closeness emboldened me to lift my hand and press it to the trunk.

I didn't even hear Chastidy start the blessing.

The moment my fingers grazed the bark, a connection flooded open—not violent or dangerous—but intentional and very much waiting for me.

I expected Nyxarra and the caged room, but I was met with a much different scene. My eyes widened as the darkness cleared to bring forth a shaded emerald green garden. It was a mere circle of space with walled vines on all sides and a soft mist blanketing the place where the sky would normally be.

"Hello?" I called out, not nervous exactly, but apprehensive. Was this Sylvaern? It was obviously not Nyxarra because I didn't feel her magic at all.

Then in a blink, a woman appeared, causing me to step back quickly in surprise.

Her muscular stature was nearly triple mine, and her build was that of a lethal predator. She was covered in draped fur, and her brown hair was pushed back from her scarred face and critical dark gaze. She was *terrifying* and beautiful all in the same breath, and her power pushed at me in a way that made my wolf want to break out of my skin.

"Vaelithra." The word left me as I dropped to my knees without meaning to, gripping the ground underneath me. *Who else could it be?* I hissed at the amount of magic surging against my skin, unable to hear what she was saying as my ears rang to the point of pain.

Suddenly the energy calmed and a soft golden glow filled the space. I lifted my head in relief and watched her shrink to my own size, offering me a look I couldn't fully explain.

"My apologies, mortal. I often forget how delicate you are."

Or how *strong* she was.

"It's okay," I managed, standing up straight and forcing myself to hold her gaze despite being more than a bit scared. She looked me over in confusion before arching a brow.

"You're the mortal that Nyxarra has made her champion?"

My pride stung at her loosely veiled surprise, but I nodded once. "And you're one of the gods stuck behind bars with her?"

"Yes," she answered. "I have come to trust Nyxarra, so if you are the warrior she has chosen then that will have to work. Although...wasn't there more than one of you?"

"My three mates," I explained. "They're part of the bond."

"Not just any bond." She offered a knowing smile. "But one with a god scar. Marked by more than one god—very unique indeed. That part was my idea."

"The scar on our bond was your idea?"

"It was. When you released Nyxarra, I saw the opportunity to strengthen the bond that already existed between you and your mates, to make it something *more*. To allow you to harness and channel power against what is to come."

Relief hit me. Our bond had existed before divine intervention. And now I knew the identity of the unnamed god who was on our side. I could have assumed, but having confirmation of both helped.

"What's to come?" I asked. "You mean Ivan?"

"Ivan is nothing but a pawn."

*A pawn?* Maybe in a god's eye, in the second of time we existed compared to them. To everyone else? Ivan represented an excruciating existence and daily torture.

I must have been obvious in my reaction because the goddess offered me a conciliatory nod. "That isn't to say what he's doing isn't horrific, but he's feeding much more than his own ego."

"Kaevor—"

A bar of gold magic flexed around my mouth to silence me. I watched Vaelithra with wide eyes as she spoke. "Don't call on him."

I understood, signaling with a nod before the bar fell.

"But yes, Ivan has been feeding *him* in exchange for power, although he believes he's feeding Nyxarra," Vaelithra explained, as if it was simple and not the answer we had been looking for this entire time.

"How are you here then?" I asked while looking around.

"Nyxarra has more allies than I ever did—apparently I don't come across as *friendly*—and Sylvaern seemed to be in a good mood," she mused, glancing upward with a slightly narrowed look. "But how I'm here doesn't matter. You're growing closer to your goal, and with it there must be absolute clarity."

"On how to defeat Ivan?"

"Yes, but more than that. You have to stop him from performing the ritual. If you do not, chaos and war like this world has never seen will spill into Thornfell. *He* has had many years to plan."

My fists tightened with nerves. "How?"

"You must defeat his mortal factions to reach the ritual. They will try to stop you. And your bond, infused with the power of two gods, must be used to defeat both Ivan and *him*."

It was all of the answers I needed and yet not enough.

"You already have the way to harness and channel power against him."

"But how?" I pressed. "How do we use it?"

"The god scar is the key, you need only to—"

*The garden lurched.* The mist above me thinned and Vaelithra's expression shifted, an alarmed expression crossing her face.

"They are pulling you back," she said simply. "Go."

"Wait—"

But the emerald green was already dissolving at the edges, gold light bleeding through until there was nothing left but warmth and the smell of moss.

I blinked.

The dome of glass was above me. The tree was still beneath my hand but no longer moving. I became aware of Ravik's hands on my shoulders, turning me toward him, his voice low and controlled. It always got this way when he was trying to hide the fear I could feel moving between our bonds.

"Gracie. Look at me."

I did.

Then I looked past him to Thornar and Basir, bags abandoned outside. My voice was urgent but firm as I tried to explain.

"Vaelithra told us what we need to do."

# CHAPTER 20

# GRACIE

I COULD HEAR Thornar assuring Chastidy that I was fine as Ravik and Basir guided me from the temple. Our bond buzzed with a mix of concern and excitement—I knew they could feel the *relief* I felt at finally having answers. Not all of them, but enough. The fresh air brushing across my face had me letting out a steadying breath as Thornar caught up to us, my brain going a million miles an hour.

"What happened?" Ravik demanded, trying to pull me to a stop.

"Let's walk while we talk," I suggested. "I need to clear my head a bit." More than a bit.

I trusted my mates knew where we were going as Ravik took the lead, Thornar and Basir on either side of me.

"What could you feel through our bond?"

"It felt more calm than when you talk to Nyxarra," Basir said.

"But you were seizing so bad that you started bleeding out of your nose and the priestesses nearly called for emergency medical intervention." Ravik's voice was tight.

"That doesn't make sense," I whispered more to myself than to them. Did the physical effect have to do with the power of the god who'd called me there?

"We could see small snippets but couldn't hear anything substantial," Thornar added. I nodded in understanding, the large city blocks oddly perfect for a conversation that had to float between us, unheard by the crowded busy streets.

I told them everything as we walked, or as much as I could before we reached Alpha Kaliyah's home. About Vaelithra being the one who could be trusted, how insanely powerful she was, and the scar on our bond being her and Nyxarra's design. Confirmation that Ivan was feeding power to Kaevorak unknowingly, believing all this time it was Nyxarra receiving his offerings. How the Cold Moon Pack and Grimfur Skulk most likely stood between us and stopping the ritual. All of it filled the space between us as we walked, my mates absorbing it in silence.

The part I kept returning to was the part I *didn't* have.

Vaelithra had been cut off mid-sentence. The god

scar was the key, but the concrete answer we actually needed—like how to use it—was still missing.

"I'm sure she'll find a way to contact you again," Ravik said firmly. "Especially if she felt there was more to say. Although I want to know how our intervention will affect her. If it's to stop *him* from being freed, wouldn't it affect her the same?"

I nodded. That was something we had to ask about. It was possible she was doing it for the greater good, but we couldn't be sure.

"We shouldn't have interrupted," Basir said quietly.

I squeezed his hand. "I would have done the same." Especially if my mates had looked like they were in pain, let alone seizing and bleeding.

"I did find out something interesting though," I said, my brows lifting. "She said our bond already existed before any of this—that's why she chose to put a god scar on it."

Thornar flashed me a huge smile. "Well I could have told you that, little flame."

Ravik glanced back in agreement. "There was no way my reaction to you was anywhere in the realm of normal."

"I climbed through a bathroom window to meet you." Basir's words pulled an unexpected smile from me.

Thornar barked out a laugh. "Did you just make a joke?"

Basir's lip lifted just slightly as I leaned into him, feeling my body release some of its tension. We still didn't have all the answers, but I felt much better having a path forward and even more motivated to continue gathering our forces.

"It should be the building coming up," Ravik said after turning left, traveling along another city block. At the far end was a three-story townhome of white marble, the front gated with heavily armed guards.

Was this Alpha Kaliyah's home? An office?

My gaze moved to the street around us, mostly empty except for perfectly manicured parks and landscaping—but in the distance, I saw *it*.

"The trade conference building," I murmured as I came to a stop. I could feel my mates pause as well, but my eyes were glued on the structure.

Less than a month ago I'd been brought there as a captive, to be sold and traded like property. Now I was here meeting the Alpha on equal footing. I shook my head, letting the weight of that settle before moving forward with my mates toward Alpha Kaliyah's property.

Ravik kept me tucked to his side as Thornar went ahead and Basir followed behind, none of them shying away from the armed guards at the gate. It was clear they knew who we were before Ravik said anything because no questions were asked before the gates opened to reveal a front yard lush with plants and small creatures roaming about.

"Where to?" Ravik called out to a soldier coming down the front steps.

"Alpha Kaliyah is in her garden and would like to meet with you there. You can leave your bags on the steps—they will be kept safe."

Thornar let out a dissatisfied sound, but he and Basir dropped our bags. The soldier then gave another command. "Weapons must be left as well."

This time it was Basir who made a sound of discontent, but he removed two knives from a pocket on his pants that I hadn't even seen, tossing them into the air before catching them with practiced ease and stowing them with the rest of our belongings.

Thornar hadn't budged, his gaze narrowed on the soldier. "I'm not going in there without a weapon."

"Then you can't go in," the soldier said, placing a hand on his own gun.

"Thornar," Ravik said. "We can handle ourselves without firearms. It's not worth it."

Thornar's jaw was tight. I watched in shock as he finally shrugged off his jacket and began to unload his weapons. My mouth fell open as he removed not one —not three—but *five* guns before placing them in the bag. He shook his head and turned back toward us, looking disgruntled, until he caught my expression.

"So many guns," I whispered. "Where did you even hide them?"

Thornar smirked and nodded toward the garden. "Don't worry, I'll show you later, little flame."

Honestly, I couldn't wait.

As we rounded the property and caught sight of the walled garden, I was reminded of the vision I'd been in less than an hour ago. Climbing vines covered every surface and stone paths wound out from the gate we walked through, cutting across beds of herbs and flowering plants.

It was quiet, more than I would have thought possible, the noise of the city completely absent. A large wooden table covered in gardening tools sat at the center, and beyond it a row of fruit trees lined the far wall. Seated in one of the chairs, her silver-streaked hair catching the morning light, was Alpha Kaliyah Greene.

"Ravik Gentry, Gracie Holloway, Thornar Veydran, and Basir Morcant," she greeted. "Please join me. I trust you had a good train ride?"

"Yes," I answered, getting far more comfortable with these conversations than I used to be. "It was a beautiful area to travel through."

"We try our best," she said, looking pleased as everyone sat—Ravik closest, right next to me, Thornar and Basir across the way. "How is my good friend Lacey?"

My eyes widened at her relaxed, unknowing tone. Did she not realize…

Kaliyah broke into a laugh. "I know, I know. She views us as enemies, doesn't she?"

"Competition, I'd say," Ravik smoothed over.

"Don't tell your father," she said conspiratorially, "but she's my favorite out of all the other leaders." My smile grew, loving the twist of events.

"I'm sure she would be surprised to hear that," Thornar said.

"No, no." Kaliyah raised her hand. "She knows exactly how I feel. After all, we didn't date at university for no reason."

My mouth dropped open. "You dated?"

"She didn't say?" Kaliyah mused, shaking her head. "I've tried time and time again to convince her to give us another shot—especially since neither of us ever found others. But she's too stubborn."

"That explains a lot, actually," Ravik murmured as I tried to sort through the implications

"But you aren't here on this lovely morning to hear my sordid dating history," she said with a charming smile. "You're here to talk about Ivan Rivers."

His name instantly sobered the mood.

"Well, first." She put down her cup of coffee and leaned forward, looking directly at me. "I have to apologize, Gracie. I assumed Ivan was being his horrible self, but I didn't realize what immediate danger you were in at the time. I'm sorry for not stepping in when it happened in my own territory."

A flash of Ivan's hand coming up to hit me at the trade conference had my body tensing. I offered her a stiff smile. "It's okay. I'm just thankful to not be there anymore."

"And thank you for allowing us to fly out of your territory to handle it," Ravik added. "I know it brought you into the line of conflict."

Kaliyah nodded and sat back. "It did. But conflict with Ivan doesn't scare me. His need for power? That does. I fear that he will not be easy to defeat."

I could feel my mates shift into a more tactical mindset.

Ravik spoke up first. "So far we have secured allied forces from Nightstar Flight and Bloodrose Sloth territory. After this, we hope to do the same in the South."

"The question of my help is *not* a question," Kaliyah said with surety. "It's a matter of details. What of the Blazefur Pride?"

I was so relieved by her words that I couldn't contain my grimace at her question.

"He sent someone to kill us in our hotel," Basir said bluntly. Kaliyah looked completely unfazed. She adjusted her tunic slightly, her gaze dropping to her coffee in thought.

"I heard rumors that he and Ivan had made a deal, but that was two years ago. I doubt it was due to that."

She tapped her fingers on the table. "I'll reach out. We recently made a new trade agreement, so I'll use it as leverage to figure out whether he simply wanted you gone or if he's truly an enemy."

"Thank you," I said, but she waved me off.

"No gratitude is needed in war. We need to know his pride won't appear out of nowhere." She folded her hands and spoke candidly. "You still need the South. Waylon Kane has the largest territory in terms of population. We need him on our side—his numbers are among the only forces that can hold Grimfur Skulk, assuming you plan to take it over on your way north."

"Yes, I agree," Ravik said. "We appreciate your commitment. We worried that after the rescue mission you would want to clean your hands of this."

"Truth be told, I've been waiting for an opportunity to disrupt Ivan's operation. I already have eyes in Grimfur Skulk territory—they're due back in the morning. If you'd like to hear what they have to say, I welcome you to stay the night."

"We would appreciate that," Ravik said.

"I do have one request though," said Thornar.

I looked at him curiously as Kaliyah tilted her head in an unspoken question.

He cleared his throat. "Is it possible to get my guns back?"

# CHAPTER 21

# GRACIE

I'D NEVER EXPERIENCED a city at night, at least not one like this. Ironsun had a controlled and polished air that was different from this chaotic beauty. From the time we left Alpha Kaliyah's house, I'd been captured by the atmosphere and sights of the city, the streets still alive at this hour.

While they hadn't called it a date, that was exactly what tonight felt like. And wrapped in a sweater dress, boots, and a coat, I felt like someone who deserved to be here, walking these streets with her mates.

"There are *so* many people," I said as we neared what appeared to be an open-air market. I could see the tops of the stalls from here, but the heavy crowds blocked sight of everything else.

"It's called a night market," Thornar said. "You're going to love it, little flame."

His enthusiasm enthralled me, and while Ravik kept to my side protectively, none of my men seemed on edge—each of us looking around as we went down three stone stairs into the market center.

*Wow.* I was caught off guard by the way my senses —especially now that they were enhanced by my wolf —perked to life.

Colorful stalls and flashy outfits. Two different types of music playing upbeat tunes from opposite ends of the marketplace. The scent of sugar and something warmer.

I tightened my hand in Ravik's, grounding myself while feeling extremely eager to explore.

The sheer number of options and directions had my head spinning, and I was thankful when Thornar stole me from Ravik and led me toward a series of stalls. Ravik and Basir were close behind, falling into step and talking about something I couldn't quite hear.

"Looking for anything specific?" I asked Thornar as we approached the first stall, filled to the brim with candied citrus treats and beautifully crafted chocolates. The five tables following that stall also had treats, and I felt almost overwhelmed by the options.

"Something for us to snack on later," Thornar mused, kissing my temple. "I hate staying at other people's houses. I never feel right going to grab something from the kitchen."

"I could see that, especially if you wake up in the middle of the night wanting something sweet."

A loud clang drew both of our attention to where massive copper pots were lifting into the air, the shopkeeper tipping them to pour molten sugar onto a wide table. Thornar leaned close, his lips brushing my ear.

"Then again, I have other ideas of what to eat if I want something sweet at night."

My cheeks went bright red as I smiled up at him. Thornar chuckled at my reaction, and when Basir appeared to lead me toward the copper pots, I looked back at the man. He offered me a wink that left me feeling like I was on cloud nine.

"What are they making?" I asked, leaning into Basir.

"Candy, I think." We watched them stretch the sugar and color it, and I was so captured by it that I didn't realize I was leaning over the table until I almost knocked over a jar. I straightened it in my hand before becoming more curious and picked it up.

It was a small glass jar with a cork, tiny suns decorating the glass, filled with hard candies in amber and gold. A woman spoke up from behind the table. "Those are made from honey, harvested from the farms right outside the city—they're delicious."

I bet they were. I offered her a bright smile, thinking of how much Thornar would love them, before it hit me: I couldn't buy them for him. *I had no money.*

I had no idea how it hadn't occurred to me before, but I literally had no way to buy anything. My brow furrowed as I began walking down the table.

"Glow?" Basir prompted.

"Do I need a job?"

My question brought Basir to a full stop as the other two caught up, offering him a confused look. I was confused too, at their reactions. Why were *they* confused? Had I asked something weird?

"A job?" Basir rumbled.

"Yeah." I looked around. "I just realized I can't buy anything. I don't have money."

Ravik arched his brow. "Gracie, you have access to whatever money you could possibly need."

I blinked and looked down at the ground, frowning. "Okay...but I feel like I need my own money. Because that's yours, right?"

Thornar, who had been silent so far, let out an amused hum. "Good luck with this one, little flame. I would say this conversation is better left for later."

"Why—*oh!*" I laughed as he turned me under his arm like we were dancing, but I could tell that my question had bothered, or maybe concerned, Ravik and Basir.

"This one looks interesting," Thornar said, leading me to another stall.

Thornar was a master of distraction because *interesting* was an understatement. The stall was surrounded by a brisk, almost unnatural air, and the clean metallic taste told me they were working with stone and metal. I brushed away mineral dust floating in the air as we found our way to the table.

*Carved animals.*

Except that didn't do the stall justice. Each small crafted creature was a piece of art. I crouched down to look at them, staring at each detailed face, as Thornar picked them up and commented on how heavy they were. He even went so far as to start asking the stall owner questions about the process to make them. But it wasn't until I reached the end of the table that something *truly* caught my eye.

Basir. Except it wasn't really him. A black wolf carved from obsidian, perfect down to the etched fur. I picked it up, holding it at eye level with a smile.

"What's that?" Thornar asked. Over his shoulder I saw the other two walking toward us, carrying a bag and seeming far more relaxed.

"Basir." I cracked a smile as Thornar looked over the figurine.

"That is extremely impressive," he admitted, then winked. "Don't tell Basir you think that looks like him though—can't let the bastard get an ego."

I shook my head, smiling as I set it down. *An ego? Basir? Literally could never happen.*

The next few stalls were much the same, switching between stonework and leather—even some armor—though most of it didn't stand out to me. I did stop to look over a thick leather bracelet with dark stitching in a pattern running the full length. It was simple, just a knot closure, but I had the odd urge to have Ravik try it on.

The only thing stopping me was the way he hovered a few feet away, as if trying to give me space to look around. I would have preferred all of my mates as close as possible, but maybe they felt like they had to stay on watch.

"What are those?" My breath caught as we came to a stop in front of a simple but beautiful stand decorated in what could only be described as tiny masterpieces. The scent of greenery and flowers wrapped around me, and a woman along with a young girl stood behind the table.

"These?" The girl asked, her voice confident. "They're flowers!"

Except they were so much more than that.

I approached, awestruck, as I examined the pendants on thin gold chains hanging over the table. Inside each one, suspended and preserved in clear resin, was a stunning blossom.

I picked up the one with a tiny pink mum and felt something shift in my chest. Pressing flowers made me feel as though I could preserve part of nature's beauty—something I'd lacked for so long—but this?

*It was so special.* No matter where I was, I would always have a piece of something so incredibly alive. Something that could survive the cold, desolate territory of the Cold Moon Pack.

"Those are some of our favorites to make," the woman said. "We make at least a dozen every month."

"My friends and I trade them at school," the girl added.

"You should get it, *lux mea.*"

I closed my hand around the necklace. "You think?"

A nod and a low rumble came from his chest as he looked toward the woman. "How much?"

"Only ten—oh, this is way too much." The woman's voice was filled with shock, clutching the money my mate had handed her. Ravik offered her a small shake of his head, then looked back down at me. "Happy?"

"Yes," I whispered, but for so many more reasons than just the necklace.

After thanking the woman and her daughter, the four of us made our way to a nearby restaurant, my gaze dropping to the necklace at my throat. All of my mates had taken a moment to admire it, and I could tell they loved it nearly as much as I did.

Maybe not quite as much. But close.

"I bet we could learn how to make those," Thornar mused. I wasn't sure I was that talented, but I wouldn't mind giving it a try.

Once we ordered food, I noticed Ravik had placed three bags on the table. I offered him a questioning look. "Did you find something you liked?"

"I found something you liked," he explained and unpacked the bags—to reveal the three items I had spent the most time looking at. My cheeks flushed pink as I looked each one over then looked up at the three of them.

"I do like them...but I was actually picking them out for you, which is why I brought up the job thing," I said, placing them in front of each of my mates.

Thornar broke out in a laugh that had me softening as he reached across to grab my hand and kiss the top of it. "Thanks, little flame. These look delicious." He didn't hesitate to open the container of sweets immediately.

"I know it's a bracelet, so I'm not sure you want to wear it but..." I hesitated as Ravik inspected the leather, but he shook his head and held out his wrist.

I wrapped the bracelet around his wrist, thrilled that it looked so good on him—not to mention that something about having my mark on him was so right.

"I love it, Gracie."

Ravik's words brought a big smile to my face as I looked over to Basir. His gaze was on me, but the wolf was already secure in his hand, his thumb smoothing slowly over it.

"Do you like it?" I asked.

Basir's bond with me warmed with what felt like so much overwhelming...love? *Was that possible?* He offered a single nod before pulling my chair so I was tucked right against him, his nose buried in my hair.

"Thank you, glow."

# CHAPTER 22

# BASIR

I COULD FEEL the weather turning. It may have been early autumn, but the dawn air had a bite to it. Gracie was buried in blankets, but I had checked that having the window open this wide wouldn't wake her. As I'd found myself many times before, I was sitting in my mate's window rather than in bed with her. I told myself it was so the others could have room. Both of them had already woken for the day, though, and the truth was more complicated than any justification I could come up with.

*I didn't trust myself.*

I didn't normally, but after she'd given me a gift? I couldn't risk my control.

The figurine was still in my hand, warming under my touch. I hadn't put it down since she'd given it to me at dinner.

For most of my life, I'd lived under the rule of my wolf, and it had made it easy to focus on survival over everything else. It had made it easy to forget about the pain I caused—and the pain I was forced to endure. And when I was unshifted? The control I held onto allowed me to feel detached from those moments.

So to see a representation of my wolf fit in the palm of my hand was unsettling in a way I hadn't expected.

So why couldn't I put it down?

Because Gracie had given it to me. It was the first present I'd ever received. In the past, Ravik and Thornar had given me things, but never like this. She had chosen this *for* me.

My eyes closed as I tried to dispel the emotion rising up, but with her so close and her scent filling my lungs...I knew that was impossible. *I was so fucked.*

I knew what was happening. I knew what I was feeling. It was just the first time I'd ever experienced it, and I was terrified. Scared that I would fuck it up and scared that I would somehow taint her. That I would somehow extinguish the fire that was growing within her.

I wasn't worthy of Gracie's love, but that didn't stop mine from growing.

Gracie shifted in the bed to pull the covers up further around her, so I slipped the figurine into my pocket as I moved from the window, silently closing it behind me. Moving toward the fireplace, I stoked the embers while trapped in my own thoughts. About her and about the previous night. My brows furrowed. What a perfect example of me not being worthy.

*Gracie felt like she needed a job.*

My wolf shifted under my skin, the dissatisfied and disgusted feeling radiating down to my bones. My reaction was embarrassing. Her words shouldn't have bothered me so much, but for her to question for even a moment if she was provided for...

I didn't like it. I really didn't like it.

It made me feel as though I wasn't doing my job, and while each of us had our hands in different ventures across Ironsun, it was clear that Gracie didn't understand the resources available to her. I didn't want her to see a difference between her money and our money. I didn't want her to even think about money.

It was an insane thought process, I knew that. But knowing it didn't help how I felt.

Ravik had managed to calm me, barely, but I could tell he didn't like the idea. It had been Thornar's perspective of it later in the night which had made me feel moderately better.

Gracie *should* be able to work, but because she enjoys it—because it interests her—not for money.

He was absolutely right, and despite the fact that he regularly made me want to lose my mind, I relied on Thornar's point of view. Ravik as well. Each of them read Gracie in a way that I hadn't figured out but hoped to. Gracie deserved so much more than I could probably give her, but I was going to try my hardest to at least give her everything she needed.

Maybe there was some type of compromise we could find with the job.

Down the hall, I heard the chime of a grandfather clock, signaling that it was six in the morning. Alpha Greene's house was quiet as I left the bedroom, the guards stationed in the foyer offering me nods of greeting but nothing else.

As I made my way to the kitchen, I passed a vase of flowers. I plucked three of them, putting them in my pocket. I was unsurprised to find Thornar in the kitchen, already making a tray up for Gracie.

"Good timing," he said, placing a cup of tea on the tray. "I was about to take this up."

"I'll do it," I offered. "Where's Ravik?"

"Coming back from a run. I think he was wasting time before the meeting." That was not surprising and probably a good idea. I had been fighting the urge to go on a shifted run for days now.

I wanted to be part of the meeting, so I made quick work of going back up to the bedroom and placing the tray down for Gracie. We had decided to let her sleep, knowing we could easily update her on any intel, and with a day of travel ahead it was important she was well rested. Pulling back the curtains so the morning light could eventually filter in, I walked over to the table where the journal Ravik had gotten her sat.

Taking the flowers out of my pocket, I pressed them between the pages before stepping back.

I stood in the middle of the room for a long second, looking toward my mate, before giving into the urge to go to the side of the bed. Leaning down, I pressed my lips to her forehead. Her scent was still in my lungs as I found Ravik and Thornar both in the kitchen.

"Where are we meeting them?" I asked.

"Garden, she's already out there," Ravik said.

I followed the two of them out, trying to brace myself for information about the Grimfur Skulk. I did my best to forget the damn place existed, let alone think about whatever was going on there now. As we reached the garden, I clocked that Alpha Kaliyah was sitting in the same chair as yesterday, but now there were two women with her.

Both looked like they had been through hell.

"Here they are," Kayliah said, sitting forward. "Join us. I know these two want to get to sleep after so much travel."

I had a feeling it hadn't been in a jet either, considering their clothes were covered in dirt, their faces drawn and exhausted. I placed both of them in their mid-to-late thirties. If I didn't have a trained eye, I would have assumed they were ordinary citizens, but their critical gazes said they were something more.

"This is Ravik Gentry, future Alpha of Ironsun, and his Enforcer and Beta," Kayliah introduced before motioning to the two women. "These ladies are some of my best intel operatives—you can call them Ashley and Rachel—and they just returned from behind Grimfur territory lines. Please, tell us what you found."

*Fourteen days.* It was fourteen days until the ritual, and I hoped they had information that could help us. The only other option was their intel would make everything considerably worse.

"Alpha Ivan and Alpha Graeme have been transporting citizens from the farthest corners of the Grimfur Skulk territory into the Cold Moon Pack," Rachel explained, reaffirming what we already knew.

"Have there been reports to local authorities? Riots?" Ravik asked. "If they're shipping buses of people up north, there has to be some type of public outrage."

"There is," Ashley agreed. "But people are scared. They aren't using Grimfur Skulk military, although local authorities aren't responding to calls to aid either. Ivan and Graeme have enlisted one of the city-based crime syndicates to take people in the dead of night. They started first with their shockdust clients and have expanded past that."

My entire body went stiff and I was speaking

before I could stop myself. "Which crime syndicate? And why would they follow Ivan Rivers?"

"He's paying them, naturally, and supplying them with shockdust for free," Rachel explained. "The group is named Cinder Ring—CR for short."

I sat back in my chair as if trying to distance myself from the name. They continued talking around me, but I wasn't fully hearing them. The Cinder Ring had grown that large in a decade? To be a group recognized by an Alpha from another territory?

My gaze dropped to the table as I tried to steady myself. Underground tunnels. Sewers filled with rats. Tables covered in shockdust. I could still feel the sensation of rope against my skin as I waited—hoped —that my parents would come back.

But they never did. Cinder Ring was who they'd sold me to in order to pay off their debts. It was the syndicate that had infected my childhood with despair. The syndicate that I'd run shockdust for.

"Basir." Ravik's voice broke me from my stupor. I realized the arm of the chair I sat in was creaking underneath my fingers, where I was grabbing it with a white-knuckle hold.

"Excuse me," I said, standing to go inside. I was sure Ravik and Thornar would offer some type of explanation for me. I couldn't afford to sit there, not with so many eyes watching.

I didn't have a plan, but the moment I walked into

the kitchen, I came to a full stop. Gracie stood there, looking around in confusion, wrapped in a fluffy robe with her slippers peeking out from under her sweatpants. Her hair was messy and her gaze sleepy, and she looked as if she wasn't fully sure why she was down in the kitchen.

"Basir?" she asked. "Are you okay? I felt something—"

I had her in my arms before I'd decided to move. The second her head was resting against me and I could feel every inch of her, my chest cracked open. The anxiety and panic spilled out of me as she clung tighter. My inability to control my emotions had woken Gracie, and she had come looking for me.

"I'm worried," she whispered. "What's going on?"

"Nothing," I said, my voice muffled by her hair. "Nothing that hasn't already happened. I'm sorry I woke you, glow."

Gracie didn't push, but she did melt further into me.

"Morning, little flame," Thornar said a few seconds later when he and Ravik walked inside.

Gracie peeked her head up but didn't leave my arms. "Morning. Did you guys just have the meeting?"

"Yeah." Ravik nodded, offering me a look. "When we're on the road today, we can update you."

"When are we leaving?" she asked. "We're going south, right?"

"Yep, Stark Flight territory," Thornar said, then offered his hand. "Now come on. Let's go eat breakfast upstairs before it gets cold."

It was painful to let Gracie slip from my arms, but I let her go with Thornar as Ravik stood next to me. "You good?"

"Cinder Ring is who I ran shockdust for." I said.

Ravik understood. "Hopefully we won't have to see those bastards, but if we get Stark Flight on our side, we may get a chance to destroy them."

One could only hope.

As we made our way toward the stairs, I said, "I'm not looking forward to going south."

"Why?" Ravik asked.

"Because that's who Ivan tried to sell Gracie to."

# CHAPTER 23
# GRACIE

It had been easy the past few days to forget about the reality of our world. Who my men were and what they were capable of. I couldn't ignore it now, though, the midafternoon light barely breaking through the tinted windows of the armored SUV we were in, a convoy of seven cars ahead and behind us.

The lightness of last night and the slow morning was replaced by clipped questions and answers. The car was silent as we left city limits, and I felt my stomach twist with nerves. This trip wouldn't be easy. I wasn't nervous because I thought I would be hurt—I knew my mates would protect me. I was nervous because of what they would do *to* protect me.

At the same time, the moment grounded me. These men were dangerous, but they were also my mates—and just as they had accepted me, I accepted them. Even if that meant the car was filled with more guns than I would have otherwise preferred.

I remembered the black armor and gear Ravik had worn the night he, Thornar, and Basir had rescued me, but seeing them in it again was something else. Weapons were strapped to their bodies, every glint of metal catching my eye.

I was dressed similarly, except my clothing seemed more focused on protection. The pants were a stiff material with pockets, and the boots were hard, the toe completely solid. Underneath my jacket and over my tank top was a heavy vest that I knew was bullet-proof. I was completely protected in more ways than one.

Alpha Kaliyah had already sworn she was an ally, but this morning as we prepared to leave, she didn't shy away from showing it. After having to ditch the jet, we were traveling light with only the tonics, some other vital supplies, and basic clothes. Knowing that, she had made sure that we had everything we needed to make it to the southern border, which also happened to be the border line of her territory and the Grimfur Skulk territory.

"Will the vehicles come with us all the way to the border?" I asked Ravik, who was driving.

"Yes. Alpha Waylon said he would meet us with his own forces, but apparently the border has been plagued with attacks for years now, and recently they've escalated."

Which was also why we couldn't fly. The closer we got to Ivan's reach, the more eyes were on us and for all the wrong reasons.

"It's not that far of a drive," Thornar said, sitting next to me while sorting through bags. "We should make it quickly, but we have to be prepared for whatever greets us."

"I'm positive they know we're traveling," Basir murmured. I pulled on our bond gently, knowing he was still feeling tense. He'd explained everything to me before we left, and I understood his anxiety more than he probably realized. Both of us were going to be asked to face the monsters of our past.

"How?" I asked with a frown.

"There are always spies, even in the most secure of situations," Thornar pointed out. I nodded in understanding.

How hard must it be to live like that, constantly wondering who would betray you? Then again, I supposed I'd felt similar in those moments at the Cold Moon Pack...but that was because everyone was trying to survive.

It was nearly two hours later, the road passing by in a blur of green hills and cliffs, that we finally began to slow. My wolf bristled as the silence in the car shifted. Out the windows I could see that the border intersected with a forested landscape.

I may not have known much about war, but on the night of the attack, Ivan's men had hidden their trucks by driving through the forest leading up to our village. It seemed like a good place to hide.

Up ahead the cars began to stop and turn, framing the wall and gate to either side. Only our car would be going through.

Except when we finally pulled up, there was no one there to greet us. Silence permeated the air as Thornar turned on his radio, the static breaking through.

"Any signs of the usual patrol?" he asked. No one had gotten out of their cars yet.

"No," an unfamiliar voice answered. "But there are bootprints leading up to the gate from this side." Thornar sighed in annoyance, and I wrapped my arms around myself.

"My guess is that they already knocked out the guards on the other side," Ravik said, the mic clearly able to pick his voice up so the other soldiers could hear him. "They're waiting for us to get out."

"I don't see much other choice. You feel comfortable with this?" Thornar asked. His voice was smooth, but there was something bubbling underneath it— almost *excitement.*

The guy on the other side chuckled. "Yeah, we're good."

"Wait for us to get out. We're going to secure Gracie." Thornar turned off the mic.

"Alright, little flame." Thornar turned to me while handing weapons to Ravik and Basir. "I'm going to need you to do something for me."

"Okay." I bit down on my lip, trying not to portray my nerves.

"They're going to start shooting the minute we get out," he said, adjusting his own vest. "I need you to sit in the driver's seat but with your head down. The car is armored, so it should be okay. But if shit starts to get dangerous—you start seeing explosions—I want you to drive your pretty ass out of here."

"What...*what?*"

Thornar chuckled at my shocked reaction. "We'll be back before you miss us. But I don't want you just sitting in the back. I want you to be able to get out of here if you have to."

"Is there another way so you don't have to go out there?" I asked the three of them, my wolf nearly letting out a whine of distress. I had no doubt my mates were capable, but the idea of them going directly into danger was something my entire body rebelled against.

"Unfortunately not," Basir said.

"The roads behind us are clear," Ravik said. "I want you to reverse out before turning right—there are cliffs the opposite way about twenty miles back. Avoid those."

Reverse. Turn right. Avoid the cliffs. Got it.

I cleared my throat before admitting, "I can't drive."

Ravik and Thornar didn't seem surprised by the admission, but Basir made a thoughtful noise. "Have to teach you that."

"Come up here." Ravik motioned and I climbed over the center console, Ravik pulling me onto his lap in the driver's seat. Despite the dangerous circumstances, I couldn't deny the way my body heated under his touch.

He quickly showed me the *reverse* and *drive* gear shift, as well as the brake. I tried to memorize all of it, but our bond was already humming with something eager and it was hard to focus on anything else.

When Thornar opened the door to get out, I didn't get to say a word before they were all moving from the car. I slid my hands around the wheel and tried to make myself as small as possible.

Unfortunately for my nerves, Thornar was right.

The second they stepped foot outside, shots rained down from the trees. I ducked down, not wanting to see how many people it took to make that *many* shots go off at once. When the car jerked as if it had been hit, I squeezed my eyes shut, trying to calm myself.

The sound of shots ringing out reminded me so much of the Cold Moon Pack. My skin prickled with awareness, and with each yell, each shot, I felt panic crawling up my throat. Not only because of the memories playing out in my head, but because my mates were out there.

My wolf forced a whimper through my lips, nearly driving me to shift. To go protect them.

I didn't think they needed it though. The excitement coming through the bond, especially from Thornar, had my stomach flipping. I could smell smoke and blood. The leather under the wheel was slick with sweat. My eyes burned with restrained tears.

When I felt Thornar shift into his wolf, like an explosion going through our mate bond, I felt the bloodlust that saturated it.

My head snapped up, needing eyes on him, and *by The Eight*—I wished I hadn't.

Bodies. Ours. Theirs. Over fifteen people down. In the center of it were Ravik and Basir, firing on a group of men on top of the stone wall that acted as the border between territories.

Thornar was to my left, facing off against a gigantic lion and three foxes.

He was enormous in his wolf form, bigger than I remembered, and he moved through them like they had never been a threat in the first place. Blood spurted as his teeth and claws shredded through the foxes before going after the lion, and every hit landed through our bond like a shockwave.

I could feel his wolf. Not Thornar, not the man who called me *little flame*—just the wolf.

Part of me wanted to look away. But I couldn't because some primal piece of me recognized what he was doing and why. *Thornar was making sure nothing and no one survived this.*

A loud bang tore a scream from my throat, and I snapped my head up to find a man on the hood of the car, pointing a gun right at my head through the window. A bullet was lodged between the two of us, stuck in the glass.

I didn't think. I just acted. I threw the car into drive and floored it.

My vision went spotty as the SUV slammed into the gate, my head thrown forward to collide with the airbag. Some sort of powder filled the air, and blood *covered* the window. The man's face was pressed against it, his body trapped between the gate and the car.

I had no idea how long I sat there staring at the man's face, feeling dazed and confused—it could have been seconds or hours—but eventually the door was pulled open so hard it rocked the vehicle.

Familiar voices called my name in panic, and warm, rough hands gently removed me from the car. My eyes closed as I murmured under my breath, trying to figure out where that soldier had come from.

I hadn't seen him. Until he was dead. Or maybe I'd killed him. I had killed him. *I'd killed someone?*

"Little flame."

My eyes slowly opened. Thornar's gorgeous face was over me, but the sky beyond him was covered in blood. *The sky was covered in blood?* That wasn't right.

"Look at her eyes," Basir hissed. "We'll need to check for a concussion." His words faded as I continued to stare up at Thornar.

"Are you okay?" I whispered, my throat thick. "I saw you fighting them. I felt you fighting them."

Thornar's jaw tightened as he offered a nod, his hand smoothing over my cheek. "Don't worry about me, Gracie. Let's focus on you."

"There was a lion," I murmured, the fight flashing before me again. "Lion shifters don't live over here, right?"

Ravik, who must have been standing close by, turned and said something to one of the soldiers as Thornar looked up at Basir. They exchanged a look, but my eyes were already closing so I wasn't able to decipher it.

"Keep them open," Thornar encouraged. "We're moving the car from the gate. The envoy from Waylon was taken out, so we're going to drive one of the cars to the closest station."

*Move the car.*

My eyes widened as I inhaled sharply.

"I killed him. I killed a man."

# CHAPTER 24

# GRACIE

"I'm sorry, sir, we won't be stopping until we reach the capital." The woman's voice was firm but kind. "The best we can do is a medical kit."

"A medical kit should be fine," I said. Ravik didn't look convinced, though, and I could feel Basir's guilt, as if he somehow should have predicted this. In my mind, being unable to stop was a *good* thing—I wasn't really in the best condition to be moving around.

The woman offered me a thankful look before leaving our cabin. It was clearly some type of first class cabin, featuring a bathroom and a bedroom, as well as a lounging and dining area. Apparently this long train ride was something of a destination trip for people traveling between territories.

"Ridiculous," Thornar murmured. "What would one stop hurt?"

I smiled up at him. He sat next to me on the couch, his massive frame warm against my side. He'd managed to wipe the blood from his face during our drive, but the minute we'd gotten on the train he'd showered. The others had as well. I'd changed clothes, but I didn't trust myself to stand upright just yet. My body was a bit shaky.

"I really do feel okay," I promised, looking directly at Basir. "My body hurts, but it's probably from the impact." I stopped myself from saying that I'd been through worse.

Basir ran a hand through his hair, still pacing. "We have to teach you how to drive."

I nodded, giving him an understanding look. I knew he needed a solution right now.

"We should start traveling with a healer," Ravik said, his gaze on me. "Are you positive you don't want to stop? We can make them—"

"No." I leaned forward to grab his hand. "I really just want to rest."

Both my body and my brain. Also my heart.

I thought coming to terms with killing a man would have been harder. But like the man Basir had killed in the Blazefur Pride territory, my mind had already found its way to a justification. *I had been protecting myself.* It was true, and it went a long way to appease my guilt. Although I couldn't help but wonder who wouldn't have someone coming home tonight.

The car ride to the train station had been quiet, but as my adrenaline faded, my body started processing what had happened. I began to feel everything, including an overwhelming sensation of sadness and guilt.

They had chosen to attack us, those members of the Grimfur Skulk military. But at the end of the day, they were still following someone else's orders. Couldn't the same be said about the soldiers that accompanied us, some of whom wouldn't be going home to their families? Probably. Or maybe they didn't think about it. Maybe they didn't care. And then there were the ones who hadn't chosen any of this. Pulled from the streets and thrown into a war that was never theirs to begin with. My head pulsed in confusion as I tried to sort through all of it.

I wasn't sure what to think anymore, and that hurt my heart more than anything.

In the Cold Moon Pack, it was easy to see in black and white, the extremes of power simple to understand. But now? Not so much. Sure, the soldiers who followed orders were doing so to survive, but what of the obligation *not* to kill people? Did that matter in war? I was learning that it may not.

"You have a bruise," Thornar pointed out, gently tilting my chin and examining my forehead. I hadn't looked at myself in a mirror, but I knew my body was roughened up—I could feel it. I just didn't care right now. I was relieved to be inside a contained and safe train car.

"Could have been worse," I admitted. From the corner of my eye I noticed Ravik stand to go talk to Basir, whose tense form still paced the cabin.

Thornar's gaze moved over my expression. "It could have been, but you didn't let that happen, little flame. You took care of the problem. You kept yourself safe."

Pride flooded through our bond, and unexpected tears filled my eyes. Thornar was right.

I rested my hand on his chest as I spoke softly. "I didn't think about it; I just acted. It feels wrong to not feel more guilt, but everything is so much more complicated when it comes to *all* of this."

Thornar was quiet for a moment. "Both sides believe they're right. That's the nature of it." His thumb traced along my jaw. "My morality isn't the purest, little flame—that was never a secret. I kill, and there are times I enjoy it. And when it's someone who's hurt people who couldn't protect themselves?" Something dark settled in his expression. "I don't lose sleep over that."

I didn't find that frightening. Should that worry me?

"That makes sense," I said, thinking of how he'd moved today—without holding back.

"Did I scare you today?"

"Scare me? Not exactly. I was overwhelmed by the situation because it reminded me a lot of my time in the Cold Moon Pack. But I was taken off guard by what you were feeling. The scale of it."

"I won't feel guilt for protecting what's mine," he said, his hand moving to rest against my face. "And neither should you."

"It doesn't scare me, the lengths you'll go to protect the people you care about," I told him honestly. "It makes me feel safe."

Relief filled Thornar's expression before he dipped his head and pressed a slow kiss to my lips. His voice was rough as he pulled back. "I don't just care about you, little flame. What I feel for you is much larger than that."

My throat caught as I stared up at him, feeling my cheeks heat, unable to help the joy rising in my chest. "Larger than caring about me?"

"I love you, Gracie." He said it so simply, and my heart felt like it was beating in my ears. Before I could say a word, tell him how I felt back, he dipped his head and kissed me once more. I clung to him as he finally pulled back.

"I love you too." My voice was a whisper between us. I loved him. Thornar *loved* me. It was that simple and that overwhelming.

"I told you I'd have to marry you if you keep looking at me like that."

Thornar's reminder of the first night I met him pulled a smile from me. Snuggling closer to him, I let out a deep exhale.

"It's confirmed," Ravik said, coming to sit down as Basir set a plate of sandwiches between us. "Alpha Kaliyah's soldiers followed the footprints back to their trucks. The Blazefur Pride logo is stamped all over it. It wasn't just a rogue lion shifter."

The words sat for a long minute before I spoke.

"So Alpha Chace is not a friend."

"Absolutely not." Basir's words were final.

"So Nightstar Flight, Bloodrose Sloth, and Scarlet Sloth are all allies," Ravik further explained. "Obviously, the Cold Moon Pack, Blazefur Pride, and Grimfur Skulk are not."

"And Stark Flight has by far the most citizens." I understood now why we needed them. The territories would be evenly split if they joined Ivan.

We needed that fifth territory on our side.

IT WAS A FEW HOURS LATER, dinner having come and gone, that I found myself curled up next to Ravik as he read through something on his tablet. I had explored every inch of the cabin, taken a nap, and a long shower once I felt up to it. We wouldn't arrive until early morning so I hoped to get more sleep, but until then I was unsure what to do with myself.

Thornar was already knocked out on the bed, stretched out and extremely relaxed, and Basir was sitting near one of the windows watching the dark landscape go by.

"What are you thinking about?" Ravik's voice was relaxed and curious.

"About what to do," I admitted, peeking over his tablet. "What are you doing?"

"Honestly?" he mused. "Thinking about where we could go if shit goes south in Thornfell."

My brows went up before I frowned. "I don't want to leave."

Ravik nodded and inhaled. "Neither do I, *lux mea*. Sometimes it's the best option, though, especially if it means keeping you safe."

Tilting my head, I looked at the map on his screen, trying to give the idea space to breathe. "Where would you want to go?" I barely knew what was across the country, let alone the seas.

"Possibly Florwyn—it's right across the Eastern Sea—and the fact that it's made up of so many smaller countries instead of one centralized power would make it easier to hide." Ravik's thought process made sense as he hovered over the spot on the map. "It also has a range of climates and probably the largest diversity of shifter types." He tilted his head. "Unfortunately there are other types of magic there—ones I don't have as much experience with."

"Other types?" I asked curiously.

"Forest gods and spirits," he explained. "The ones that existed before The Eight. Most pixies and fairies come from one of their lineages."

Pixies and fairies? Much like merfolk, I'd heard of them, but Thornfell was so saturated with shifters that I'd yet to actually experience anything else.

"Have you ever met a pixie or fairy?"

"Unfortunately," Ravik muttered. "We went over there to talk with one of the clan leaders and had to deal with an ambassador that was a fairy. He was an asshole."

I snorted with laughter, which pulled a small smile from Ravik before he continued. "Still one of the better options. There are only two others I would seriously consider."

"Which?" I asked, looking over the map.

"Goldmere or Eldwyn. The first has a dense rainforest we could get lost in and allies we have specifically sought out, but it's complicated by their politics."

"They have poor leadership?"

"No..." Ravik considered my question before answering, "The rainforest is a living entity and has a say in everything. There are also flora-species— imagine a person or creature made entirely of plants, with a deep connection that allows them to speak *for* the forest."

Oh. That was a lot to imagine and genuinely fascinating.

"And Eldwyn?" I asked.

"Peaceful but with a strict hierarchy that is essentially unbreakable. Less breathing room for negotiating our stay, especially considering our own power," he said. "Dragon shifters are the dominant species but there are other, far older, powers at play."

"I would love to eventually see all three of these places," I said. Despite not wanting to leave Thornfell, I couldn't deny the picture he painted had my curiosity piqued.

"We will, *lux mea*." He zoomed out on the map. "Any others catch your eye?"

For the next hour I peppered Ravik with questions about the other continents—Coralis, Pyraen, and Skarhold. I listened to every piece of information, even the parts that were hard to wrap my head around. Hope and excitement stirred in my chest with every word. *I wanted to see it all.* Coralis and its merfolk, Pyraen and its storm elementals, even Skarhold and the deep sea shifters that lived there.

When it was finally time to go to bed and I crawled into the soft sheets next to Thornar, I was more determined than ever to get Alpha Waylon on our side.

To make all of those dreams come true, Ivan had to be handled.

I couldn't be free until he was gone.

274

# CHAPTER 25
# GRACIE

THE FIRST THING I noticed when I stepped off the train was that the wind was warm, despite being near the coast. I shielded my eyes from the morning light as Ravik led me off the station platform and into the shade.

"Wow."

I felt as though I'd been transported to an entirely different universe, let alone world. I moved to the edge of the high cliff we stood on—a purposeful end to the train line—to get the best view possible. To look at the capital city of Stark Flight territory.

Whoever had designed or chosen this overlook had done so with the purpose of showing each and every visitor the grandeur of the capital city. In the morning light everything was lit up in gold, and the wind that moved over the water rustled the leaves of the gigantic trees that the city was built on.

Although, *on* wasn't quite the right word.

The city itself was built into enormous ancient trees that were seemingly rooted deep underwater. Their trunks and roots acted as walls and foundations, with structures carved directly into them both vertically and horizontally. Warm amber light emanated from the buildings that stretched all the way to the top of the canopy, where dragon shifters soared past, looking small against the scale of the city.

Islands were scattered around the edges of the city, the land between them mostly wetlands. Below the trees, small vessels proudly displaying flags of purple and gold moved through the waterways. They were so tiny, comparatively.

"I'm surprised the dragons preferred water," Thornar said openly.

As if in answer, a dragon flew overhead and let out a roar, sending a tremor through the land. My eyes shot up in awe. The scale of everything—including the dragons themselves—made it feel impossible to truly take in. I'd seen paintings and pictures of dragons before, but seeing their jewel-toned colors fill the sky was something else entirely.

"How do we get down there?" I asked, noticing both Basir and Ravik looking around.

"Well, since we can't fly," Thornar murmured,

sounding almost disappointed, "I would say those aerial trams."

My gaze moved to where he was looking and saw that a short distance away were aerial trams, similar to gondolas, designed to carry passengers down into the city. I was walking toward them before I could stop myself—but Ravik caught me around the waist.

"What's wrong?" Basir asked.

Ravik rumbled. "I prefer being on the ground, not hanging several hundred feet above water."

Thornar chuckled. "Come on, Ravik. It won't be that bad."

And it wasn't—for me at least. But from the time we stepped onto the aerial tram and took our seats, Ravik had remained motionless, and I could feel the unease through our bond. He had pulled me onto his lap, and considering it gave me an even better view, I hadn't even tried to get up.

The city revealed itself further as we descended, each minute pulling us closer to the arrival platform. What had looked like a dense canopy of wood and light from the overlook was an entirely different world up close.

Bridges wide enough to drive a vehicle across ran between roots. Balconies carved directly into the bark held washing lines and window boxes. A dragon passed so close that I felt the air shift, its wingspan blocking out the sun for a full second before it banked lazily toward an upper branch, where it landed with a grace that shouldn't have been possible for something that size.

Ravik's grip on me tightened. I offered him a sympathetic, concerned look.

"You don't like heights?"

"I don't like situations I can't control, *lux mea.*"

Looking over his shoulder toward the city, I leaned closer. "We're about halfway now, so that's not too bad."

"You know, they take this entire Yvelis worship to a new level," Thornar pointed out.

"What?" Basir offered him a questioning look.

"God of bone and transitions." He waved his hand and cracked a smile. "This is a very *transitional* way to get into the city."

A laugh bubbled out of me as Ravik buried his head against my shoulder with a groan. I squeezed his hand wrapped around me and continued to watch as we descended. I was so eager to get down there that I had to stop myself from bouncing as the aerial tram *finally* came to a stop.

Faster than my mates, I was out and looking around. Before us was a marketplace that seemed to stretch on forever into the tree. The stalls were carved alcoves filled with goods I didn't recognize—dark gleaming stones, dried herbs that smelled of salt, and piles of fabric in deep jewel tones.

I immediately noticed that the people of Stark Flight moved differently too, unhurried but watchful. They seemed to catch every detail of what they were looking at, and I realized that dragon shifters carried a very different energy than pack wolves. There was no instinctive awareness of one another. They didn't seem to even greet each other in passing, every individual existing in their own contained world.

A flash of light to my left pulled my attention, where a winding path carved down into the tree led to what appeared to be a temple. Its stone and bone doors glinted in sunlight as people moved in and out of the spiritual center.

Even from here I could feel the ancient power radiating from it, and I found myself glad that it wasn't calling to me in the same way it had in the Scarlet Sloth territory. I didn't necessarily want to meet Yvelis —at least not yet.

"Ravik Gentry." A low voice had my head snapping to the right, a prickle of awareness causing me to still. I'd been around a lot of danger in my life, so there was absolutely no doubt that the two men walking toward Ravik were dangerous. So much so that I moved to be between Basir and Thornar.

"Caelan, Soren, it's good to see you both." Ravik looked unsurprised and even happy to see both men, offering the first a handshake before doing the same for the second. Both were as tall as Ravik, but neither had the warmth and grounding that my mates had.

They made me distinctly uncomfortable.

"We were sent to lead you up to the castle," Soren explained, his eyes moving over to the three of us in a lazy, indifferent way. "Thornar and Basir, it's good to see both of you."

"Is it?" Basir hummed, looking suddenly amused.

Soren offered a shake of the head but ultimately let it go, choosing to focus on me. "You brought your...mate?"

"Yes." Ravik said seriously. "*Our* mate."

Caelan made an amused noise. "Never would I have thought you'd be the sharing type. What's your name?"

"Gracie," I said evenly, trying to not portray my nerves.

"Good to meet you," Caelan said politely. I didn't offer the same in response because I honestly wasn't sure if it *was* good to meet them.

"Alright, you four." Soren nodded upwards. "Dad is waiting. Let's go."

Ravik led the way, and once we had a bit of distance, I asked Thornar and Basir my question.

"Who are they?"

"Waylon's youngest sons," Thornar explained with an annoyed sigh. "Ravik has known them for a long time. But..."

"I don't like them," Basir stated.

Thornar chuckled. "Something you've made abundantly clear."

"What's wrong with them?" I asked. "Is it because they're dragons? My wolf reacted so strongly when I met Waylon."

Up until this point my wolf had been quiet, but in the past she'd distinctly rejected being around dragons. Or maybe just *his* line of dragons. Interesting.

"No," Thornar said. "It's because they're psychopaths."

*Oh.* "Like…"

"Killers," Basir leveled. "Just under the guise of being part of a special military unit."

I was thankful that my mates were also scary so that I didn't have to worry about individuals like Soren and Caelan.

The scale of the tree revealed itself slowly on our ascent. The path wound in a slow upward spiral lit by lanterns hung at intervals from iron brackets driven into the wood. The higher we climbed, the more the city fell away below us, visible only through gaps in the bark.

Though what I'd thought was only bark was mixed with layered growth, decades upon decades of compressed material turning into something that felt like stone. My hand grazed the surface as we walked. It was warm under my fingers, faintly vibrating, as if something deep inside was still moving.

It must have taken us twenty minutes to get to our destination at the top of the stairs. Except as I reached the last step...I fell back slightly, unsure of what I was seeing.

It was a castle, but not like any I'd ever seen.

A gigantic dragon skull faced outward, acting as the archway into the castle, the teeth all intact except for the front two. The eyes were glass orbs stained purple and gold like the Stark Flight flag hanging above the door, and as we moved forward I found myself trying to take in the scale of it.

How did a dragon get this big? Had it been a shifter? *Something else?*

The surface underfoot shifted as we stepped inside, stone giving way to bone. I cringed. *So that's where the other two teeth had gone.* Basir put a hand on my back and offered a look that said he understood.

"Are those ribs?" I asked my mate in a hushed whisper. Thornar had already moved ahead, hands clasped behind his back, studying the beams overhead with what looked like genuine interest. Ravik stood at ease between the Kane brothers, exchanging quiet words with Caelan.

The space was vast, making my words echo in a way that I had not intended. Lanterns hung from the vertebrae, filling the room with a warm contrasting light. Fresh flowers stood in ivory vases every few feet and staff wearing deep purple and gold linens moved through the hall toward sets of heavy doors.

Before Basir could answer my question, someone came running up behind us. Ravik stepped back to be more firmly in front of me, but the man ignored us, rushing past to get to Caelan and Soren.

He was a frazzled man, speaking in quiet urgency. "I have been searching for both of you everywhere. You cannot be late, and they are waiting for you in the south wing. Right now!"

Soren sighed, but Caelan offered a nod of understanding. He looked toward Ravik. "Just walk straight to the double doors. He's waiting for you."

"Sounds good." Ravik said. "It was good seeing both of you."

"You'll be seeing more of us this summer." Soren smirked. "We've got the Solakrin Trials."

As the brothers disappeared to the left, we continued to the doors ahead.

Why did the Solakrin Trials sound familiar...

# CHAPTER 26
# GRACIE

"Ravik Gentry, welcome," the steward at the door said. His purple linens were fitted with gold buttons and a crest on the lapel, similar to the staff moving about the castle but elevated. His expression was polite but firm, his hands clasped in front of him.

"Alpha Waylon knows we're here, I assume?" Ravik asked, pulling me gently into his side.

"Yes, he is expecting you. Please follow me."

With those words, the jewels embedded in the wood glowed with light and the doors opened in one sweep, giving way to a *stunning* hall.

The room was filled to the brim with people who barely noticed the doors had opened. They laughed and moved about the space, some even dancing to the music. None of them seemed in awe of the space they were in, but I had no idea how.

The hall was a very long room that peaked at the top, the walls covered in bone and wood, and from the rafters hung crystal chandeliers of purple and gold that cast stunning rays of light onto the floor.

Castle staff carried food from table to table, the seated faces smiling and happy to receive more. I felt completely underdressed in my tactical clothing. Every woman and man present was dressed in heavy, expensive clothes and jewelry. From their power signatures I could tell that, no matter who else lived in the territory, everyone here was a dragon shifter—down to the castle staff.

The bones that formed the structure of each room may have felt eerie at first, but the joy and ease of the people filling the space made it feel anything but. There was a formality, sure. I could see it in the guests' polite and polished mannerisms. But the atmosphere was relaxed and so incredibly happy. I didn't even move forward at first, just soaking it all in.

I hadn't expected this at all.

"At the back, in the center," Ravik said, and I realized he was pointing out where Alpha Waylon was. I nodded as the steward led us forward. People offered us curious looks but otherwise went about their celebration.

Was it a celebration? Or was this just a normal lunch for them?

Before the crowd shifted, I caught a glimpse of

Waylon already in conversation. He was leaning toward whoever was speaking as though what they were saying genuinely mattered to him.

Then a break in the crowd made it easy to fully lay eyes on the dragon shifter. On a raised platform, a few steps off the ground, he sat with a woman who appeared to be around his same age.

Thornar let out an amused sound. "They don't look bad for being a few thousand years old."

A thousand or more? My eyes widened as I looked over Waylon and his possible mate. Just like the last time I'd seen him, he looked to be only in his mid-fifties, his angular face carrying almost no wrinkles except around his eyes and mouth. Green scales covered his olive-toned cheekbones, and his black hair was loose, hanging down to his waist against his purple robes.

There was a confidence to the way Waylon held himself that wasn't arrogance so much as the quiet certainty of a man who felt he had never done wrong. That he'd always made the right choice. Whatever that meant.

"Who are all of these people?" I asked.

"Family. He and his mate have upwards of forty children, and naturally some of those have children of their own," Thornar said.

"Forty?" My voice came out almost choked. Basir

shook his head, seeming to find it just as insane as I did while Thornar flashed me a smile.

"You don't want forty kids, Gracie? You sure?"

I nearly wheezed, breaking into laughter. I shook my head immediately because the idea of children, while appealing in theory, was not on my immediate horizon. Freeing Thornfell of Ivan had first place firmly and tightly in its grasp.

Now that he'd mentioned it, though, I could absolutely see how they were family. I could see it in the young and old alike, their facial features similar and their mannerisms even more so, and at the center of it all were Waylon and his mate.

*Queen* would probably have been a better title for her, though. Her head was tilted back in laughter, her black hair shimmering under the colored lighting. Much like Waylon, she had scales on her face, and I was starting to think it was a show of power. None of the children had them, but many of the older adults did.

It also couldn't be understated how different this was from even the Ironsun Pack, and a universe away from the Cold Moon Pack. No one feared Waylon here. They viewed him as a leader, yes, but they didn't fear him. Maybe those outside these walls did, but not the people he surrounded himself with daily. I was fascinated by how you even kept track of a family this large!

Although I supposed my family was growing every day as well.

The steward brought us past the crowds, and Waylon turned his dark gaze on us. His mate did the same, offering me a friendly smile. I felt a weird sense of misplaced guilt. Was it uncomfortable for me to be here? Ivan had tried to sell me to Waylon—she had to know that, right?

"Ravik Gentry!" Waylon exclaimed. "You've arrived, and you brought friends!"

"It's good to see you, Alpha Waylon. My father says hello." Ravik offered him a nod of greeting, his hand tightening around my waist protectively. I could feel Basir and Thornar on either side of us.

Waylon made his way down toward us, his mate still talking to a woman standing next to her. "How is your father?"

"Good. Busy as ever." Ravik chuckled, not giving any hint to his father's diminishing health. "You've met my Beta and Enforcer, Thornar and Basir? And this is our mate, Gracie."

Waylon let out a hum of understanding. "I thought I recognized this young lady. You were accompanying Ivan Rivers last time."

"Yes. I was living in the Cold Moon Pack territory."

Waylon's gaze searched my face, and his expression softened. "I'm glad to see you're no longer in his care. I heard how he treated you at the conference—

what you endured—through my operatives. You deserve better than that."

Emotion welled in me at his sincerity. "Thank you. I appreciate that."

His gaze moved over my mates before settling back on me. "I hope you don't mind me asking, but once I rejected Ivan's suggestion...how do I put this politely... Were your mates involved in the arrangement Ivan had in mind for you?"

Ravik's chest rumbled at the insinuation. I shook my head, feeling a defensive bristle rise out of my wolf. In theory I appreciated him checking, but he hadn't worried about the effects of his rejection at the TTC, so why now?

Before traveling from territory to territory, a question like the one he'd posed would have left me overwhelmed and flustered, certain I had done something wrong. This time I felt composed, because I knew the truth and felt confident in it. More than that, I no longer feared every person I came across who held power. I was slowly learning that I had my own.

"No." It was a firm and sincere answer, my voice steady. "They were the reason I got out. I met them at the trade conference and they came to save me from the Cold Moon Pack."

I knew I didn't need to explain past a *no*, but I wanted that thought corrected.

My mates said nothing. I could feel that they were

proud of my answer but still stung by the question. After a moment of weighing my answer, Waylon nodded and looked at them.

"I hope you understand why I needed to ask," he said evenly. "We don't tolerate anything like that in Stark Flight."

"And I insisted on knowing," Waylon's mate said as she floated down toward us, offering me a soft and understanding look. "You must be Gracie Holloway. I'm Waylon's mate, Bishu."

*Now I was nervous.*

I offered her a smile of greeting as she continued, "Alpha Haiden contacted me and told me you'd be coming. She said you were the one to listen to." The compliment melted my nerves away.

"It's wonderful to meet you. I do hope you'll listen to what we have to say," I said.

"Speaking of that." Waylon glanced over our shoulders, and I noticed the eyes on us, the interested murmurs carrying across the hall. "They are much too interested in what's going on up here."

"Very nosy bunch," Bishu mused. "Let's retire to the private sitting room."

"Lead the way," Ravik suggested.

The room they led us into was simpler and more homey than the hall, cushioned surfaces and incense filling the space. Fresh air drifted in on a breeze from an open window that faced the ocean, and I fought the urge to walk over and breathe it in properly. When Waylon and Bishu motioned for us to join them at a round table, I sat as close to that window as I could manage.

"We were surprised you risked coming here," Waylon admitted. "We heard what happened at the border, the envoy we lost before you arrived. I assume the issue was taken care of?"

"Yes," Thornar said. "But with it came a larger one. The Blazefur Pride is assisting them."

"That doesn't surprise me," Bishu said. "Chace has always been a prick."

My eyes widened at her unexpected language, but I tried to hide it by nodding in agreement. I was gathering that there was a general consensus on the man. Waylon offered her an amused look before his gaze roamed over all of us.

"You're here to pull us into a war."

"Yes," I answered resolutely, feeling as though this was the moment I needed to be most vocal. "I'm not sure how much Alpha Haiden explained, but what we're facing with Ivan isn't just a threat to the neighboring territories. It's a threat to all of Thornfell."

"She didn't explain much," Bishu conceded.

"Ivan and Graeme don't have the numbers to counter even *one* of our military branches," Waylon said. "I don't understand how he can be a threat. We will need you to paint us a picture."

"He'll have even fewer people soon," Ravik said, "because he's planning to sacrifice all of them in a ritual during the full moon."

That seemed to hit a chord. The two of them exchanged a look before Waylon sat back. "The Stark Flight is a deeply spiritual territory. After thousands of years it's the one thing I've learned will survive any war—the belief in the unknown."

"So war and territory disputes don't worry us," Bishu agreed. "This ritual, though—that does worry me. What does he hope to accomplish?"

"For a decade now, he's performed monthly sacrificial rituals to Nyxarra," Basir explained. "He hopes to sacrifice thousands for the same goal. To amass power."

"We believe he thinks it will allow him to ultimately subjugate more people to his rule and expand outward," Ravik said, "but that type of power..."

"Can't be left unchecked."

Both of the leaders nodded at my answer.

After a moment, Waylon tilted his head. "There is more to this picture that we're not seeing. Why would one of The Eight accept that type of sacrifice? We've spoken with the six named, and I cannot see them accepting that."

Of course they had. Anything less from a thousand-year-old dragon would have felt strange.

"You're right," I agreed. "There is more, but it's

hard to explain and even harder to know who we can trust with the information. What we can say is that the ritual *has* to be stopped. We want you to help us make that happen."

I hadn't expected to sound so certain of it. But I was.

Waylon let out a low hum and looked up at the ceiling. "Trust. I understand your qualms. But if we are to be allies, we need to know exactly what threat lies before us. Other Alphas may be content with the non-spiritual, but my mate and I don't make decisions without full knowledge and guidance."

"I have a suggestion," Bishu said. "You feel as though you can't speak the words to tell us, but what if they were read? In Stark Flight, our spiritual counsel comes through a high priestess directly connected to Yvelis. Our god is the foundation for everything here."

"You want your priestess to do a reading?" I asked. Ravik tightened his hand around mine. I could feel the unease through the bond as I turned the idea over, but my mates had apparently decided to let me take the reins for this meeting. It filled me with pride to know they trusted me with such a vital piece of the mission, but it was also intimidating. What if I chose wrong?

At face value, I felt as though I could trust Waylon and Bishu, and I was starting to rely on my instincts. At the same time, we had no idea who was listening to our conversation. A high priestess, though, would probably be able to *feel* what was going on. To sense the danger associated with the scale of Ivan's planned ritual, even if we didn't feel comfortable putting it into words.

"Yes," Bishu said, disappearing through a door on the other side of the room. Waylon spoke with my mates, but I found myself standing to walk to the window. It wasn't something I'd normally do, feeling bound to my seat in these talks, but everything could come together or fall apart in the next few minutes.

We hadn't told them about Nyxarra—not the truth of it—or Vaelithra. It was clear they had a relationship with the gods and probably knew of the unnamed ones as well. A reading could do so much more than give the priestess an understanding of the scale of our problem. It could reveal everything, all at once, including who we were trying to keep imprisoned.

My gaze moved out over the ocean as I let my mind drift to what Ravik had told me about the other continents out there. It was a nice distraction from my nerves...at least until the door opened again.

In my life, I'd been around my fair share of high priestesses, but not a single one had a power signature like the woman walking through the door behind Bishu. My head snapped to her, but her black gaze was already on me.

I turned my body toward her as she paused in the doorway, looking around the room. Her pupils were completely absent, her icy face half-covered in silver scales. Her hair was bone white and her robes were black, the contrast stark against the comfortable room around her.

"This is Tashmin, High Priestess of the Temple of Yvelis."

My mates acknowledged her but she was still looking at me. The pressure in the air grew heavier, as though she took up ten times more space than she actually occupied. My wolf curled inward as the woman took a step closer, her robes shifting to reveal white bony feet, her nails black. I swallowed. I could hear the others talking quietly around me, but I was having trouble focusing. Something pulled at the edges of my mind.

"Child of shadows and moonlight. You've come."

# CHAPTER 27

# GRACIE

"*Lux mea*, do you know her?" Ravik's voice jolted me out of the hold Tashmin had on my attention. I could feel my mates bristling at her intense focus trained on me.

"No. Yes," Tashmin answered for me, stepping fully into the room. "I know of her. I've heard her name whispered in bones. Many of The Eight speak through them."

I wasn't sure how I felt about *many* of The Eight talking about me.

"Join us, Gracie." She looked up. "I promise I won't harm you or your mates. My power, siphoned from Yvelis, is not unlike Nyxarra's flavor of power." She was trying to comfort me, but it wasn't entirely working.

"We will give you room." Bishu stood, and Alpha Waylon joined her. Their priestess offered a nod of thanks as the two rulers made themselves comfortable in a nearby sitting area.

I moved toward the table, not loving the idea of Tashmin near my mates without me close. My wolf pressed against my chest, and I held back a growl that threatened to break out. *I needed to take a breath.* This woman didn't mean us harm. Probably.

Slowly, settling into her seat, Tashmin looked toward Waylon and Bishu. "I am to understand that you want a reading to give assurance that the threat is real and not just on a mortal level?"

"Yes," Waylon responded.

"I can tell you that it is, but this should allow me to see the scale," Tashmin said, confirming my suspicions. She returned her gaze to me. "It will probably tell me much more than that. You understand?"

"Yes."

"Little flame, is this—"

I reached over and gave Thornar's hand a squeeze. I caught the look passing between my mates, the calculation in weighing whether one of them should stay outside the vision to guard the rest of our group.

"Together," I said, before any of them could offer it. My instincts were telling me that it was essential we did this together.

"If there is anyone we can trust," I added quietly, "it's those with a close connection to The Eight."

Tashmin seemed to approve of my words and instructed the four of us to sit next to one another, hands flat on the table.

I watched as she put out black candles one by one, pulling them from a bag at her feet. Between the candles she laid out bones, small and delicate, covered in runes.

The air shifted with anticipation, and I realized this was the first time my mates would be purposefully stepping into the divine with me.

"As I light each candle, you'll feel a pull of power. I encourage you to close your eyes and follow it."

I sat at the end of the line and watched anxiously as she lit each one. A deep hum came from her throat and her lips moved fast at the same time, sending an odd vibration through the air. The pull of power was intense, and I felt my mates' unease and apprehension melt into something closer to awe. When she got to me, I let my eyes fall shut, giving into the instinct to trust Waylon and Bishu and their priestess alongside them.

This time, rather than falling into darkness, a door opened in front of me. I inhaled, bolstering myself, and stepped through it into a crypt. Four stories high, stone tombs covered the walls horizontally on each side, the walls embedded with bone. My mates stood waiting for me, the silent tension between us making me worry they felt as overwhelmed as I had the first time.

"They can't speak or move here." Panic rose within me as Nyxarra's voice brought forth her image, a shadow shifting into female form. "Not until we let them."

"You don't want them to talk?" I frowned, stepping protectively in front of my mates. I looked back to see they were, in fact, frozen.

I *hated* it.

Nyxarra eyed them before lowering her voice. "What I want isn't important. I'm not running this show." The venom at the end of that made my heart ache for her. More so, I could feel her magic being drained, her signature growing weaker each time we came across one another.

"I'm trying to fix this." It was a promise she hadn't expected. Her eyes closed, and I watched a single tear slip down her face before she disappeared in a wall of shadows that collapsed around her.

With what sounded like a crack of thunder, the air split open and Vaelithra dropped from above in a crouch, making the ground shake. This time she arrived in a less intimidating form, joined by three ghostly wolves prowling the crypt behind her. But it didn't stop me from moving back to protect my mates better.

Her gaze met mine first, a smile crossing her face before she looked at my mates.

"You heard my call," she said approvingly.

"I'm actually getting a reading from a high priestess, and when she opened the channel we dropped in here. So yes? Sort of."

Her laugh was genuine as she looked around the crypt. "Yvelis, by the look of it. That's wonderful. He's...interesting." Her presence was more relaxed this time, as though she felt we were on her time rather than borrowed.

"Oh, how could I forget." She snapped her fingers, and suddenly my mates were vocal. Thornar groaned, shaking himself out, and Basir appeared at my side, an arm wrapping around me possessively. Ravik moved to stand next to me, angling slightly in front of my body.

"So these are the mates at your side." Her gaze moved over them critically. "I'm beginning to understand Nyxarra's confidence."

I knew she was seeing their outward strength, and I felt a familiar prick of insecurity—of not being enough despite being chosen by gods. It didn't make complete sense, but the feeling was there, building inside of me.

"What you were saying to Gracie before, about the

bond scar," Ravik prompted, not wasting a moment. "We need to know how to use it to defeat Ivan."

Vaelithra snapped her fingers and one of the wolves prowling the crypt came to lay at her side. She settled onto the floor next to it, and I moved to join her without being asked, somehow knowing that was what she would expect. Once we had done that, the two remaining wolves positioned themselves around our circle, and I felt her power spark and move through the air like a phantom wind.

"We must speak quietly," she said. "We are shielded here for now."

After a prolonged moment of silence, she continued. "The bond scar doesn't defeat Ivan—that is a mortal job. The bond scar is a living counter-ritual to what Ivan is trying to enact."

My mates and I leaned forward, reaching for every piece of information we could. Her voice stayed hushed and serious. "Ivan's ritual severs and consumes the natural bond that each of my creations —my shifters—has to this earth. It pulls from that connection and feeds Kaevorak through destruction and desecration. It erases any sense of shared growth."

Was that why the Cold Moon Pack had been so bare? So desolate?

"The god scar is the rarest of bonds, especially when shared by multiples. Its very essence opposes what Ivan is trying to do—think of it as an antidote to a poison, rather than a weapon."

"How can our bond of four compare to his ritual of thousands, though?" Basir asked.

"I hope you reach him before the ritual starts, but if not, not all hope is lost," she said candidly. "The bond, in all its forms, was one of my many gifts to shifters. It predates anything Ivan can possibly comprehend. When you pull on your bond, it will stir others—those with pack bonds, family bonds, or mating bonds—and they will fuel you further."

"So the presence of so many will actually help us," Thornar said, his voice tinged with something close to relief.

"Ivan is pushing against forces he doesn't understand," she answered. "I've stood by before, watching Kaevorak make mistakes, but what he plans to do if freed is not something we can risk. Even if it means sacrificing my own chance at freedom."

Hadn't we wondered exactly that? What she had to gain?

"You do this for the greater good?" Ravik asked, his skepticism barely veiled.

"I do this for the greater future," she countered. "I hope that Nyxarra and the others can aid in my freedom once Ivan is dealt with, but I can't allow that to cloud what we must do now."

I took a slow breath, sitting with her words. The

way she was putting it gave me real hope that we weren't as far from a solution as we'd feared.

"So how do we use the bond when the time comes?" I asked.

"That requires a bit more…nuance. You first need to ensure it's fully formed." Her gaze moved over the four of us and lingered on me. "You need to be marked by each other. After that, it's not as clear. Bond magic manifests in ways even I can't always predict." She paused, smiling. "Much like your wolf."

"My wolf?"

"Didn't you notice the change?" she mused. "That was all Nyxarra's influence."

Something about that made me sit straighter with pride—that the change in my wolf was truly a divine representation of my bond with a god. *Our* bond, actually.

Suddenly, a plume of smoke that smelled of ash and debris filled the crypt, faint but unmistakable, and the sensation of eyes on us began to make my skin crawl. Her wolves tensed before moving toward her and merging into her. Vaelithra went quiet.

"He searches for us." Her words made my stomach clench, and each of my mates shifted into more defensive positions. Ravik's hand tightened around mine, ready to move if needed.

"We must go." Nyxarra's voice drifted through the air, soft and distant.

Vaelithra rose, and we joined her. When she spoke again it was in a more guarded tone. "This won't be the last time we speak. For now we must stop here, but remember what I said."

*The bond scar is a counter-ritual. But the bond itself needs to be fully formed.*

We didn't get a chance to say goodbye before the room faded at the edges and gave way to darkness. Something heavy and uncomfortable settled over me. After what felt like an eternity, or maybe just a few seconds, my eyes opened to find Tashmin staring at us with wide surprise.

Blood tracked from both her eyes in thin red lines down her hollow cheeks. Not only her though. Waylon and Bishu looked equally shaken. And when I looked at my mates, Thornar was looking over a split in the wood of the table where he'd white knuckled it so hard it had broken. Ravik's right ear was bleeding as he stared at me with worry, his hand moving to wipe away crimson from under my nose. Basir was already standing, shifting and pacing, trying to shake the way his control had been ripped away from him.

"How?" My question was soft but pointed to Waylon and Bishu. I could *feel* that they had seen and experienced everything. Tashmin stepped back for a moment to collect herself as Bishu and Waylon joined us at the table.

"We have a connection to Tashmin—we can see

many of her visions. Her entire family line has been connected to ours," Bishu explained.

"And that was a particularly vivid one," Waylon added.

Ravik spoke up, giving me a moment to breathe. "Do you see how important this is now? Do you understand what we're dealing with?"

When the two leaders looked at one another, I could see it—the calculation of how much devastation this could cause. Tashmin looked between them and spoke plainly.

"If Ivan completes that ritual, we will all die."

Her words hit hard. Bishu closed her eyes and Waylon's jaw tightened, his expression less disagreement than barely contained anger.

"We have interacted with The Eight," Waylon said. "But never have we dealt with the two unnamed, or spoken with any of them so openly. The bond you have, while I don't fully understand it, is the clear answer to all of this."

"We can try to explain the bond if that would help," I offered.

Bishu shook her head. "By allowing us to do the reading, even allowing us to witness the vision—which you unintentionally gave us permission to do—you earned our trust. We understand the stakes."

My eyes widened. "Does that mean we can count on your help?"

Waylon leaned forward, placing his hands on the table, and spoke in a reverent tone. "Knowing that The Eight have called you, placed their trust in you to face a far larger evil than Ivan Rivers, is more compelling than any strategic argument you could have made.

"You have our unconditional support."

# CHAPTER 28
# GRACIE

Out of all the guest rooms we'd stayed in, this was possibly the most interesting. The room was circular and domed, the living space and bed sharing one large open area with no separation in between. There was only one additional door, off the entrance, that led to a bathroom suite. The rest of the space gave the sensation of being inside a tree...which, I supposed, we were.

The bark-like walls were covered in murals of battles that seemed to be pulled from mythology, the detail work in each one genuinely fascinating. Lanterns hung from the curved ceiling, and everything was done in deep purple fabrics that were plush under my fingers. I'd been sitting in the middle of the room on a chair, looking up at the ceiling, for at *least* five minutes.

"The healer should be here before we leave for dinner," Ravik said while running a hand through his damp hair. My mates had let me shower first, all of us wanting to wash the grime of travel off, before leaving me to relax in a comfortable, soft robe.

I'd only recently changed out of it into a dress for the evening. It was a pale pink chiffon, layers of it wrapping around me, the neckline sitting off the shoulder in a way that was both comfortable and elegant. Despite how I usually felt in clothes like this, the sensation of being out of place or not worthy didn't come. I felt beautiful.

"Dinner," Thornar mused. "Four feels a bit early—makes me think we aren't eating right away."

Considering how hungry I was, I hoped that wasn't the case. Luckily the room had a few snacks, but after taking my tonic it always felt better to have something more substantial.

"We don't have to spend this dinner convincing anyone to help us, though," I pointed out. "We can just relax and enjoy ourselves."

At least for tonight.

I didn't think any of us had expected the meeting to go the way it did, but I was thankful. With only thirteen days left on the countdown, we would need to move quickly, and having so many allies gave me real hope.

So while we could enjoy ourselves tonight, come

morning we would need to push forward and make a plan.

A knock sounded at the door, and Basir, who'd just walked out of the bathroom freshly showered and dressed, made his way to answer it.

"It's the healer," he announced. The door opened to reveal two people—an older man and a younger woman who, from looks alone, I assumed was his daughter. He had silver hair and she had blonde, but they shared the same angular face and pink scales near their temples.

"Hi there!" She looked right past my mates to me. "This must be our patient."

"Yes." I offered her a smile as she took the lead, breezing past my mates to sit beside me. She extended her hand, and I took it.

"My name's Lucy; I'm my dad's assistant. He'll be the one helping you." She motioned to her father, who was moving at a slower pace, Basir stepping aside to let him through. When he reached us, the man offered me a friendly smile and settled into the chair across from me.

"Gracie, I'm Healer Thorne." He nodded in greeting. "I've been told you may have a concussion. Can you tell me what happened?"

"She was in a car accident," Ravik said. "The vehicle slammed into a wall."

*And a person.*

Lucy winced. "That sounds awful."

Her father glanced at her with quiet adoration, as if her concern for others alone made him thankful for her. I got the sense he was just glad to have her alongside him.

"May I have your hand?" Healer Thorne asked. I nodded.

For the next few minutes the room was quiet as his power moved through the space, settling around my head, shifting my hair slightly. When he pulled back he offered a smile. "Good news—I don't sense any cranial damage and no sign of a concussion."

"Thank fuck," Basir said under his breath. I looked up at him and felt our bond pulse with relief so strong it caught me off guard. I had known he was worried, but not to this extent.

Lucy beamed at me. "Is there anything else you'd like to ask while he's here?"

"I don't think so," I told her. She nodded and offered her arm to help her father stand.

"If you think of anything or need anything, don't hesitate. We're just down on the third floor."

I watched them leave after a quick goodbye and sat with the feeling their presence had stirred in me. It made me wonder how my dad and I would have interacted, if he were still alive.

Right at that moment, though, my stomach made it *very* obvious that I was hungry.

All three of them looked at me in concern, and I couldn't help but blush. Ravik shook his head, sweeping me up from the couch and heading toward the door.

"Gotta tell us when you're hungry, little flame," Thornar pointed out.

"We've been busy!" I said in my defense. The fresh coastal breeze hit us the moment we stepped out of the suite into the open-aired hallway. I tapped Ravik's hand, and he let me slip down. "Plus, until we sat down I didn't realize how hungry I was."

"I'm honestly surprised we were invited," Thornar said. "It seemed like a family thing. I won't say no, though—the food looked amazing earlier."

It had. My stomach almost grumbled again as we followed the hallway down two sets of stairs before turning left. Earlier, while being escorted to our suite by Bishu herself, she had shown us where the garden dinner would be held and promised to send up clothes. Walking through these halls now, I felt like I fit in more comfortably than when we had arrived.

I was significantly more thankful for the invitation as we reached the large bone archway that led out into a raised garden overlooking the ocean. *This was beautiful.* I had no idea what was supporting it structurally, but as I stepped through I was caught between two things at once: the tree rising behind us toward the sky and the ocean sprawling out below and around us. It wasn't a view I could ever fully get over.

The air was warm against my skin, conversation and laughter carrying across it, as we made our way toward a gathering of nearly fifty people—all lounging, enjoying drinks, and listening to music. There was no announcement or greeting; we simply arrived and melted into the crowd. I allowed myself a steadying breath as the tension in my shoulders began to release. There had been enough announcements in the past week to last a lifetime.

There was no call for when food began, either. Platters and trays simply appeared at the table we had claimed, comfortably seating the four of us with one spot open. Up front, only ten feet away, a series of performers recited poetry against a backdrop of classical music. It was a little too quiet to hear easily from where we sat, but it added to the sense that despite being surrounded by people, we could just be ourselves.

"Where are our hosts?" Thornar asked, handing me a small plate of three different items. I didn't hesitate to try all of them. The first was some type of bread topped with vegetables and a kind of seafood, the flavor both salty and earthy.

"Over there, I think," Ravik said, looking toward the far end of the garden where the largest cluster of people had gathered. "They must really enjoy a good party if this is their regular dinner."

"And considering the lunch they already had," Basir agreed.

I found it special. If I ever had a family of my own, I hoped I'd be surrounded by them just like this.

The atmosphere settled between the four of us, our bond humming with both contentment and something a little wistful. Thornar leaned forward to listen to the poetry. Ravik put his arm around my chair and pressed a kiss to the side of my head. Even Basir seemed at ease, his hand reaching out to intertwine with mine.

None of them had said so, but I suspected the wistfulness came from missing home. I was starting to miss Ironsun myself, and I'd only just begun to find my place there. Stark Flight territory was special, but much like my mates, Ironsun grounded me in a way I wasn't sure could be replicated anywhere else.

For nearly an hour the party moved around us. I had managed to eat enough that I was significantly full, and my mates were happy...*except for Basir*.

"I'm going to grab more of those," he said, his tone brooking no disagreement. I had mentioned I liked one of the dishes—thin slices of fish grilled with pineapple on a skewer—and now he wanted an entire plate of them for me. I didn't bother arguing, just reached up and squeezed his hand in thanks.

I watched him round the table toward the tree wall where the staff were gathering and had just begun to turn back to Thornar when my wolf went rigid.

It wasn't a sound. It wasn't something I saw.

There was a distinct change in the air, a sensation of terror building in my chest before I knew why. My wolf didn't warn me. She just moved and took me with her.

I was jumping over the chair before I knew it.

The shift overtook me without warning, fur and bone replacing chiffon and flesh, as I tackled Basir. Taken off guard, he stumbled forward and out of the way.

I felt the impact before I understood it. My body jolted as the air cracked around us.

I hit the ground.

"She's been shot!" The voice came from somewhere distant, already fading.

Shot? Is that what I'd intercepted? I had stopped Basir from being shot.

The ground was hard and my body felt cold, my wolf unable to hold our form as she melted away, my human form reclaiming me. It wasn't agony. It was an icy numbness. The bond between my mates and I felt unstable, as if it couldn't hold its shape any better than my wolf could. All I could see above me was the evening sky.

Then two warm, rough hands found my face, a voice cutting through everything else.

"Glow."

I tried to find Basir's eyes...I finally found them.

Then the garden, the lanterns, the warmth of the evening...all of it folded in at the edges.

And then darkness—

*Howling Fate* is available for order today!

On the following page, *you'll find* **The Thornfell Registry:** The Eight, Territories & Command, and Genealogy & Relations.

The **Hunter's Moon Ritual** Series:

- Howling Love
- Howling Desire
- Howling Fate

# THE THORNFELL REGISTRY

## THE EIGHT

- Astaruun [AH-stah-room]
- Nyxarra [Nick-ZAH-ruh]
- Vorrakar [VOHR-uh-ka]
- Thaloryn [THAL-oh-rin]
- Sylvaern. [SILL-vairn]
- Yvelis [EE-vuh-liss]
- Vaelithra [Vay-LITH-ruh]
- Kaevorak [KAY-voh-rack]

## TERRITORIES & COMMAND

- The Cold Moon Pack Territory
  - Alpha: Ivan Rivers

- The Ironsun Pack Territory
  - Alpha: Deegan Gentry
- The Scarlet Sloth Territory
  - Alpha: Kaliyah Greene
- The Grimfur Skulk Territory
  - Alpha: Graeme Sharp
- The Stark Flight Territory
  - Alpha: Waylon Kane
- The Bloodrose Sloth Territory
  - Alpha: Lacey Harrison
- The Nightstar Flight Territory
  - Alpha: Haiden Murphy
- The Blazefur Pride Territory
  - Alpha: Chace Wall

# GENEALOGY & RELATIONS

- The Holloway Family
  - Cal Holloway
  - June Holloway
  - Owen Holloway
  - Gracie Holloway
- The Gentry Family
  - Deegan Gentry
  - Malara Gentry
  - Ravik Gentry
  - Banthor Gentry

  - Solenne Gentry
  - Siguun Gentry
- The Veydran Family
  - Dane Veydran
  - Anwen Veydran
  - Thornar Veydran
  - Elowen Veydran
- The Morcant Family
  - [NAME REDACTED]
  - [NAME REDACTED]
  - Basir Morcant

# M. SINCLAIR

M. Sinclair is a USA Today Best-Selling Author who can be found writing or thinking about her characters and plots nearly every moment of the day. With over 65 published works since her debut in 2019, her work spans from paranormal to contemporary romance rooted in extensive world-building and deep character development. M. Sinclair believes there is enough room for all types of heroines in this world, and that being saved is just as important as saving others.

Just remember to love cats... that's not negotiable.

# PUBLISHED WORKS

*M. Sinclair has crafted different universes with unique plotlines, character cameos, and shared universe events. As a reader, this means that you may see your favorite character or characters... appear in multiple books besides their own storyline.*

## UNIVERSE 1

*Established in 2019*

### Vengeance

Book 1 - Savages

Book 2 - Lunatics

Book 3 - Monsters

Book 4 - Psychos

*Complete Series*

Vengeance : The Complete Series

### The Red Masques

Book 1 - Raven Blood

Book 2 - Ashes & Bones

Book 3 - Shadow Glass

Book 4 - Fire & Smoke

Book 5 - Dark King

*Complete Series*

A Raven Masques Novel - Birth of a Raven

Red Masques: Volume One

Red Masques: Volume Two

## TEARS OF THE SIREN

Book 1 - Horror of Your Heart

Book 2 - Broken House

Book 3 - Neon Drops

Book 4 - Snapped Strings

Book 5 - Fractured Souls

Book 6 - Shattered Galaxies

*Complete Series*

## DESCENDANT

Book 1 - Descendant of Chaos

Book 2 - Descendant of Blood

Book 3 - Descendant of Sin

Book 4 - Descendant of Glory

Book 5 - Descendant of Pain

Book 6 - Descendant of Victory

*Complete Series*

### Reborn

Book 1 - Reborn In Flames

Book 2 - Soaring In Flames

Book 3 - Realm Of Flames

Book 4 - Dying in Flames

Book 5 - Ruling in Flames

*Complete Series*


### The Wronged

Book 1 - Wicked Blaze Correctional

Book 2 - Evading Wicked Blaze

Book 3 - Defeating Wicked Blaze

*Complete Series*

The Wronged: Completed Series


### Lost in Fae

Book 1 - Finding Fae

Book 2 - Exploring Fae

Book 3 - Freeing Fae

Book 4 - Loving Fae

*Complete Series*

*UNIVERSE 2*

*Established in 2020*

### **AMONG SHADOWS**

Book 1 - Court of Betrayal

Book 2 - Court of Deception (TBA)

# PARANORMAL & FANTASY SERIES

THESE SERIES ARE NOT CURRENTLY AFFILIATED WITH A SPECIFIC M. SINCLAIR UNIVERSE.

### **HUNTER'S MOON RITUAL**

Book 1 - Howling Love

Book 2 - Howling Desire

Book 3 - Howling Fate

### **PHASES OF THE MOON**

Book 1 - Lunar Witch

Book 2 - Blood Witch

Book 3 - Shadow Witch

Book 4 - Unblessed Witch

*Complete Series*

*THE STORM DRAGONS' MATE*

Book 1 - Blitz

Book 2 - Flicker

Book 3 - Surge

Book 4 - Flash

*Complete Series*


*THE DEAD AND THE NOT SO DEAD*

Book 1 - Queen of the Dead

Book 2 - Team Time with the Dead

Book 3 - Dying for the Dead

*Complete Series*

The Dead and the Not So Dead: Completed Series


*SILVER FALLS UNIVERSITY*

Book 1 - Lost

Book 2 - Forgotten

Book 3 - Discovered

Book 4 - Pursued

Book 5 - Found

*Complete Series*


*I.S.S.*

Book 1 - Soothing Nightmares

Book 2 - Defending Nightmares

Book 3 - Defeating Nightmares

Book 4 - Loving Nightmares

Universe Standalone Novel - Mating Monsters

*Complete Series*

# *CONTEMPORARY UNIVERSE*

*Established in 2021*

**THE SHADOWS OF WILDBERRY LANE**

Book 1 - Perfection of Suffering

Book 2 - Execution of Anguish

Book 3 - Carnage of Misery

*Complete Series*

Complete Collection: The Shadows of Wildberry Lane

**THEIR POSSESSION**

Book 1 - Sheltered

Book 2 - Searched (TBA)

## STANDALONE NOVELS

Peridot (Jewels Cafe Series)

Time for Sensibility (Women of Time)

Of Claws & Chaos (Forgotten Kingdoms)

### WILLOWDALE VILLAGE COLLECTION

Voiceless

Fearless

Sightless

### SEASONS OF THE HUNTRESS

Winter Huntress

## COLLABORATIONS

### MONARCHS OF HELL

(M. SINCLAIR & R.L. CAULDER)

BOOK 1 - INSURRECTION

BOOK 2 - IMBALANCE

BOOK 3 - INHERITANCE

*Complete Series*

### FALLEN DESTINY

*(M. Sinclair & R.L. Caulder)*

Book 1 - Wings of Stars

Book 2 - Wings of Pain

Book 3 - Wings of Hope

*Complete Series*


**The Vampyres' Source**

*(M. Sinclair & R.L. Caulder)*

Book 1 - Ruthless Blood

Book 2 - Ruthless War

Book 3 - Ruthless Love

*Complete Series*


**Rebel Hearts Heists Duet**

*(M. Sinclair & Melissa Adams)*

Book 1 - Steal Me

Book 2 - Keep Me

*Complete Duet*